BY JASON FRY

STAR WARS

The Essential Atlas

The Clone Wars: Episode Guide

The Essential Guide to Warfare

Star Wars in 100 Scenes

Moving Target: A Princess Leia Adventure

The Weapon of a Jedi: A Luke Skywalker Adventure

The Force Awakens: Rey's Survival Guide

The Force Awakens Incredible Cross-Sections

The Last Jedi: Expanded Edition

The Servants of the Empire Series

THE JUPITER PIRATES

Hunt for the Hydra

Curse of the Iris

The Rise of Earth

🟫 MOJANG

MINECRAFT™
THE VOYAGE

MINECRAFT™
THE VOYAGE

JASON FRY

DEL REY
NEW YORK

Published in the United States by Del Rey, an imprint of Random House, a division of Penguin Random House LLC, New York.

DEL REY and the HOUSE colophon are registered trademarks of Penguin Random House LLC.

MINECRAFT is a trademark or registered trademark of Mojang Synergies AB.

LIBRARY OF CONGRESS CATALOGING-IN-PUBLICATION DATA
Names: Fry, Jason, author.
Title: The voyage / Jason Fry.
Description: New York: Del Rey, [2020] | Series: Minecraft
Identifiers: LCCN 2019058056 (print) | LCCN 2019058057 (ebook) | ISBN 9780399180750 (hardcover) | ISBN 9780399180767 (ebook) | ISBN 9780593159231 (international edition)
Classification: LCC PZ7.F9224 Voy 2020 (print) | LCC PZ7.F9224 (ebook) | DDC [Fic]—dc23
LC record available at https://lccn.loc.gov/2019058056
LC ebook record available at https://lccn.loc.gov/2019058057

Printed in the United States of America on acid-free paper

randomhousebooks.com

4 6 8 9 7 5

Book design by Elizabeth A. D. Eno

This one's for Sam Jones, a writer, thinker,
and storyteller to keep an eye on.
After you change the world, kid, you owe *me* a dedication.

MOJANG

MINECRAFT™
THE VOYAGE

CHAPTER 1

THE HOUSE BY THE SEA

Of Stax Stonecutter and his three faithful companions

In a house by the sea there lived a young man.

In a few minutes I'll tell you about the young man, who after all is the hero of this story. But first you ought to know something about the house, because it's important to our tale as well.

The house wasn't a palace. You probably wouldn't even call it a mansion. But it was big, and most people who saw it thought it was beautiful. It was built out of black-and-white speckled diorite, pink granite, and glass. The diorite and the granite had been carefully polished, so the first rays of the morning sun made the house seem to glow, like it was lit from within.

The house had been built into the side of a green hill dotted with white birches, so it looked like it was part of the landscape, instead of something artificial that had been stuck in the middle of it. And the land around the house had been carefully reshaped to make it pleasing to the eye.

If you approached the house by sea, you'd step off your boat at the end of a broad green lawn, with a line of birch trees to either side. To your right, you'd find a low hill covered with flowers of every color: roses and peonies and tulips and cornflowers and daisies. To your left, beside another low hill, you'd see pens for cattle and pigs and chickens and sheep, and above them you'd find lovingly tended rows of crops: wheat, beetroot, and carrots, and the squat squares of pumpkins and melons. Ahead and above you, you'd see the house. To reach it, you'd pass between the white birch trees, perhaps thinking they looked a little like soldiers on parade, walk around a cheerful fountain that splashed and burbled in a square of green lawn, and climb a broad flight of polished diorite steps until you stood at the front door.

The young man who lived in the house was named Stax Stonecutter, and he was the third in the line of Stonecutters to call it home. Stax's grandmother, the first Stonecutter anyone had ever heard of, had built a simple dwelling in the side of the hill many years before—little more than a cave chopped out of the dirt and rock. It was her son, Stax's father, who'd enlarged the house and planted the trees and flowers and made the Stonecutter home into an impressive estate.

Stax's father and grandmother were dead now, buried alongside the rest of his family in a place of honor in the back garden. Stax lived alone, or almost alone. Three cats lived with him: a black one with golden eyes, a gray-striped one with green eyes, and a Siamese with blue eyes. They were called Coal, Emerald, and Lapis, after some of the rocks and minerals the Stonecutter family had mined from the ground over the years.

Stax loved Coal, Emerald, and Lapis and considered them company enough for a happy life. In recent years he'd begun to talk with them, even though they never offered answers beyond swishes of the tail, purrs, or the occasional meow. Visitors to the Stonecutter estate had grown used to coming across Stax somewhere on the grounds, planting flowers or pruning tree limbs while chatting companionably with one or more of the cats, who more often than not would be asleep in the sun.

The people who lived near the Stonecutter estate thought this behavior was a bit strange, but then everything about Stax struck them as at least a bit strange. His oldest neighbors remembered Stax's grandmother as a skilled miner who never shied from marching into a dark hole in the ground and returned weighed down with rich minerals and marvelous treasures. The younger ones recalled Stax's father as a great adventurer, a smiling man who loved traveling the world and meeting new people. Stax's father had loved tales and he was pretty good at telling his own stories, and at convincing people he'd just met that they'd be happier if they bought the stone that the Stonecutters had mined and cut into polished blocks.

All of the neighbors, regardless of how old they were, agreed that Stax was nothing like his grandmother or his father. He went to the Stonecutter office every few weeks to take care of family business, but as far as anyone knew he'd never traveled through the forests or across the plains, or set out on a journey from the Stonecutter boathouse to visit any of the lands his father had told such wonderful stories about. Everyone agreed Stax was skilled at mining and cutting stone, having learned this craft from his father and grandmother, but he never expressed interest in finding new mines and seeing what they might contain. People who went to visit Stax at the big house by the sea said he was pleasant enough if you talked with him about cats or flowers, but if you tried to have a conversation with him about anything else, pretty soon he'd get a faraway look in his eye and start to fidget, and a few minutes after that he'd make some excuse—and not always a convincing one—and go back into his house.

The kind neighbors felt sorry for Stax, who'd become an orphan when he was just a teenager, and asked what was really so wrong with being a homebody who was more interested in cats and flowers than in mines, which, miners would be the first to tell you, were always dark, often smelly, and sometimes dangerous. But the less kind neighbors said Stax was lucky the other members of his family had worked so hard for so many years so he didn't have to work hard at all. And as the years went by and Stax got a little odder with each one, the less kind neighbors came to outnumber the kind ones.

Now, there's no way for me to know how old you are. You might be eight, or eighteen, or eighty-eight, or even eight hundred eighty-eight. (All right, you're probably not eight hundred eighty-eight.) But no matter what the answer is, you know that it's easy for people to be unkind about things they don't actually know a lot about. So let me tell you about one day in Stax Stonecutter's life: the day he came to think of as the last normal day he ever had, because it was the day before everything began to go so terribly wrong. Maybe if you know about that day and what came after it, you'll be able to make up your own mind.

CHAPTER 2

THE LAST REGULAR DAY

Breakfast with the kitties * An unwelcome visitor *
Duties on the estate * A job for an axe * Things are put
right, however briefly

This particular day began with a sunny morning. Stax woke up late, in the upstairs bedroom that had once belonged to his father, the one whose floor-to-ceiling windows were shielded from the morning sun by the bulk of the hill behind the back garden. He rubbed the sleep from his eyes and carefully lifted up Coal, who was sleeping on his chest, and then Emerald, who was sprawled across his knees. Neither cat woke up when set gently down amid the rumpled sheets, though Emerald gave a big yawn and stretched himself into a long, contented furry bow. Stax looked for Lapis and found the Siamese was already awake, sitting at the foot of Stax's bed and giving herself a bath.

"Good morning, kitties," Stax said cheerfully, which earned him a purr from Lapis and a twitch of Coal's ear. Still sleepy, Stax put on his robe and stretched, one hand ruffling his tousled hair.

From the upstairs bedroom, a ladder led down to the main floor of the house, while a door opened onto a balcony overlooking the back garden. Before he opened the door to the balcony, Stax peered through the windows, in case a zombie or spider might be lurking nearby. But he wasn't very worried. It was some time after dawn, late enough for any dangerous night creatures to have burned up or sought shelter from the sun. And the Stonecutter estate was dotted with lanterns set on diorite columns, carefully spaced to discourage evil things from approaching the house. There *had* been a spider lurking above the balcony one morning, one of the big ones that had a cluster of red eyes and was covered with black bristles. That had given Stax a fright and left him out of sorts for the better part of a week. When had that happened? *Last summer*, Stax thought, though he wasn't entirely sure that it hadn't been the summer before that.

This time, there was no spider or any other monstrous thing to disturb the peace of the morning—just bright sunshine and a warm breeze. Reassured, Stax left the door open and leaned against the balcony railing, looking down into the back garden. Below, he could see the edge of the diorite swimming pool his father had built, half in sunlight and half in the shadow cast by a ceiling of rock and dirt. The water looked cool and inviting, and Stax decided that a dip in the pool would be an excellent way to end what he suspected would be a hot afternoon.

Next to the pool, a wooden hatch sat on the edge of a lush green lawn. That was the entrance to the Stonecutters' richest mine, with its deep central shaft. Farther away, under the oldest birches and near a sparkling blue waterfall, lay the graves of his parents and grandparents, surrounded by flowers. Stax's eyes rose to the ridge on the far side of the back garden, and the diorite pillar that stood atop it, crowned by a brightly lit lantern. That marked the edge of the estate; beyond it, to the west, was a crescent-shaped bay, fringed with a beach and thick green forests.

If Stax followed the shoreline, a day's walk would take him past a Stonecutter mine on an island offshore, and then to a small house set into the side of a mountain surrounded by scrubland and acacia trees: a no-frills outpost his father had set up as a base for raising cattle and exploring the tunnels and lava tubes beneath the mountain, furnished with little more than a bed, furnace, chest, and crafting table. Stax hadn't visited it since he was a child, and wondered if the outpost was still there. But of course it was—why would anything have changed?

"No reason to go all that way, though, right Lapis?" Stax asked, reaching down to pet the Siamese, who was butting her head against his shins. "Not when there's so much to do here. Starting with getting three hungry kitties breakfast!"

He dressed and climbed down the ladder, emerging in the middle of the house's main floor. Ahead of him, through a wide wall of glass blocks, lay the lawn and fountain, with the line of birches leading down to the sea. To the left was the Stonecutter trophy room, with its high ceiling, and next to that, a small, low-ceilinged bedroom overlooking the lawn. Behind him was the door to the back garden and a combination storeroom and work-room, with chests against one wall, and furnaces, crafting tables, and looms against the other, as well as a ladder leading down to the enchanting room, another storeroom, and the pool. To Stax's right, past a cluster of couches and chairs, was another wall of glass framing a door leading out to the south lawn. Stax could just see the roof of the boathouse, tucked snugly against the hill and the sheep pen.

As Stax prepared breakfast, Coal, Emerald, and Lapis all made their way down from the upstairs bedroom to twine themselves around his ankles, meowing as if on the verge of starvation. He prepared fish for them, sliced off a chunk of bread for himself, slathered it with honey, and ate it while inspecting the east lawn, then the south lawn, and then the back garden. All looked as it should, which was to say all looked the same as it had yesterday, and the week and month before that.

Except.

"Hmm, kitties, that isn't right," said Stax. He put the half-eaten chunk of bread down on a table in the back hall, below the frames holding a stone pickaxe and sword, and climbed up the ladder to the bedroom. Then he made his way out onto the balcony and stared out at the ridge.

Birches crowned the top of the ridge, sprouted from the terraced slopes, and left much of the back garden in cool shadow. That was what Stax's father had wanted—he'd liked the birches' white trunks and narrow, bladelike dark green leaves, and had pointed out to Stax how their white bark marked with black whorls mimicked the diorite walls of the house, making the back garden and the lawn feel like a continuation of the Stonecutter home rather than something separate from it.

But now Stax saw clearly what he thought he'd glimpsed downstairs. There was a different shade of green peeking out among the birch leaves atop the ridge, and below it, a hint of dark wood.

"Now, how did I miss that?" he asked himself, having forgotten that Coal, Emerald, and Lapis were still downstairs, happily reducing their fish breakfast to bones. "An oak tree has grown up into the view. We can't have that, now can we? What would Father say?"

Stax stood on the balcony for some time, first considering the oak tree and then carefully scanning the ridge and the hills around the back garden, in case some other invader had escaped his attention. But all else was as it should be.

"Well, that's it, then," Stax said. "We'll have to revise the day's to-do list."

But he didn't head out to deal with the tree right then, or indeed for the next few hours. Instead he wandered the shore of the estate, taking a moment to peer out at the icebergs in the distance, and whacked away at stray tufts of long grass. He wondered if the flowers on the low hill would be more attractive if he mixed in some lilacs for more color. Or perhaps he should reshape the hill completely, making it symmetrical and creating terraces for planting.

Stax decided reshaping the hill was too big a job for one day, particularly such a hot one, but promised himself that he'd consider the idea again in a few weeks. He checked in on the cows and the chickens, gathering milk and eggs for the larder, and finished his rounds by hopping the fence to stand amid the Stonecutter flock of sheep, which included white ones but also ones with red, yellow, blue, and orange wool. He must have left the door to the house open behind him, for while he was in the sheep pen the cats joined him and alternated between purring and mewling for attention.

"I think we need a purple sheep," Stax said, eyeing the red and blue sheep munching grass in the corner. "Don't you think so, kitties? An estate needs a sheep of every color, after all."

Coal chose that moment to meow, and Stax shook his head.

"Dye a white sheep purple? Well, we could do that, I suppose. But more proper to do it the natural way, don't you think? Anyway, I'm not sure if we have any purple dye in the storeroom."

The more Stax thought about it, the more he was sure he was correct, and they had no purple dye. He knew he could find the recipe for purple dye in one of his father's books in the enchanting room, down by the pool. That reminded him of a swim, which seemed like a pleasant activity to break up a hot afternoon; the sun was midway down the sky, but it was still uncomfortably humid, with no sign of rain. And looking at the sky reminded Stax, once again, of the oak tree that had grown up where it didn't belong.

He vaulted back over the fence, thinking Grandmother wouldn't have approved of taking such a shortcut instead of using the gate. This time he made certain to shut the door of the house behind him, though Lapis, as usual, had to take her time deciding whether or not she wanted to come in.

It was nice and cool in the storeroom, and Stax's resolve wavered as he mopped his brow.

"That oak tree will only be a tiny bit taller tomorrow," he told Emerald, who had curled up on the furnace and looked ready for another nap. The gray-striped cat closed his eyes contentedly, yawned, and began licking between his toes.

"Oh, I suppose you're right," Stax said. "Hard work today means leisure tomorrow. Hmm. Wonder where I heard that. Certainly not something Father or Grandmother would have said. Hard work today, *more* hard work tomorrow. That sounds more like them, now doesn't it?"

The tool chest opened with a wheeze of hinges, revealing its carefully arranged contents: swords and axes next to shovels and hoes. There were stacks of armor and quivers of arrows and coils of bowstrings. Pairs of shears sat next to compasses and planks of exotic wood brought back from Stax's father's expeditions.

Stax selected a diamond-bladed axe, testing its edge and quickly pulling back his finger. He slung the axe over his shoulder, giving Emerald a companionable ear rub, and headed for the back door. He thought about removing a diamond chestplate or at least a helmet from the armor stand in the trophy room, but immediately decided against it. He hadn't sighted a creeper on the ridge in many months, the day was oppressively hot as it was, and surely the axe would be sufficient protection against any unexpected hazard.

"Though an axe wouldn't be the right tool for that job, now would it?" he asked Coal, who was trotting across the lawn next to him, tail held high. "Grandmother would have a fit!"

Stax glanced guiltily at the shady place in the garden where the Stonecutter gravestones stood, but a few minutes later he had climbed to the top of the ridge, peering up at the sun, which was now nearing the horizon. There was the oak tree ahead—a young tree, only recently grown from a sapling to fight its way through the shade of the birches and stretch its limbs to the sun.

"Wrong place for you, I'm afraid," Stax said apologetically, giving the young oak a little pat and looking to make sure Coal had chosen a safe distance for snoozing. He swung the axe at the oak's trunk, the deep, heavy *thwack* echoing off the hill and the gleaming white-and-pink walls of the house. A few strokes and he'd hewn the tree through, allowing him to take aim at its limbs and leaves, until he was standing on the stump, sweating freely now, surrounded by leaf litter and debris.

"There's a good day's work done," Stax told Coal, whose only answer was to stretch a little farther in search of sun. Stax hopped off the oak's stump, cut it down, and began to gather the wood he'd chopped, whistling cheerfully until the place where the oak had stood was clean and neat. Maybe it was his imagination, but Stax thought he could already even see the grass growing over the bare patch on the ground.

The sun was now touching the distant hills to the west, and its light left the placid surface of the sea dappled with pink and orange. The shadows had crept across the back garden, toward the cheerful lights of the house.

"I guess we'll make it an evening swim, then," said Stax, holstering his axe.

Before his swim, he fed the cats, added the oak to the house's supply of timber, and returned the diamond axe to its proper place in the storeroom. He thought about taking one of his father's swords with him out to the pool, but decided against it; the back garden was well lit, and in the unlikely event of trouble, the door to the enchanting room was just a quick dash away.

And so Stax snoozed idly in the pool, his elbows up on the polished diorite, while the cats played in the garden and the stars wheeled overhead. And, as he'd predicted, no trouble found him.

It was the last night he'd be able to say that.

CHAPTER 3

THE VISITOR

An unexpected caller * A tour of the estate *
Unwelcome questions are asked and reluctantly
answered * Into the mine * A promise of more company

Stax should have known the visitor was trouble when he came to the wrong dock.

Visitors who had business with Stax knew to land their boats at the end of the lawn, in the shallow cove Stax's father had carefully squared off for such arrivals. This let Stax see that visitors had arrived, but it also showed off the estate at its best: Before conducting business, visitors would walk between the lines of birches, pass the fountain, and ascend the diorite stairs.

Everyone arriving on business knew that, because of course they didn't come unannounced. They would go to the Stonecutter mining office first, and speak with someone there, and that person would hurry off to the estate to tell Stax of the new arrival. That was the way it had been done in his father's time, it had worked well then, and Stax had seen no reason for anything to change.

This visitor came unannounced too.

So it was that Stax was finishing breakfast in the house and explaining to Emerald that no, he couldn't have another cod when he spotted a boat made of dark wood approaching the southern shore.

"What's this now, kitties?" he asked, mildly annoyed, and looked across the lawn to see if another boat was arriving in the cove, where it belonged. But there was nothing there.

"What's this?" Stax asked again, as the boat neared their little family dock and the person inside shipped his oars. He was definitely going to land.

"What a bother," said Stax, checking to see if his robe was clean and deciding it was clean enough. "What a bore."

He was still muttering variations on this as he opened the south door—he got to "inconvenience" and "imposition" while pulling on his right shoe—and started across the lawn. The sheep, not used to seeing him at that hour, offered bleats and baas of curiosity, or at least as close as sheep get to being curious about things.

The hill fell away to the water on the south and west side of the sheep pen, and on the west side Stax's father had built a trim little boathouse of birch, with a dock extending out into the water. It was Stax's favorite place on the estate, and on many mornings he and the cats liked to eat breakfast out on the dock, after which the cats and sometimes Stax would enjoy a brief snooze.

Sandstone steps led down to the water from the south lawn, and as Stax strode down them the visitor stepped out of his boat and turned to face him. He was slim and not much older than Stax, with bright blue eyes that were always in motion, jumping from Stax to the boathouse to the larger house at the top of the hill.

Something else struck Stax as odd: The visitor was wearing a suit of mismatched armor—a gold chestplate above diamond leggings and leather boots—and his clothes were a riot of clashing colors and looked like they didn't fit. Some of his garments were too small, to the point of looking uncomfortably tight, while others were baggy and saggy. A diamond sword hung at his hip but his belt was too big, and he kept hitching it up as he took in his surroundings.

"Good morning," Stax said, remembering he should be polite before shooing the visitor away. "I'm afraid I must have forgotten our appointment, Mister . . . ?"

"Oh, we didn't have an appointment," the man said with a smile that struck Stax as faintly mocking. "Boring things, appointments. I go where I want, when I want. And now I'm here."

That sounded faintly rude, and Stax didn't like it. His father probably would have turned it into a joke, but then his father loved visitors and meeting new people, and at some point while living alone Stax had decided he wasn't fond of either. Or rather, he hadn't quite decided that but had started acting as if he had, until they'd become one and the same thing. That can happen to people who spend too long with only themselves for company, and I'm afraid it had happened to Stax.

So instead of making a joke, or turning the conversation somewhere different, Stax stared at the new arrival and crossed his arms over his chest.

"And your business is . . . ?" he asked.

"You might call me a collector," the man said, his eyes studying the house with his intent blue gaze. "Of experiences."

"I don't see how experiences can be collected," Stax said.

Now the man laughed, a braying guffaw that went on an uncomfortably long time.

"I'm sure you don't, Stax Stonecutter," he said.

Stax had made up his mind that he didn't like this unannounced visitor, but it was mildly reassuring that the man knew Stax's name. That suggested he at least had some reason for arriving on the dock. He tried to think of how his father would have handled this situation.

"You have me at a disadvantage," Stax said. "You know my name, but I'm afraid I don't know yours."

"That's because I haven't said it. But since we're going to be well acquainted, it's time I did. Fouge Tempro, at your service."

And Fouge Tempro gave Stax a low bow, then looked up with a grin that struck Stax as unsettlingly similar to the look a predator might give a particularly plump meal. And what did that mean that they were going to be well acquainted?

Stax reluctantly decided his father would have treated this Fouge Tempro like any other potential business partner, even though he had arrived unannounced and was behaving strangely, even rudely. "Never let a poor first impression get in the way of turning a profit," his father had said—or at least that sounded like something he might have said.

Stax didn't like the idea—what he most wanted to do was order the man to go away, and this minute—but he forced himself to behave the way he thought his father would have.

"Well, now that we know each other, how I can help you, Mr. Tempro?" Stax asked.

"By giving me a tour of your home," Fouge said. "It's an impressive property. You must have worked very hard to make it what it is."

"Well, yes," Stax said. "Er, that is, my father did most of the work, to be honest. My job is more to keep things running."

"And what does that require?" Fouge asked.

"Why, well . . . hmm." Stax wasn't quite sure what to say. Cutting down the occasional oak tree and plucking tufts of tall grass from the lawn didn't seem like the kind of work that would impress a potential business partner.

"The house mostly runs itself, to be honest," he said. "As does the business. Really, Mr. Tempro, you should have stopped by our office before your visit. There you could see samples of the minerals we mine, as well as blocks we've shaped and polished. I assure you our workers are the best in the business. Stonecutter by name, stonecutter by trade—that's what we say!"

This forced cheerfulness sounded ridiculous to him, but Fouge was barely listening.

"Offices, bah," he said. "Offices are where people go to die, once they've given up and accepted what the world thinks they should be. For a collector like me, the home is the key to understanding a person's soul. So, lead on, Mr. Stonecutter!"

And he gestured at the house, as if their roles were reversed and Fouge was the one who lived there and Stax the visitor asking for a favor.

Stax was so flummoxed that before he quite knew what was happening he was leading Fouge around the grounds, showing him the allée of birches and pointing out that the fountain's central pillar was made of glowstone, which lit up the lawn at night.

Now, if you're like me, you're probably thinking, NO, STAX, DON'T! CAN'T YOU SEE THIS IS A HORRIBLE MISTAKE?

And, without skipping ahead too much, I can tell you that Stax spent many, many lonely nights and anxious days thinking something very much like that. But Stax had grown up happy and comfortable, without ever having been touched by evil, and like most people who grow up that way, he thought that meant evil never would touch him. He would figure out that he was terribly wrong about that, but by then of course it would be too late.

Fouge said little during the tour of the grounds, which made Stax wonder if he were bored. But being in his familiar surroundings made Stax feel more at ease, and slightly less irritated at having his peace interrupted. And anyway he was genuinely proud of the estate, from its energetically squawking chickens and multi-hued sheep to the drifts of flowers that carpeted the terraced hills. Before too long he was enjoying giving the tour, at least a little, and he opened the front door and invited Fouge inside.

Coal, Lapis, and Emerald heard the door open and sauntered out of the bedroom, where they'd been sleeping in a puddle of sunshine. But all three cats stopped at the sight of Fouge Tempro, their tails suddenly held low.

"Hello, kitties," Stax said brightly. "We have a visitor!"

One of the things about Stax that annoyed his neighbors and the workers at the Stonecutter office was how Stax seemed much more at ease talking with his cats than with other people. He was more cheerful with the cats and somehow better at making conversation, even though, as far as his neighbors knew, the cats had never held up their end of the bargain.

This time, however, the cats' opinions were clear. Coal hissed at Fouge, her black tail swollen into a bottle brush.

"Now, Coal, mind your manners—" Stax began, but before he could finish all three cats shot off in different directions, making themselves scarce.

"Huh," Stax said, scratching his head. "I don't know what got into them."

"Animals don't like me, and I don't much like them," Fouge said matter-of-factly. "Lead on, Mr. Stonecutter. Lead on."

Fouge had no more to say about the inside of the house than he'd had about the grounds. His eyes skittered over the paintings, the furniture, and the flowers in their pots, betraying no apparent interest—until Stax led him to the trophy room.

"This room is on the site where my grandmother spent her very first night here," Stax said. "That was just a hole hacked out of the hillside. Grandmother didn't even have a bed. She huddled inside all night, listening to monsters howl on the other side of a dirt wall. And look at it now."

Stax looked proudly around the room at the polished diorite-and-granite walls, the gleaming suits of armor that had belonged to his grandmother and father, the framed blocks of precious metals that symbolized the Stonecutters' good fortune, and the massive map that covered an entire wall.

"You should have left the hidey-hole as it was," Fouge said. "As a reminder."

"Oh, I don't need a reminder," Stax said. "That's what this room is all about."

"It's certainly impressive," Fouge said, walking up to the map and craning his neck to see it better, his eyes tracing the blue squiggles of rivers through green swathes of forest and jungle. "But what are all these flags I see on this map?"

"Outposts of the family business," Stax said. "Some are houses—none as impressive as this one, mind you. Others are little more than a hollowed-out space with a bed, a furnace, and a crafting table. My father created a network of them for his business dealings."

"What a busy man your father was," Fouge said. "What happened to him, then?"

"He died a few years ago," Stax said. "His boat was lost on a trip back from our southern operations, just a month after Grandmother's death. And my mother passed away when I was a boy. So it's just me."

"Hard to be all alone in the world, with no one to watch out for you," Fouge said.

"I miss them, every day," Stax said. "But I can take care of myself."

"Can you, then?" Fouge asked, but he wasn't even looking at Stax; he was intently studying the map. He pointed to a green flag at its center. "We're here, are we not?"

"That's right. That's the Stonecutter peninsula. Home."

"And this would be the ice field I had to navigate to reach you," Fouge said, tapping a section of the map just east of the peninsula. "Hazardous seas, Mr. Stonecutter. But of course you'd know that, seeing how you live so close to the icebergs."

"Oh, I've never taken a boat out there. Too dangerous. Too risky. What would be the purpose of a journey like that, Mr. Tempro?"

"To see what's practically at your front door," Fouge said, then shook his head. "Never mind. What about this flag here, up in this orange area to the north? That must be an interesting spot."

"Badlands, by the look of it. Never been there either," Stax said, a bit stiffly. "The folks in our office could tell you more about the outposts, if that's what you're interested in."

"It seems you've never been much of anywhere," Fouge said, and Stax opened his mouth to object, thinking that was the final straw and this was his chance to order this disagreeable man to leave.

But before Stax could get the words out, Fouge smiled broadly.

"But then who can blame you for staying home, when you live surrounded by such beauty?"

That was the first polite thing Fouge had said. Stax decided to look at the bright side—it was good that the man had finally remembered his manners. Stax nodded modestly, but Fouge had already turned to look out into the back garden, his eyes moving from the pool to the hatch in the lawn.

"That hatch leads to the main Stonecutter mine," Stax said, a bit reluctant but determined to do what was right for the business. "Would you like to see it?"

"Very much so," said Fouge, and Stax led him out the back door into the backyard, then opened the hatch. He climbed down a ladder that ended at the top of a narrow stone staircase, then waited for Fouge to join him. It was cool belowground, with a faint ripple of a breeze rising up the stairs.

"This way," said Stax, and picked his way down the stairs, his footsteps echoing in the narrow space. About ten blocks down there was a landing with a door and a narrow window looking into a storeroom that contained mining tools and other supplies. From there the staircase turned and descended deeper into the ground, but was no longer enclosed by a wall on the right.

"Watch your step. Sometimes visitors get a little disoriented here," Stax warned as Fouge picked his way down behind him.

"Why would they—oh," said Fouge, and one hand reached reflexively for the wall. "Aha."

Below them, a vast shaft plunged into the depths. Its opening was twenty blocks wide on each side, the walls rough-hewn stone, with a narrow staircase clinging to them. Down, down, down ran the steps, looking like a thin thread that had been glued to the rock. Torches had been hammered into the walls at irregular intervals, and Stax could see the speckles of their orange light down in the darkness. A rising wind made the flames gutter and their clothing ripple.

"How deep does it go?" Fouge asked, his back against the wall.

"All the way to bedrock—as deep as you can mine," Stax said, then pointed up at the roof. "And that's the bottom of the pool, believe it or not."

"That would make me nervous, sitting over so much nothing," said Fouge.

"Oh no, it's very safe," Stax said, taking a nonchalant step over to the edge of the staircase and peering down into the depths.

"Shouldn't you be careful, Mr. Stonecutter? You might take a bad step."

"I'm used to it," Stax said. "This is my backyard, remember? I spent my teenage years down here, learning the family trade. Figuring out the best levels to mine, how to avoid lava and water, techniques for finding the richest veins. Those sorts of things."

"I'd be nervous someone might give me a push," Fouge said, and Stax's heart jumped at the realization that he'd turned his back on his strange visitor. He took a hasty step down, out of Fouge's reach, but looked up to see the man still had his back pressed against the wall.

Stax told himself he was being ridiculous. The man was rude and strange, but that didn't make him a criminal, let alone a murderer.

"A Stonecutter can't be afraid of heights, Mr. Tempro," Stax said. "Or enclosed spaces, for that matter."

"I can imagine," Fouge said, taking a cautious peek below them. "So this is where the vast Stonecutter wealth comes from."

"Oh, I wouldn't call our wealth 'vast,' and we have a lot of mines besides this one," Stax said. "But yes, this was the first one. Grandmother started the digging, mostly for coal and diorite. Then she and my father expanded operations, tunneling all the way down to bedrock and excavating the mine complex just above it. From the central shaft—that's what we're standing in—tunnels run on for hundreds of blocks in every direction."

"It must be easy to get lost," Fouge said.

"Oh no, it's actually nearly impossible. We have a system, you see. The feeder tunnels are always two blocks wide, so you can tell you're in one. Then the branch tunnels are a single block wide, and arrayed in a grid around the feeder tunnels. Like twigs around a tree limb, or limbs around a trunk. But really, it's simpler if we go down so you can see for yourself."

Stax beckoned to his guest, and for a moment Fouge did look out and down, at the line of stairs snaking its way ever lower around the edges down the shaft. But then he paled and retreated to the relative safety of the wall.

"Surely you should bring a weapon, if we're to go down so far," Fouge said.

"In Grandmother's mine?" Stax asked. "Oh no. I've never carried one—not when I learned to mine back in the day, and not on inspections now. And no armor either. All that weight would just be a burden, and climbing these stairs is tiring enough."

"And here I thought you were never reckless, Stax Stonecutter," Fouge said, his eyes glittering. "Yet it turns out you go gallivanting through the lightless bowels of the world without so much as a little knife in your hand or a tin pot on your head to keep your skull from getting cracked."

Stax laughed. "The mines used to be perilous, true. Grandmother would tell tales of fighting skeletons in the dark that would make your hair stand on end. But any caverns were cleared out or sealed off long ago, and the shaft is inaccessible from the outside. Nothing can get in except through that hatch up above us. And I assure you everything is well lit, Mr. Tempro. It wouldn't do to have evil things taking up residence on the premises, now would it?"

"No, I imagine it wouldn't," Fouge said. "I thank you for the tour. It's been most informative."

And then, without waiting for Stax, he headed back up the narrow staircase.

By now Stax had grown used to his visitor's abrupt manner, and figured it was Fouge's fear of heights that had caused him to retreat to the world of bright sunshine and green grass. As they reentered the house, Fouge seemed lost in thought. But his eyes settled on the well-worn stone pickaxe and blunt stone sword in their frames.

"Quite a place of honor for a pair of broken things," he said.

"Those were Grandmother's. She made them that first night, in her dirt hidey-hole," Stax explained. "They were worn almost down to nothing by the time she hit her first vein of iron, but Grandmother never threw anything away. Father put them here, to remind us of where we'd come from."

"Ah," Fouge said, and ran a pale finger over the pitted edge of the blade.

"I'm sure that seems odd to you," Stax said. For in truth, he'd always thought the old pickaxe and sword looked shabby, and he'd thought about putting them away in a storeroom and finding something else for that space—perhaps a bright, cheery painting or an arrangement of flowers.

"It doesn't seem odd to me at all," Fouge said. "In fact, I'd call them the most valuable items in the house. I can't wait for my associates to get a look at them."

"Associates?" asked Stax, who was very much looking forward to being rid of Fouge.

"Oh yes. I've worked with them for years. Very capable fellows," Fouge said, striding through the living room. "They're tough in a fight and loyal because I pay them to be. I thought I'd bring them by day after tomorrow."

For a moment Stax felt like he was falling. But then he got his bearings, and as they crossed the south lawn he shook his head at Fouge in what he hoped was a stern manner.

"I have to insist that our future dealings go through the office. That will be much more efficient, for both of us."

"But it won't be more efficient," Fouge said, striding down the sandstone stairs to the boathouse and the dock. "It won't be, at all. My business is here, with you."

Stax wondered what his father would say in *this* situation — and reluctantly decided he'd say Fouge Tempro was a difficult and demanding customer, but a customer nonetheless. But it was distasteful, to say the very least, to think of yet more strangers in his house, and another morning spoiled. Particularly if Fouge's associates had the same deplorable lack of manners as their boss. What if they tracked in mud, or stepped on the flowers?

"No, the day after tomorrow simply won't do," Stax said, stalling for time. "I'm frightfully busy, you see. There's much to do on the estate, and I simply couldn't clear my schedule. It's quite impossible."

Fouge smiled his unpleasant smile, the one that made Stax think of a wolf that had cornered a lamb.

"Yes, it's obvious you're a very busy fellow, Stax," he said. "What's on your overflowing to-do list, then?"

"Well, um, there are cornflowers to be planted on the ridge," Stax said. "And the birches need to be trimmed — they're frightfully shaggy. Three flowerpots need to be made, and I don't have any clay in the storeroom, so that's a whole expedition right there. And, well, look right there, that plank on the deck is cracked. Needs replacing."

"That *does* seem like a lot of work," Fouge said. "And how long will these labors take you, do you think?"

It occurred to Stax that none of this was Fouge's business, and he shouldn't have discussed any of it with him. But it also occurred to him that it was too late to do anything about it.

"Oh, that's probably a week," Stax said, thinking a week would surely be too long for Fouge to wait. He would have business elsewhere, and he would leave Stax in peace, and pretty soon the entire unpleasant morning would fade from memory.

But Fouge just smiled and gave Stax a little bow.

"A week, then. I'm looking forward to it, Stax Stonecutter."

Stax forced himself to smile back, and say something polite and meaningless as Fouge rearranged his baggy, ill-fitting garments and grasped the oars of his boat.

But Stax wasn't looking forward to it, not at all.

CHAPTER 4

FIRE AND RUIN

A lazy morning interrupted * Terrible things * The cats'
hiding place discovered * Stax has a question

And then something happened that's unfortunate but under-standable, or at least I think so: Stax forgot.

Oh, he didn't forget for the rest of that day, or the next. In fact, he was agitated much of the time on both those days. Every stray moment—and Stax, as you've learned, had a lot of stray moments—his thoughts returned to Fouge Tempro, and how rude he'd been, and what a nuisance his associates would doubt-less prove to be, and what the nature of his proposed business might be, and whether doing business with Fouge might mean having to put up with him being a frequent visitor, and why he had to put up with visitors at all, and even thinking about all that was more than Stax could bear.

But the next day Stax planted a drift of cornflowers on the

ridge, above the allée of birches, and was pleased by the splash of blue it added to the hillside. The day after that he fixed the cracked board on the boat dock, while Coal, Lapis, and Emerald snoozed on their backs with their bellies pointed up at the sun, and it was such a nice day that Stax thought of his disagreeable visitor only three or four times. Then the day after that Stax trimmed back the shaggy birches, and hardly thought of Fouge at all. On the fourth day after Fouge's visit, Stax couldn't think of anything he needed to do—he'd entirely forgotten about the flowerpots and the expedition to fetch clay—and so he spent the morning fishing from the dock while the cats meowed encouragement, and then he spent the afternoon puttering in his father's library.

Stax was used to being reminded about his business appointments by the Stonecutter office, which would send a messenger out to the estate to prevent an important visitor from finding Stax, say, mucking out the cow pen. (No, really; that had happened not once, but twice.) But Stax had never gone to the office to warn them about Fouge, because thinking about Fouge upset him too much. So no one there thought to ask about the possibility of a return visit, or warn Stax that something bad might happen.

Stax forgot, and the next couple of days slipped by, tranquil and torpid and free of not just trouble but even the thought of it.

A week after Fouge's visit, Stax was sitting by the little table on the end of the boathouse dock. He'd finished a leisurely breakfast, with a smear of honey remaining on his plate, and was skimming *Optimized Mining Practices for Locating Emerald Deposits*, a book from his father's library that was even more boring than its title might suggest. Coal, Lapis, and Emerald lay in lazy S figures around him, next to the picked-over bones of fishes.

When he saw the first boat in the distance to the south, Stax thought it was a cloud near the horizon. But this cloud kept growing, and pretty soon Stax saw it was a boat, and that there were other boats behind it—more than a dozen, in fact.

"Why can't that horrible man use the cove like he's supposed to?" Stax asked the sleeping cats, who ignored him, unless a sleepy flick of Emerald's tail counted as an answer.

As the boats drew closer, Stax became more uneasy. He could see Fouge standing in the lead boat, his blond hair shining in the sun, and he was pretty sure the man was smiling that unsettling, predatory smile of his. The other boats were festooned with banners—black-and-purple, red-and-gold, green–and–sickly pink—and filled with rough-looking men and women, the sun flashing on swords and axes.

Lapis was the first of the cats to awaken, and she hissed and growled low in her throat, her tail held back behind her.

"It'll be okay, kitties," Stax said, getting to his feet. But he heard the doubt in his own voice, and realized he no longer believed that.

Move, he told himself. *Go! Run!*

But he couldn't make his feet move. He felt frozen, like he was trapped in a dream where he kept trying to run but found himself stuck in place.

The cats shot off up the stone stairs when Fouge's boat ground against the side of the slip with a groan of wood. Fouge stepped nimbly onto the dock as the other boats bumped up against the steps. Their occupants leapt out into the shallow water, looking up at the house and laughing.

"Stax Stonecutter," Fouge said. "So good to see you again. I'd introduce you to my associates, but well, there're quite a lot of them and they're going to be very busy. And you'll have time to get acquainted later."

"Now see here," Stax managed. "This has gone quite too far. I insist that you visit our office. That's the proper way to—"

Fouge had been listening silently, with a slight smile on his face. As Stax lectured him, he picked up *Optimized Mining Practices for Locating Emerald Deposits* where it lay on the table, glanced at it, and then tossed it into the sea.

"Hey!" Stax cried out, staring at the book where it was bobbing, facedown, in the swells. "That's Father's book!"

"And now it belongs to the deep," Fouge said. "A trophy for puffer fish, maybe. A plaything for dolphins. Who's to say?"

"You have no right—"

"Look at my associates' weapons, Stax," Fouge said. "Gleaming iron, sharp arrowheads and shafts, and diamond honed to a razor's edge. Those give me the right to do as I please, as long as I'm strong enough. And ultimately, in this world, that's the only right that matters. Ladies and gentlemen, take Mr. Stonecutter in hand and make sure he has a good view."

"A good view? What are you going to do?"

But Fouge was opening the boathouse door and directing some of his associates inside, while other bandits climbed the stairs to the house.

"You're going to rob me?" Stax demanded.

"For starters," Fouge said, and gestured for several raiders to follow him up the stairs. Two burly men seized Stax by each wrist and dragged him along behind them. He heard glass shattering and looked back to see a raider had bashed his sword through the boathouse's window, while another had brought his axe down on the railing of the dock.

"Help! Robbery! Help!" Stax yelled, but he lived alone, far from his neighbors, and so there was no one to hear and no one to help. Fouge didn't even look back, and the raiders just laughed as they hauled him up the steps and forced him inside the house.

Fouge's associates had already been at work in the trophy room and the storerooms. A line of raiders passed by Stax, their arms filled with iron ingots and diamonds. They'd ripped down the map in the trophy room and carried it out in pieces, and Stax saw his grandmother's armor departing, one diamond piece at a time.

"Got a bottleneck here at the door, boss," grumbled a black-bearded man. "Too many what's goin' out while too many others is goin' in."

"So make a bigger door," Fouge said.

The man nodded and barked orders and the raiders smashed down the glass walls, leaving the house open on all sides. That freed them to carry out paintings and furniture and tools, like a swarm of furious ants serving their queen. Stax watched in horror as raiders worked in pairs outside to chop down the birches and rip out the flower beds, while others broke down the fences keeping the cows and pigs and sheep penned up. Confused and frightened, the sheep raced in all directions, bumping into one another and bleating in distress as the raiders laughed and jumped at them to spook them further.

"Leave my animals alone!" Stax yelled.

"Or you'll do what, little man?" asked a grinning bandit carrying away a stack of his father's books.

Nothing. There was nothing he could do, not against such numbers. There were too many of them, they were all heavily armed, and they were veteran warriors, while Stax had rarely lifted a blade to deal with anything that wasn't vegetation. He sank to his knees in despair as the destruction raged around him.

He was still there, limp with shock, when Fouge arrived half an hour later, whistling cheerfully as he yanked Stax's grandmother's stone pickaxe off the wall, along with its frame.

"Stax, come with me," he said. "You're not going to want to miss this part."

When Stax said nothing, Fouge ordered two ruffians to drag him to the back door. Fouge pointed to where a pair of his bandits were standing by the diorite swimming pool, bundles of red explosives in their arms.

"Do you know what that is, Stax?" Fouge asked.

"TNT," Stax said hollowly. "It's used for mining. Or rather, it's used by fools who don't care about putting themselves or others in danger."

"Oh, we'll be careful. Now watch."

Fouge nodded and the two bandits lit arrows, then fired them at the TNT. It ignited, with the detonation knocking both raiders backward. Stax raised his arms reflexively against the blast. He heard a roar of overstressed stone and then the bottom of the pool collapsed, sending water pouring through the breach into the Stonecutter mine.

"I've just created the Overworld's deepest swimming pool," Fouge said. "Wouldn't you say so, Stax?"

That was when Stax caught sight of a black shape in the shadows by the now-wrecked pool. It was Coal; the explosion had frightened her out of whatever hiding place she'd found.

Stax forced himself to look away, hoping Fouge wouldn't spot her. But Fouge had seen the black cat, just as he'd seen Lapis and Emerald, who were huddled behind Coal, all of them wild-eyed with fright. He gestured to the raiders.

"No!" Stax cried out. "Do what you want to me, do what you want to the house, but don't hurt my cats! They've done nothing to you!"

"Well, neither have you," Fouge said.

One of the raiders crouched down and reached out to the cats, a wide smile on his face, and made *psst-psst* noises of enticement. Stax opened his mouth to yell a warning, only to have Fouge clamp a hand over it.

"Stax!" he said mildly, wagging a finger. "That's *cheating!*"

Stax stared in horror as the cats shrank back from the raider's outstretched hand. Silently, he begged them not to fall for the trick. They hesitated, uncertain, and then Coal hissed and spat. A moment later all three cats had shot up the cracked diorite stairs and vanished into the shadows of the garden.

Stax closed his eyes in relief, but Fouge just shrugged.

"Our work is almost done, anyway," he said. "In fact, it's time for the finale, Stax."

They dragged Stax out into the yard, now marred by pits and littered with broken birch limbs. He watched as the raiders bashed down the diorite-and-granite walls and tore up the stairs. The animals had fled or been carried away, the fountain was shattered and befouled, and the fences had been toppled.

"That ought to do it," Fouge said. "Set the rest on fire."

A raider poured lava from a bucket into the center of the living room, then hurried out as the remains of the carpet caught fire. Fouge nodded and marched away, down the sandstone steps. The planks of the dock were floating in the water and the little trim boathouse was a burning, roofless shell. The boats sat low in the water, overloaded with goods pillaged from the Stonecutter estate. At Fouge's orders, Stax was forced into one of the boats and made to sit by a big, black-bearded ruffian at the oars. The man was wearing Stax's third-favorite shirt, the yellow one with red dragons on it.

"Comfy, Stax?" Fouge asked. "I hope so. We have a long journey ahead of us."

Stax looked at Fouge and found his face outlined by the burning boathouse, a red halo of fire. It was twilight and bright cinders were drifting through the air like little stars.

"Why?" he managed to ask.

"You know, everyone always wants to know that," Fouge said. And then he shrugged. "It's funny."

Stax stared at Fouge, waiting, and it wasn't until the bandit leader had climbed into his own boat that he realized that there wouldn't be more. Fouge had given him the only answer he was going to get.

CHAPTER 5

INTO THE UNKNOWN

An inhabitant of the ice * A journey through
rough seas * Fouge discusses the world *
A night around the campfire

It was quiet on the water, with no sound except the *shoosh* of oars in the water and an occasional grunt from the raiders at their work. Night fell, and soon the stars were spilled out over Stax's head, shimmering constellations slowly wheeling above him.

The raiders' path took them between giant spikes of ice that rose from the ocean around the Stonecutter estate. Stax shivered; it was a warm night, but occasionally drafts of cold air swept down from the ice floes and over the water. Looming above them, the ice seemed to glow with its own light, which was a gentle, pale blue. Stax could hear faint creaks and groans in the night around him. At first he thought it was the raiders, tired after their grim work, but then he realized it was the ice shifting and settling, the equivalent of a sleeper turning over in an effort to find a comfortable position.

It's beautiful out here, Stax thought to himself. *And I never knew it.*

If you're thinking that's a strange thought for someone who'd just been kidnapped and seen his home reduced to ruins, a moment later Stax had the same reaction. He wondered why he wasn't screaming, or trying to fight the black-bearded raider, or doing something. But everything still felt slightly unreal, like he was dreaming.

And the pillars of ice really *were* beautiful.

A moment later, though, something growled in the darkness — a low warning sound that Stax could somehow tell was made by something large and powerful. He peered into the gloom, trying to spot its source, but was confused by the echoes bouncing around in the labyrinth of ice slabs.

Next to the boat carrying Stax and the black-bearded ruffian was another one, rowed by a smaller, sour-faced man.

"That'd be one of them white bears," the black-bearded raider grunted to his colleague. "Give it space. That noise means it's got young with it. They're vicious things — tear yer head clean off."

"That's exactly what you all deserve," grumbled Stax, which earned him a smack across the face.

"You *dare* — " Stax spluttered.

"Oh, I dare," the black-bearded raider said. "Gimme a reason, fancy boy, and I'll end yer adventure right here."

Stax shrank away from the raider, who went back to his rowing with a last warning glower.

"Can't see a thing out here," the sour-faced rower complained. "We could be right on top of that beast and not even know it. Foolish choice, travelin' by night."

"Yeh don't like it, take it up with the boss. Orders are that we keep movin'."

The boat slowed. Stax could see the pale shapes of the other boats, but they were hard to tell apart from the drifting ice — or the mysterious white bears.

Part of him hoped he'd be able to see the attack, if it came; he would take a grim satisfaction in watching a furious bear sink the boats and tear into the outlaws that had destroyed his home. In fact, he realized he could raise a ruckus in hope of drawing the bear's attention. But then he thought of himself bobbing helplessly in the icy water, surrounded by bodies and wreckage and having to choose between freezing to death and walking into a predator's teeth and claws.

No, Stax decided, he would wait. He would wait and hope for a chance to get away, or get revenge, or do something other than sit there as a helpless prisoner. His house — whatever was left of it — was behind him, just on the other side of the ice field. He would be able to find his way back, and comfort the cats, and find shelter. And then he'd figure out how to track down Fouge and his raiders and make them pay.

But he wouldn't be able to do any of that frozen in the water or in a bear's stomach. So he told himself to be patient and then leaned forward and scanned the gloom of the ice field, trying to find the bear.

When he did, he drew back in shock and surprise. He couldn't see the bear itself — just a suggestion of a great white mass — but a torch held by a raider in another boat was reflected in its eyes, which shone in the darkness ahead of them, like two great lanterns.

"There!" Stax said, his voice urgent, his finger outstretched.

"Quiet, yeh miserable stupid—" the black-bearded raider began, but then he saw where Stax was pointing and stopped. Hasty, hushed conversation was made, and the raiders cut to their right, seeking another path through the blocks of ice. Stax kept his eyes fixed on the bear, and the great eyes remained fixed on him, with the huge beast growling continuously until the boats were past it.

The boats made slow progress through the labyrinth, and eventually Stax felt his eyelids drooping. His chin began to sag onto his chest, and finally he fell into a fitful, uncomfortable doze. The night passed that way, interrupted by brief glimpses of dark water around them, and the ceaseless stars above them.

Stax woke up completely when the boat scraped across sand and gravel, grinding to a halt. Someone was shaking him roughly. It was the black-bearded raider, and he looked weary and mean after a night's work at the oars.

"Out, yeh," the man snarled. "No time for freeloaders."

Blinking, Stax found himself on a bleak gray shore beneath a bluff of exposed dirt. Above the dirt were gray mountains rising into clouds tinged pink by the dawn. He looked back across the water, hoping to spot the ice field, but saw nothing but the sea, dotted with the raiders' other boats.

"Where are we?" he asked dully. His neck hurt abominably from being slumped in the boat all night, salt had left his eyes stinging and his clothes stiff, and his wrists were raw and chafed from being bound.

The raiders just ignored him, barking out orders. A few clambered up the bluff, axes in hand, to chop down trees. They let Stax walk in a small circle on the beach, trying to work the stiffness out of his legs.

"Well, good morning, Stax!" called a cheerful voice.

Stax looked over and saw Fouge grinning from his own boat, beneath a black banner.

"Dangerous seas ahead," Fouge said. "You don't get seasick, do you?"

Stax felt his anger rise up, but before he could yell or make a rush at Fouge's boat, helplessness seemed to overcome him and suddenly his arms and legs felt impossibly heavy.

"That's right, you don't know if you get seasick," Fouge said. "Because you've never been anywhere. I guess we'll find out, won't we?"

"Question, boss?" grumbled the black-bearded raider.

"What is it, Miggs?"

"Can we camp here?" Miggs asked, wiping his dirty hands on what was no longer Stax's shirt. "My rowers are tired and could use a rest."

"No," Fouge said immediately. "These waters are crawling with drowned, and where those things are lurking, worse things aren't far behind. If we make good time, we can camp tonight."

"But, boss—" Miggs began.

"I said no," Fouge said sharply. "Presumably you understand what 'no' means."

Fouge signaled to his own rower. They began to pull and soon his boat had dwindled to a pale dot against the gray sea.

"Yeh heard the boss. Hurry it up!" Miggs yelled, and the raiders came back down the hill, carrying chunks of timber.

He turned his baleful gaze on Stax. "As for yeh, back in the boat. I'm tired of rowin' yeh around while yeh sit there and do nothin'."

He gave Stax a shove in the back, hard enough that he almost fell.

"So just leave me here, then," Stax said. The little spit of land looked grim and uninviting, but anything was better than whatever Fouge and his raiders had in mind for him. "I've nothing else you can steal, and I'm just slowing you down."

"Wish I could," Miggs growled. "But the boss says otherwise. He's got plans for yeh, fancy boy."

The other raiders began to laugh, a sound that Stax didn't like at all.

Miggs's boat joined a line of craft rowing across the dark gray sea beneath a low sky with clouds like old iron. The sun shone wanly through them, and Stax shivered. Dark clouds hid the sun and it began to rain.

"Don't yeh dare lose sight of the next line of boats!" Miggs yelled across the water to the sallow-faced man, his muscles straining at the oars. "We'll be lost out here forever!"

The boat lurched sideways and Stax slipped off the bench. He huddled in the bottom of the boat, immediately soaking his legs and rear end. Within minutes he was violently sick, heaving and spitting.

The sallow-faced man laughed, and Miggs glowered at him. "Stick to yer rowing, Kivak," he growled. He gave Stax a look of disgust, but was too busy to do anything else. When Stax's stomach was finally empty, he just groaned and clung to the bench, only half-conscious. After an hour or so he was able to drag himself back up to a sitting position. He remained there, wet and miserable, as the boats spent hours crawling through the water.

The sun shone dully near the horizon to the right of the boat. Stax supposed that meant they were going south, and tried to remember where the sun had been at various times during the journey. But it was hopeless—a jumble of impressions and brief glances. He had no idea where they were, or the path they'd taken from the estate. They could have been anywhere.

They were heading for an island, he saw now—a spit of beach in the middle of the emptiness. He could see torches moving back and forth across it, and boats on the shore. Miggs's boat ground to a stop and he and Kivak dragged Stax out by the back of his shirt, leaving him on his knees in grit and muck. Stax forced himself to stand up, but the land seemed to be heaving up and down, like he was still on a boat. Disoriented, he staggered a couple of blocks up the beach and half-sat, half-collapsed on the sand.

The camp was buzzing with activity, with raiders setting torches out in a ring, building a fire, and crafting beds. Fouge stood in the center, the setting sun throwing his elongated shadow across the beach.

"Stax!" he said, with that same fake cheer that made Stax want to scream. "You must be tired. We can't treat an honored guest so poorly, now can we?"

And before Stax quite knew what was happening, he'd been dragged to his feet, the ropes around his wrists had been cut and he was sitting in front of the campfire on a log. Someone pressed a slice of meat into his hands, burnt and blackened from the fire. He sniffed at it: pork. Other raiders were tearing into mutton, chicken legs, and beefsteaks, the juice running down their chins. They were laughing now, the stress of the long ocean passage temporarily forgotten.

Suddenly it occurred to Stax where the food must have come from and he thought about flinging his meal into the fire. But his belly rumbled and he stopped himself. He was starving, and there was no point doing the raiders' cruel work for them. He forced himself to eat, chewing mechanically and staring into the fire, while trying to ignore the crude boasts and insults that passed for conversation among the raiders.

Stax wondered where they'd all come from. They were human, but very different in terms of skin color, size, and dress. There was a mix of men and women, and they ranged from short and wiry to intimidatingly large and muscular. Some had long black beards, while others were bald, their heads covered with tattoos. All of them carried weapons, from bows slung over shoulders to swords and axes. Some were missing eyes, fingers, and even arms.

"Quite a merry band, don't you think?" asked Fouge, settling down on the log next to Stax.

Stax thought about once again asking the raider boss why he'd done what he'd done, but doubted he'd get an answer this time either. And then he thought about ignoring Fouge, but found he couldn't do it.

"What . . . what are you going to do with me?" he finally asked, wondering if the raider would answer.

"You know, I haven't decided," Fouge said, then got to his feet. "Mr. Stonecutter wants to know what we're going to do with him. Any ideas?"

The raiders laughed.

"Drown him in the surf," said Miggs. "I'm tired of him."

"Stake him out for the creepers," suggested a tattooed woman with an eye patch. "And in the morning—KABLAMMO! We'll see how many pieces he's in."

"Leave him here," said Kivak. "Lovely place. Garden spot of the entire Southern Sea."

It went on like that for a while, with each suggestion more barbaric, while Fouge smiled and nodded.

"Any of those ideas appeal to you?" Fouge asked Stax, when the raiders finally ran out of suggestions.

"No," Stax said. "Well, yes, actually. Leave me here."

"Here?" Fouge looked around the island. "There isn't a tree or even any grass. I don't think you'd last very long, Stax."

"What do you care if I die?"

Fouge smiled that predatory smile of his. "Stax, Stax. If I wanted you dead, it would have been a minute's work back at the house. But no. I don't know why I feel this way, but something tells me you have some purpose, some role left to play in our little drama."

"Purpose? Role? Haven't you done enough to me?"

Fouge pursed his lips, considering. "No, I don't think I have. But hey, what a start, right? A couple of days ago you were sitting in your house doing nothing, and here you are having a great adventure. You've done more in the last day or so than in your entire life, wouldn't you say?"

"Great adventure?" Stax sputtered. "You destroyed my house, stole my things, and kidnapped me. That's not an adventure."

"Well, it is for *us*," Fouge said. "We go where we want and do what we want. You should have tried it, all those years you sat there in your house on the hill."

"You're robbers and killers," Stax said. "If everyone did what you've done, no one would live in peace. The world would be an awful place. Is that the kind of world you want?"

Fouge just laughed.

"But Stax, that's the world we live in already," he said. "If I had my followers douse the fire and those torches, do you know how long we'd survive? Within an hour, terrible things would come out of the sea and drag us beneath the waves, or creep out of some hole and put their hands around our throats and squeeze the life out of us. And our story would be over, just like that."

He leaned back and gestured to the sky, where a few stars glimmered through the veil of clouds.

"Look up there, Stax," Fouge said. "Do you think the stars care about you and your house? About me and what I've done, or what I will do? Will the waves break any differently on this miserable bit of sand? Will the sun rise at a different time, by way of protest?

Will the rain come down harder? The world doesn't care about any of us, Stax. The mightiest person is but a momentary nuisance compared with what you see up there. So yes, Stax: Do what you want. It's the only way we'll ever matter."

Stax just shook his head. "You're a monster."

"We're all monsters. The difference is some of us admit it. Now get some sleep, dear boy. We'll be setting off at dawn, so you'll need your rest."

Fouge barked an order and a moment later one of the raiders set a bed down on the sand. Stax looked at it in disbelief, but Fouge just bowed and grinned and strode away from the fire.

Stax poked at the woolen mattress reluctantly, figuring one of the raiders had put some kind of vile creature inside it as a macabre prank. But it was just a mattress, stuffed with wool that was a little stiffened by salt and begrimed with sand but reasonably soft and comfortable despite its rough handling. He climbed into the bed and stared up at the cold stars.

Maybe the stars don't care what happens down here, but I do. Decent people do. Fouge is wrong. Wrong, and selfish, and evil.

And cruel, Stax might have added. Not finding some awful surprise in the bed made Stax even more convinced this was some trick, a torment of Fouge's concocted to amuse him and the rest of his foul band. Stax resolved to stay awake, so he wouldn't be caught unawares. But it was warm by the fire and the bed was comfortable, and so despite his best efforts, within a few seconds he was asleep.

CHAPTER 6

INTO THE SEA OF SORROWS

A brief moment in a better place * Journeying past
forlorn shores * The howling of terrible things *
A hasty farewell

Stax sat on the dock of the boathouse, eating a piece of cake and looking out over the water. A fish jumped a few blocks out from the railing and Coal twitched an ear sleepily, then decided whatever had disturbed her wasn't worth waking up for.

Stax had baked the cake in one of the house's furnaces, after looking up his mother's recipe. He wasn't sure she would have approved of cake for breakfast, but it was good—moist, sweet, and delicious.

Though he hadn't made the recipe quite correctly, it seemed. Beneath the sweetness, there was something gritty and unpleasant in the cake. He could feel it crunching between his back teeth. Almost like it was . . .

. . . sand.

Stax woke up with a start and heard himself cry out. A red-haired woman wearing one of his grandmother's flowerpots as a helmet gaped at him and let out a shriek, then waved her hands in mock fright and laughed. Stax stared at her in puzzlement for a moment before it all came back: the raid on his house, his kidnapping, the grueling journey across the sea as a prisoner.

He was sitting up in a grimy bed on a gray, stony beach, next to a dying fire, and there was sand in his mouth.

"In the boat in two minutes or I'll tie yer hands again," Miggs said, kicking sand in Stax's direction.

Stax turned his head so he didn't get sand in his eyes, then spat out as much of the grit in his mouth as he could. He supposed Miggs's offer was what passed for kindness in the raiders' world, and he wasn't going to pass it up—not when his wrists were still red and painfully raw. He pulled on his boots and waded out to the boat, where Miggs acknowledged him with a reluctant grunt.

"Gonna be a hard day today," Miggs said. "And maybe tomorrow too. We'll be passing dangerous coasts. Yeh gimme any trouble, fancy boy, and we'll see how well yeh can swim."

"Is it true we're going through the Sea of Sorrows?" Kivak asked Miggs, and Stax thought the sallow-faced raider looked frightened.

"We'll go where the boss tells us to go," Miggs said sharply. "No need to put names on where—yeh know he don't like that. Just shut yer mouth and row."

Stax kept his eyes down, trying to avoid incurring either raider's wrath. But he repeated the name Kivak had said in his head over and over, until he was sure he wouldn't forget it: *Sea of Sorrows, Sea of Sorrows, Sea of Sorrows.*

The boats moved out, and for hours everything looked much

the same as it had the previous day: water as far as the eye could see, with the boats feeling tiny and vulnerable in the midst of all that emptiness. On this day, however, there was barely a cloud in the sky, and the sun was high and bright, a brilliant white coin in the dark blue sky. Miggs and Kivak were sweating freely behind the oars, grunting as they worked side by side in their boats.

After a time Stax spotted islands to their left, shimmering in the sunlight, low bits of land covered with trees. Then there were islands on their right as well, a chain of rocks rising out of the water. An hour later the line of islands to their right rose from the sea to become a brooding headland of gray rock. At Fouge's command the boats angled in close to this rugged coast, close enough that Stax could hear surf on the beach and the tumble and shush of the water withdrawing and dragging thousands of pebbles into the waves.

Kivak began to mutter nervously, constantly looking over at the rocks, and Miggs's eyes were wide and white in his tanned face.

"They'll come," Kivak said nervously. "Drowned will come and take us below. Like so many before us."

"Them's tall tales," Miggs said, but Stax could hear the fear in his voice. "Stories to frighten little ones."

"What stories?" Stax asked Kivak, vaguely remembering that Fouge had mentioned the drowned. "What is this place? And what are the drowned?"

"Zombies," Kivak said. "Cursed men and women who died at sea. They say these waters is full of them, on account of all the wrecks. They say at night you can see the moonlight glittering on their tridents. Only if you do, it's too late for you, because the drowned throw those things hard enough to pierce stone, and they return to the dead hand what threw them."

"Not another word, Kivak," said Miggs. "Or I'll throw yeh over the side and let yeh meet one of 'em."

Kivak subsided into muttering, but Stax was staring at the bleak shore, thinking that every gleam and bit of reflection amid the rocks was a weapon in the hand of an undead warrior.

Stax had spotted no signs of life on their journey—no villages, farms, or houses—but now he began to see buildings on the cliffs above them. But all of them were abandoned and forlorn: towers reduced to tumbles and spikes, the burned-out shells of houses, overgrown fields with fallen fences.

"What a dreary place," Stax said.

As if in response, a raider in the line of boats ahead of them turned to call out a warning, her partner waving a torch to get their attention.

"Head to port, Kivak," Miggs growled. "That's yer left."

As Kivak grumbled that he'd known that since he was a lad, Stax spotted the obstacle ahead: a ship, or at least what was left of one, jammed against the rocks. Much of its upper deck had been smashed apart, its masts were gone, and a rock had opened a gash in its bow.

"Don't look, *row*," Miggs told Kivak.

But Stax had no such duties. Filled with dread, he tried to peer through the jagged rents in the wreck's hull, expecting to see some waterlogged corpse waiting with a trident in its hand. But no enemy lurked within, and there was no sound except the splash of oars.

They continued along that lonely shore for hours, passing more shattered towers and broken ships, until Stax had grown numb to the sight of masts sticking out of the waves at odd angles and hulls reduced to clumps of planks.

The boat ahead had slowed, and its rowers waited for Miggs and Kivak to pull alongside.

"The boss says keep going," said a white-haired raider with tattooed tears on her cheeks. "We row through the night."

Kivak started to mutter, but Miggs just nodded as the boat pulled away again. And then he began to row, hard, his muscled arms shooting the boat through the water.

The sun sank in the sky and night crept over the water—a night that Stax would remember forever. The moon rose as the sun disappeared, and it cast a ghostly white radiance over the ruins on the shore and the wrecked ships along it, as well as the things that came out of the forests and up from the swamps to prowl the night.

Stax could see them all too well, and knew they could see him too. Skeletons stood sentinel among the rocks, their bony hands clutching bows, and Stax could hear the hiss of arrows in the air around them. Green-skinned zombies plodded across the beach, their groans carrying through the night, wet and thick with a horrible desire. Stax spotted the green pillars of creepers, their black mouths fixed in silent screams. And there were things he caught only glimpses of—eyes like red lamps, or ones like purple slits, enviously tracking the boats as they passed.

Kivak had left off muttering and was loudly beseeching every god he'd ever heard of for mercy. But though panicked to find himself so close to such denizens of the night, he kept rowing, his knuckles white on the oars. Miggs was silent, his eyes fixed straight ahead, as if he thought refusing to look at something meant it couldn't hurt him.

Stax had neither oar nor weapon, and couldn't defend himself or help row them out of trouble. He could only sit there terrified, wondering when one of those arrows would find its target, or a trident would come through the boat and spear them, or dead hands would rise up from the water to drag them beneath the waves. It wasn't until nearly dawn that he fell into a doze, and even then his dreams were spiked with jolts of panic.

The crews were all exhausted, slumped numbly over the oars, but Fouge refused to call a halt, and so they rowed on for hours and hours, grim and silent, beneath leaden gray skies that seemed to constantly threaten rain. It finally began to drizzle as the day neared its end, with the sun a red smear in the clouds behind them. The drizzle slowly intensified until Miggs was struggling to see the shore and wiping water away from his face.

"What does the boss mean to do, sail on until we fall off the edge of the world?" Kivak wailed from the next boat.

"Keep yer eyes open," Miggs growled. "Or we'll come to a bad end long before then."

It grew harder and harder to see, and Stax sagged in relief when word came that Fouge had finally agreed to make camp in a little bay up ahead.

The bay was sheltered, but Kivak began muttering as soon as he saw it. It was bleak and sandy, little more than a low, swampy stretch carpeted with brambles and scrub, below sandy hills. The keel of a wrecked ship was visible above the water just offshore, and in the center of the bay stood the stump of a tower of gray stone, surrounded by tumbled blocks overgrown with moss.

"That's an unlucky shore, sure as I'm a sailor," Kivak muttered, and Miggs had to shout at him to bring his boat into the shallows where the rest of the raiders were unloading their gear and Stax's stolen property and trying to build a fire.

Stax stumbled when he got off the boat, his legs stiff and

cramped. Miggs was too exhausted to pay much attention as he trudged up the beach to warm himself by the fire. Fouge was barking orders, his face grim, but forced a smile onto his face when he saw Stax.

"I think we've found your new home, Stax," he said. "It even comes with a house! Not quite as fancy as you're used to, but it's a fixer-upper."

Stax looked around the grim swamp with alarm. While huddled at Miggs's feet, he would have said he'd take his chances ashore—or anywhere besides the boat. But now that idea seemed insane.

And there was something else: a nameless dread he could feel, like a chill crawling up the back of his neck. You know how sometimes you can feel someone's looking at you, even if you couldn't say how you know? That's something like what Stax felt, only he also felt that whatever was watching was simultaneously hungry and *patient*, willing to wait for the perfect opportunity to strike. There was something wrong here, something terribly wrong, and though he was neither a warrior nor an explorer, he could feel it.

And he wasn't the only one. As he sat slumped on a chunk of stone, Stax could see the way the raiders hurried up the beach after unloading a boat, and the fear in their faces when they looked out at the water. He could see the way they shied from the shattered stones of the tower, and peered suspiciously at the wreck in the shallows. Fouge was looking around too, his gaze roving ceaselessly from the water to the top of the hills.

None of the raiders was paying any attention to Stax, and for a moment he thought of slipping up the beach and seeing if anyone noticed. If they didn't, perhaps he could keep going, and make it over the top of the hill, and then he'd have a chance to hide or run. He'd dreamed of a chance like that many times in the boat, trying to figure out just how quickly he'd be able to flee and what he might use for a makeshift weapon. But now that he actually had that chance, he felt frozen in place. Just as he knew something terrible was watching them from the water, he also knew that he'd be in even greater danger away from the raiders than he was with them.

Miggs stood at Fouge's side, speaking to him in a low, urgent voice. But the raider boss shook his head.

"Just get the fire built and everyone will feel better," Fouge insisted. "And tomorrow will bring clear skies. You'll see."

Miggs tried to say something else, but Fouge folded his arms over his chest.

"Every shore in this part of the world is a dangerous shore," he said. "But I thought you were dangerous men and women. Was I wrong about that? If anything comes out of that sea, that will be its last mistake. Now enough, Miggs. Get the fire built."

Miggs nodded and turned away, and for a moment Stax could see the disgust on the big, bearded man's face. But then he was barking orders, which the others hurried to turn into action. That night there was neither singing nor jokes. Fouge's raiders were exhausted and clearly nervous. But the fire started to blaze up as the first stars came out, and a few minutes later, with the sun reduced to a bright line on the horizon, Stax smelled meat roasting. And for a moment—just a moment—he thought the danger had passed.

That was when Kivak died.

The sallow-faced man was coming back from the campfire, gnawing at a chunk of mutton spitted on a fork, when he stopped in his tracks and a confused expression came over his face. He was standing right in front of Stax, and at first Stax assumed Kivak was about to mock him for something.

But then Stax heard a sound he would never forget: a wet, gargling groan, coming from the beach. Kivak slumped over, an oddly disappointed look on his face, and with his last breath he made a wet sound so similar to the groan coming from the dark beach that Stax shivered. Then he plopped into the sand.

"Drowned!" screeched a raider, her eyes wild. "The drowned have come for us!"

Stax looked down the beach and saw a gray-green figure clad in sodden rags, a trident clutched in its hand.

The drowned lurched forward, out of the sea, its feet squishing in the wet sand. Its skin was mottled and drab, but its eyes were a bright green, shining with an eerie light. It groaned again, and water bubbled out of its throat and ran down the front of its ruined shirt.

An arrow flew into the night, a wild shot that missed, and the raiders fell back, yelling. Then Miggs stepped forward, his sword an orange blur in the campfire. The drowned slumped to the sand, and Miggs turned to look for Fouge.

"It's only sunset!" he said. "Soon there will be more, boss. *Many* more. We can't stay here!"

Fouge looked uncertain for a moment, then nodded. Miggs started yelling out orders, and the goods that had just been unloaded from the boats were reloaded nearly as quickly, with several reluctant raiders pressed into forming a defensive line at the water's edge, swords held in front of them.

"Stax, I'm afraid our association has come to an end," Fouge said with a little bow. "Here is where we part. But don't forget the gift I've given you."

"Gift?" Stax asked, too shocked and frightened to be angry. "What are you talking about?"

"Why, the greatest gift of all, Stax! I freed you from your past. Now you can be anything you want to be. You can experience the world and make something of yourself, instead of idling away your days amid the accomplishments of others. Or, I suppose, you can give up and die here. It's your choice."

Something groaned wetly in the gloom on the other side of the ruined tower.

"Still, I'd choose quickly," Fouge said. "Farewell, Mr. Stonecutter!"

The first raiders had leapt into their boats and rowed away from the shore; now the others followed. Fouge was the last to depart, offering Stax a little wave as he stepped into the stern of his boat. Within moments, the boats were pale dots against the dark water, and a moment after that, they were lost to sight.

Stax stood alone on the shore, next to the campfire. It began to rain harder. The fire hissed and spat, fighting a losing battle against the water. Stax sat down in the sand next to it, his arms around his knees, as the rain pelted down and the last bit of sunlight vanished below the horizon.

CHAPTER 7

CORNERED

A fight in the night * Searching for refuge * Stax digs in
* A beautiful morning * Stax wonders what's possible

Stax knew he needed to run or fight or do both, but he found he couldn't get further than thinking about it. Fight? He couldn't even imagine being able to get out of the rain.

He thought of his dream of home from the other morning, before he'd awakened in the raiders' last camp, and tried to convince himself this was a dream too. Perhaps he would wake up in his sunny bedroom and find the cats reminding him that it was time for breakfast, and realize Fouge Tempro had been just a vivid nightmare, one that would soon fade to a vaguely unpleasant memory.

But Stax knew that wasn't true, and all the wishing in the Overworld wouldn't make it true. He knew that even before he heard something heavy squishing and squelching through the sand, and a growl from the other side of the campfire.

He looked up, trying desperately to blink away the rainwater that was running into his eyes, and saw a dark shape there — something shaped like a man, but that wasn't human anymore.

Lightning split the sky and he stared into the empty green eyes of the drowned, the flash of light revealing its terrible features in minute detail: gray-green flesh, so heavy that it dragged down the corners of its mouth; swollen fingers like hideous sausages; and black, jagged fingernails.

The drowned saw him too. It gurgled so eagerly that a flight of tiny bubbles popped around its lips and dark water ran down its chin. Then, as thunder boomed overhead, its arms came up and it started to stagger toward him.

Stax sat there, frozen with horror, and then he jumped at another sodden groan. This one was behind him, close enough that he could hear water bubbling in its throat.

Before he was conscious of it, he had scrambled away from the fire, and at the last possible second — the drowned that had snuck up behind him took a huge swipe at Stax, but fortunately connected only with air. Meanwhile, the first drowned had found its way around the campfire and stood side by side with its fellow undead, eyes fixed on its prey.

Stax leapt to his feet, eyes wild, and screamed at them.

"Come on, then! What are you waiting for?"

The drowned trudged through the sand, their hands reaching for him. Stax ducked, then backpedaled frantically, his feet struggling for purchase. Another flash of lightning revealed something glimmering in the gloom — a trident, clutched by a third drowned who was still waist-deep in the water.

"Oh no," Stax said.

He was so worried about the weapon that he failed to look

behind him, and backed into something soft, squishy, and cold. A terrible smell filled his nostrils: stagnant water, and beneath that something rotten. The drowned he had bumped into groaned, and the water it coughed up ran down the back of Stax's neck, making him shiver as the creature fumbled to smash him with its fists.

Stax twisted away from the dead thing and shoved it, wincing as his hands sank into the spongy flesh. His fists beat at the drowned while it swung wildly at him.

Then the drowned fell backward with a blubbering sigh. Stax staggered farther up the beach, breathing hard.

Something flashed past his ear. It was the trident—and it had nearly hit him. Stax followed its pale purple arc through the darkness as it returned to its owner's hand, guided by some dreadful magic. A blow from the fist of another drowned caught him in the back and he stumbled forward, crying out.

This is the end if I don't think of something, Stax thought. He was faster than the drowned, but there were too many of them, and if he stood his ground they would eventually batter him into unconsciousness, or the trident would find its mark. And then he would die—or become one of them, doomed to live out eternity on this bleak shore, consumed by rage and a hunger that could never be satisfied.

He ran between two of the shambling figures, certain that at any second he'd feel the trident strike home, and scrambled up the sandy hill, repeatedly falling to his hands and knees. He reached the top just as lightning flashed, revealing barren desert as far as he could see.

There was no escape that way.

Stax flung himself down the other side of the hill, hearing the drowned gurgling in confusion at having lost sight of him. Halfway down he began to dig, his hands moving frantically. In a moment he was through the layer of wet sand on the surface and flinging dry grit behind him, frantically trying to make the hole he was digging even deeper. Thunder rumbled, and as it faded he could hear the drowned's groans of frustration.

Stax kept digging, ignoring his stinging fingers and palms. He'd hollowed out a little space in the hill now, just big enough to turn around in. He clambered into it and was relieved to find sandstone above him, hard and stable. Stax began to dig down now, farther into the hill.

He stopped after a couple of frantic minutes, gasping for breath. He could see the night sky above him, outside his vulnerable refuge, and the wall of rain falling. He kept digging until he was certain he was out of reach of any arms that might come through the gap he had left.

Should he fill it in? Pack in sand until he was walled inside the hill? Stax knew he probably should; there would be nowhere to hide if the trident's owner found him. But the idea of escaping the drowned only to suffocate in sand filled him with horror. And he was exhausted, bone-tired in a way he'd never been in his entire life.

Stax huddled in the hole he had made, shivering, until he'd recovered enough that his breathing slowed and his heart stopped pounding in his ears. His fingertips were raw from scrabbling at the sand and his palms were red and scraped. Outside, the rain continued to pelt down, and he could still hear the thunder rolling—and the groans of the drowned, searching the beach.

Stax was sure that any moment he'd hear the slow, labored steps of undead feet outside his refuge, followed by a choking gurgle of triumph and hands working, slowly but methodically, to strip away his meager defenses.

But a minute passed and that didn't happen.

And then five minutes.

And then Stax lost track of how much time had passed.

And then he was blinking his eyes in confusion, because bright light was streaming through the gap in the sand. It had become a strip of blue above him, the color of the sky at morning.

Wincing at the pain in his hands, Stax carefully pushed enough sand out of the way to be able to stick his head out of his refuge. Yellow sand stretched out around him, and below him was the strip of green with its ruined tower, and the dark blue water beyond that. The drowned were gone.

Stax shoved his way through the sand and trudged down to the beach, trying to shake the grit out of his hair. Here and there in the sand were bits of loot the raiders had left behind in their haste to escape. There wasn't a weapon to be found, but Stax did spot a bruised apple and fell on it frantically, eating it core and all. He also found a few lumps of coal that hadn't been burned for fuel. And, best of all, he discovered an abandoned bed at the edge of the water, wet and salty but intact.

He had survived the night, but now what? It would be night again soon, and he had no boat or refuge. There wasn't so much as a tree.

Stax dragged the bed up the beach to dry. He looked at the wrecked tower, eyed the hull of the shipwreck in the shallows of the bay, then turned his gaze to the horizon, hoping to spot a more hospitable island he could swim to. Then he looked back at the pale keel of the wrecked boat, lying above the water.

That's made of wood, he thought. *A lot of wood.*

His eyes returned to the forlorn spike of the tower, scrutinizing it the way he might have examined a tumble of rock he encountered in a cavern far beneath the ground. He thought about the condition of the stone he could see, and measured the gaps in the tower's walls.

I bet I could repair that.

CHAPTER 8

A BUILDING PROJECT

Harvesting wood * Shoring up the tower *
A last errand before nightfall

Stax was half-convinced that some terrible creature—one of the drowned, if not something even worse—would be lurking in the shallows, waiting for him to stray too far from the shore. He waded in up to his waist, ready to retreat to the relative safety of the broken tower, then peered into the water, alert for any sign of danger.

But there was nothing. It was a beautiful day and the water was gentle and cool. If not for the terrible things that had befallen him, he might have been able to pretend he was on some carefree excursion, taking a dip after a day at the seashore or on a long hike.

Tentatively, Stax swam out to the keel of the capsized ship and heaved himself up onto the spine of pale wood. He could tell at a glance which planks were rarely, if ever, submerged because they were bleached by the sun and free of the seagrass that had colonized the wood below the surface of the water.

Stax ran his hands over the wood, looking for a weak spot, and found a place where the planks had warped slightly and sprung apart. Wincing at the pain in his hands, he began working the planks back and forth, until one gave way with a groan of distress.

One down, goodness knows how many to go.

He set the plank carefully aside on the keel next to him, and looked for another weak point. Within half an hour or so, he had a stack of planks, and the keel was starting to look like giant worms had been gnawing it. Stax rubbed his arm across his sweaty forehead and looked back at the stump of the tower, trying to calculate how many planks he'd need to fill all the gaps in the stonework.

The sun was directly overhead, about to begin its descent toward the horizon. For a moment the task seemed too big for him, and he was grimly certain he couldn't be finished by nighttime. But then he shook his head. That was no way to think. He'd do whatever he could, and if the job was still incomplete at sundown, he'd hide in the sand bank again and hope his luck held.

Stax worked all day, as the sun sank in the sky and sweat ran down his neck. He worked until his hands were raw and cramped and his back was stiff and his knees hurt. He was hungry, and thirsty, and whenever he stopped for a moment he thought of his ruined house and his lost cats and he felt despair creeping into his mind. When that happened—and it happened several times during the long hot day—he'd swim awkwardly back to the shore with a load of wood and pile it near the tower. That way, when he got tired again and looked back at the tower he'd immediately see that he was making progress.

Finally, with the sun nearing the horizon, Stax waded ashore with a last armload of wood. The inside of the tower was cool and shadowy and, he was glad to see, free of vermin, briars, or other unpleasant things. Stax thought about taking a brief rest, but knew he shouldn't; it wouldn't do to wake up and discover the sun was down and one of the drowned was putting its hands around his throat.

The first thing to do, he thought, was make a crafting table. He grabbed several planks, and ten minutes later produced a serviceable table on which he could work.

Another hour of work, and he'd banged together a door out of planks that fit into the doorway. Then it was time to begin filling the gaps in the stone. Stax sweated and hammered and sweated some more, annoyed with himself each time he made a mistake and had to start over.

The sun was an orange ball on the horizon when he wedged a plank into a gap between two stones, stepped back, and realized there weren't any more holes in the tower. They'd all been filled—in a cockeyed, haphazard way that his grandmother wouldn't have approved of, maybe, but then Stax had nothing but scavenged material and was half-starved. He allowed himself a brief moment of satisfaction, after which his eyelids started to droop.

That was when he remembered the bed.

Was he too late? He peered between the planks and saw the sun had sunk almost out of sight. No, he still had time—but only just. Pushing open his makeshift door, he hurried down the beach to where he'd left the bed, overshooting it but then spotting it in the gloom behind him. To his relief, a long day beneath the sun had dried it.

Was that a gurgle somewhere behind him? He heaved the bed

onto his shoulder and forced his tired legs to run, his feet kicking up sand, made it back to the tower, and shut the door behind him, careful not to dislodge it. He took a piece of scrap wood and jammed it into one of the lumps of coal, hoping not to break it, coaxed it aflame, and jammed the scrap of wood into a rusted sconce on the wall. Warm yellow light filled his refuge. Stax just hoped it would repel any creatures that spotted it through the cracks in the boards, instead of attracting them.

Stax lay down on the bed, moving his shoulders back and forth to rearrange the clumps of wool inside it. It was lumpy, stiff with salt, smelled damp, and the frame might give way in the night, dumping him onto the tower's flagstones. But in that moment, it felt as soft and inviting as his feather bed back home.

Stax sighed. He knew he should get up, that he should perform a last check of his hasty repairs to make sure they couldn't be battered down. But he was bone-weary, his mind fuzzy and his energy utterly spent.

I've done the best I could. I just have to hope it's enough.

A moment later, he was asleep.

CHAPTER 9

GIFTS FROM THE SEA

Stax makes an aquatic discovery *
A hated food from childhood gets reconsidered *
Remedial tool use * Laughter in the dark

Stax woke with a start, but this time he knew exactly where he was. His stomach clenched and turned over, demanding food he couldn't give it.

Stax carefully opened the door. The beach was quiet, the water serene beneath the rising sun. Stax scanned the shore for signs of trouble, a little disturbed to realize how well he'd already come to know this miserable little bay. Maybe that was his future: to memorize each hummock of mud and drift of sand, each particular of his shrunken, forlorn world.

But then if he didn't find something to eat, and soon, that problem would take care of itself. Stax kicked through the ashes of the fire in hope that he'd missed another apple or something else useful that Fouge's raiders had left behind in their hasty departure. But there was nothing.

Stax struggled up the sand hill where he'd spent the night hidden from the drowned, giving the little hollow of his refuge a brief glance before forcing himself to look away. His situation was dire, but now at least he had a roof over his head—however haphazardly patched—and a bed.

He stood at the top of the hill and shielded his eyes with his hand, gazing out into the desert and turning slowly around in a full circle. He'd surveyed his surroundings only briefly, during the night, while under attack. It was entirely possible he'd missed something: a patch of woods, say, or the mouth of a river.

"Why stop there?" Stax asked himself. "Why not a farm with a barn full of warm hay? An inn that doesn't charge travelers for rooms? A castle whose aged owner needs a young heir?"

But there was nothing but low hills of sand marching to the horizon, broken by the green spikes of cacti and the brittle sticks of dead bushes—remnants, Stax supposed, of some bygone era when these shores had been green and pleasant.

Stax mechanically gathered the sticks, thinking they might be useful as firewood, and dumped them in his patchwork tower. He stared out to sea, hoping to sight something, anything, that might deliver him.

His belly rumbled again.

Fish. Could he make a fishing pole? He'd just gathered an armload of sticks, but he had no line. At home, they'd used spider silk for fishing line, but the thought of battling a spider in the night made Stax shiver.

No, that wouldn't work. He couldn't see anything beneath the water except sand and stones and kelp.

Kelp.

A stray memory from childhood came back to him: his father,

unloading his boat after one of his trips across the sea to tour Stonecutter outposts. He'd handed Stax a chunk of dried kelp, explaining that he'd eaten it during his travels and inviting him to take a bite.

Oh, how Stax had hated it. It was tasteless at first, tough and chewy, and then the tang of salt overwhelmed everything. Stax had spat it out into the water, running his finger along his gums and across the back of his tongue in an effort to get rid of even the smallest bit of it.

Well, now he'd have to learn to like it.

Stax swam out to the overturned ship, its keel mostly stripped of planks. Now that he was looking for kelp, he could see that the wreck was surrounded with strands of it, reaching up from the seafloor toward the sun. Stax wrenched a plank free, held his breath and dove into the water, forcing himself down as far as he could go. The seafloor here was a strange gray—gravel, maybe, or clay.

Whatever it was, it would have to wait. He yanked at the surprisingly tough stalk of the kelp until he was desperate for air.

The stalk finally parted. Stax kicked for the surface, gasping when his head cleared the water, and draped the length of kelp over the ship's keel. He heaved himself out of the water and sat on the keel while he got his breath back. Pieces of kelp were floating nearby. When he'd rested a bit, he'd collect them. Though there were more of them than he'd thought there'd be.

Wait a minute.

It wasn't just kelp that he saw floating. Something shiny was out there too, glinting in the sun. A dead fish, maybe?

Stax swam out to it, worried it might sink. To his astonishment, it was a compass. He held it in his hand, awkwardly treading water, and gazed down at the red needle. He supposed it must have fallen overboard while the raiders were making their getaway.

Stax's father had carried a compass with him during his ocean journeys, and Stax tried to think back to what he'd told him about how they worked. To his frustration, he realized he didn't remember all the details. There'd been something about an origin point, and making adjustments from there, and during the explanation Stax's mind had wandered. He'd already known he had no interest in sailing all across the Overworld, and if he ever changed his mind his father would be next to him, and able to take care of the navigation.

But it was useless to get angry at himself about not having listened to a long explanation back when he was a teenager. The important thing was that Stax's father had used a compass to find his way home, and Stax now had one of his own.

Which meant he could get home. Or close enough—his father had made those adjustments that Stax couldn't remember. But close enough would be a lot better than his current situation.

The thought of being able to get home was so amazing that Stax shivered despite being in warm water. He shook the compass gently, half-wondering if he was dreaming. But no, it was very real.

Stax reminded himself that he had work to do; it wasn't as if he could just start swimming in the direction the compass was pointing. Clutching the compass in his hand, he swam back to the keel and set his new discovery carefully on one of the highest planks.

While he rested, he peered at the patchwork tower. He had plenty of wood. Enough, even, to replace some of the tower's stone blocks. That would let him use the stone for other things. Such as building a furnace. If he built a furnace, he could dry his new supply of kelp, using his precious stock of sticks and few lumps of coal. And once the kelp was dried, he'd have food.

And then . . . he was so excited that he almost tripped over his thoughts, and made himself calm down and start again.

And then I can build a boat, use the compass, and go home.

But first he needed that stone. And he needed it relatively quickly—the sun was high in the sky. At home, the days had seemed to crawl while he wasn't doing much. Now it felt like the sun was racing toward the opposite horizon the moment it rose, leaving Stax with too much to do and not enough time in which to do it.

Stax thought of when he'd been small and his grandmother had walked him through puzzles like this, asking what steps he needed to take and in what order he needed to take them. He supposed she'd never imagined that her grandson might have to draw on those lessons in a situation like this, lost and marooned far from home.

Or maybe she had. She'd been a formidable woman, with stories he'd found equal parts thrilling and terrifying. Hadn't she escaped from a nest of creepers—maneuvering them, in fact, so that when they blew themselves up they barely hurt her, but blasted a hole into a cavern that proved rich in iron ore? Hadn't she escaped a near-fatal fall by tunneling her way back to the surface in total darkness, with a pickaxe worn down to a mere nub?

Stax wasn't nearly as brave or resourceful as his grandmother had been. But maybe, he mused, she might be proud of what he'd accomplished. He had survived a night battling the drowned, after all, and turned a shattered tower into a reasonably safe refuge. And now, if he just kept calm, he could get himself home.

He clambered back onto the keel, careful not to knock either the compass or the kelp into the water, and started hunting for planks that were particularly straight and strong. He found a few and wrenched them free, checking that they were free of soft spots. Then he gathered the kelp, stuffed the compass into his pocket, and made the by now familiar swim back to the beach and his tower. Taking the straightest board and stoutest stick he could find, he hunkered down over the crafting table and got to work.

Stax wasn't sure it was quite right to call what he'd made a pickaxe—it was more of a prybar made out of wood. But it would have to do. And, to his relief, it did. By midafternoon he had assembled eight stone blocks into a furnace, and filled it with sticks gathered from the desert.

He used his torch to light the sticks, put kelp in the furnace's top slot, and waited impatiently as the kelp leaves shrank and changed from green to a dark gray color. Stax was so hungry that he burned his fingers snatching the first piece of kelp out of the furnace and had to juggle it for a couple of minutes while it cooled.

He bit into the kelp and made a face. It was as bad as he remembered: salty and chewy and thoroughly nasty. But it was also what he desperately needed. By the time the sun sank below the horizon, Stax had eaten six pieces and dried another dozen or so for tomorrow.

Something groaned outside the door, close enough to make Stax jump. With night having fallen, the drowned had returned.

"I know it's delicious, but get your own dried kelp!" Stax yelled, shocking even himself.

He heard footsteps squishing away from the door and began to laugh, a low chuckle that turned into a helpless stream of giggles.

Stax lay on his lumpy bed, one hand pressed over his mouth, but he couldn't stop the laughter.

I think I'm losing my mind.

Maybe so. But at least he wasn't going to starve to death.

No, I'm not. And tomorrow? Tomorrow I'm building a boat.

CHAPTER 10

BACK TO SEA

Stax puts his father's lessons to work * A reluctant
decision and several promises * The science of making
weapons on a beach * A brief aside about the nature of
storytelling * A melancholy nighttime chorus

The next morning, as he started building his boat on the beach, Stax found his thoughts drifting back to his family.

Stax's grandmother had always preferred to travel by land, disdaining boats as both dangerous and a waste of time. If he closed his eyes, he could still hear her complaining about them in particular and ocean travel in general: "What's the use? All that time traveling through something you can't mine! I'll go by foot and by the time I get where I'm going I'll have found two more places where we can pull a fortune out of the ground. Three, if nobody hurries me."

But Stax's father had loved boats and been comfortable in them—more comfortable, probably, than he'd been underground with a pickaxe in his hand. He'd been the one who'd taught Stax how to make a boat by carefully overlapping planks. He'd made several boats that way, to escape trouble far from home, and wanted to make sure his son had the same skills.

Stax had never imagined having to make use of that knowledge, but now he was heartily glad he'd listened to his father's long-ago lessons. Over the better part of the day the boat took shape, though Stax had to spend an annoying amount of time getting the planks to fit just right.

But finally the boat was finished. Stax walked around it, inspecting it with a critical eye; it wouldn't do to have put in all that work only to have the thing sink a minute after he put it in the water.

Or, far worse, an hour or a day after he put it in the water.

"That is one awful-looking watercraft," Stax said when his inspection was complete. He'd started to talk to himself more and more during the last couple of days, and only wished there were a cat or two to pay no attention to what he said.

The boat was indeed terrible-looking. His father had made trim, elegant boats out of birch or oak, and sometimes returned from a long voyage in a new boat made from some dark, exotic wood harvested from trees that didn't grow near the Stonecutter estate. Stax's boat was a mess, made from different woods of varied colors, most of it bleached by the sun, tinged green by water, or both. If Stax was being honest, the boat was spotty and blotchy and vaguely diseased-looking. The oars he'd made weren't any more attractive: one was a sickly yellow-green, while the other was vaguely misshapen.

"So what?" Stax asked himself. "If this boat gets me home, I'll hang it from the ceiling of the new trophy room."

Home. What Stax wanted to do—desperately wanted to do—

was get into the boat right now and start the journey back to the place he missed so badly. The idea of spending another night on this miserable shore, trapped between a hostile sea and a bleak desert, seemed unbearable.

But he knew that wasn't a good idea. He was tired, and the journey home would be difficult and dangerous. It made much more sense to begin at dawn, when he'd be rested and stronger and able to go ashore in daylight if something went wrong.

Stax knew that, but it was still difficult to accept. With a sigh, he turned away from the water and sat down on a rock, pulling a chunk of dried kelp out of his pocket. He took a salty bite and chewed mechanically, grimacing at the taste.

"If I get home," he said, his words muffled, "I am never, ever, ever eating this nasty stuff again."

Stax finished his unpleasant meal and stood morosely on the shore, kicking pebbles into the water. He decided to spend the rest of his daylight hours making a sword out of wood; it wouldn't be much use in a serious fight, but it would be better than fighting with his bare fists again. And he could use it if he was lucky enough to encounter animals somewhere on the way home — a wild cow, perhaps, or a pig or a chicken.

The thought of chicken — to say nothing of beef or pork — made his mouth water, and he spent some time daydreaming about food. Just a few days ago, a juicy steak or a plump pork chop had been a regular meal, as had a loaf of fresh bread or a potato. Now those foods seemed like the kinds of things a king might eat, in a fancy hall surrounded by servants.

Stax made himself a promise that if he ever got to eat like that again he wouldn't take it for granted. He'd appreciate each and every bite of each and every meal. Then he finished making his sword, shaping and sanding the edge until it was as sharp as one could make a piece of wood salvaged from the keel of a wrecked ship.

The sun was just touching the horizon now. To his surprise, Stax wished it were later, even though that meant the drowned would be prowling around his patched-together tower. The sooner night came, the sooner it would be morning, when he could finally depart.

Stax made some experimental thrusts and sweeps with his new wooden sword, liking the way it felt in his hand. Then he gave his boat a pat and retreated into the tower, shutting the door behind him.

Not long after the sun went down he heard the drowned tramping around on the beach, moaning wetly. But the sound had become familiar, and had lost much of its terror. If those mindless unfortunates were going to bash down his door, they would have done it already. With luck, this was the last night he would ever hear those awful noises.

Now, here's a funny thing about storytelling. You can see for yourself that there's a lot more of this story left to go before we're done, so you already know that Stax isn't going to simply sail home and have everything turn out okay. But even though *you* know this, heroes have no idea how much is yet to come in their story. Stax had done everything he could to prepare for his journey, and he really was confident that it would go well. So let's leave him there, in his bed, happier than he'd been in several days. He went to sleep with a smile on his face, despite being surrounded by a chorus of gurgling moans made by hungry things that wanted to eat him.

CHAPTER 11

A PERILOUS JOURNEY

Fatherly advice, imperfectly recalled * A camp on
another lonesome shore * The library of dreams * Alone
on the Sea of Sorrows * A light in the darkness

Stax woke at dawn and lay in bed for a moment, blinking up at the patched ceiling above him. His stomach rumbled, and he frowned at the thought that he had nothing to put in it except more dried kelp.

Then his brain shook off sleep and he remembered what today meant—that his boat was outside, waiting for him to get in and begin the long journey home—and he almost jumped out of bed, excited to get moving.

Stax had his hand on the door, then stopped. He had to take things slowly, making sure he had everything he needed before setting out across the sea. It would be very bad to discover he'd forgotten something and have to row back. Besides, the sun wasn't high enough to have driven the night's monsters into hiding or set them afire. And if it would be very bad to forget something, it would be far worse to blunder into the soggy embrace of one of the drowned.

Stax ate a piece of kelp, grimacing at the salty taste, and packed the rest away. He disassembled his bed. He checked that his wooden sword was sharp. He examined the compass he'd found and pushed it deep down into his pocket. And only then, with the sun a little higher in the sky, did he peek out of the tower's make-shift door.

He didn't see the boat he'd built yesterday, and for a moment fear gripped his heart and squeezed. But then he remembered that he'd dragged it to the other side of the tower, and found it right where he'd left it.

Stax gathered planks and stone, well aware that he'd need to find shelter on the way home, and forced himself to take another look inside the gloomy tower to make sure he hadn't missed anything. But no, he had everything. He was ready.

He dragged the boat down the beach into the shallows at the shore. It bobbed up and down in the water, showing no sign of leaks.

"Well, all right then," Stax said. "Off we go, I suppose."

He clambered into the boat, set the compass face up in front of him, and took a last look at the gray spike of the broken tower that had been his refuge, and the sandy hill beyond it.

"Farewell, horrible place," Stax said. "Nothing personal, but I am never, ever going to see you again."

He began to row, putting his back into it. The boat moved smoothly through the water, and Stax allowed himself a smile. Apparently he was better at building watercraft than he'd thought. Within minutes the stone tower had shrunk to a small dark line against the pale hills behind him.

Stax frowned at the compass, with its red needle pointing behind him, in the opposite direction of his strokes. Once again he found himself wishing he'd remembered his father's explanation and what he'd done to navigate. But Stax remembered the last stage of his journey as the raiders' prisoner, and this was definitely the direction the boats had come from.

He decided he'd worry about figuring out how to use the compass later. For now, the sun was overhead, the weather was clear, and his job was to row.

And row Stax did. Steadily and patiently, as the sun reached its zenith above him and then began to descend, until he was rowing into a smear of orange light at the horizon. He rowed as the sun beat down on him, and his shoulders ached, and his hands began to cramp. He rowed so long that he figured even Miggs would have been impressed, and maybe even grunted approvingly at him.

Thinking of Miggs made Stax angry, but that turned out to be a good thing, and the better part of an hour went by as he fantasized about tracking Miggs down and making him beg for forgiveness. Beg for forgiveness and then tell Stax where to find Fouge Tempro.

To Stax's left, the shore had turned gray and stony, rising to a line of bluffs. That was good; he remembered passing those same bluffs on the last day before the raiders abandoned him, except they'd been on his right then. He was going in the correct direction, even if that direction was the opposite of where the compass needle was pointing.

He passed the ships wrecked off the rocky shore, their wooden ribs protruding above the waves like the skeletons of great sea creatures, and the ruined fortresses and buildings on the bluff above the sea. The sight of those ruins frightened him less than when he'd spotted them from Miggs's boat; now, in fact, Stax scanned them as he passed, hoping to find a safe place to spend the night.

With the sun low in the sky, Stax chose a battered stone building on the shore, tucked below the bluffs—perhaps a storehouse that had been attached to some long-gone dock. He maneuvered his boat carefully to the shore and stumbled out of it, his hands cramped and his eyes stinging with salt. The horizon kept going up and down, as if he were still out on the water and not on dry land.

Stax could easily have collapsed into the sand and slept right there, but he forced himself to pull the boat up onto the beach and perform some hasty repairs on the abandoned storehouse; its door had rotted away, and there were holes in the roof. Stax filled in the gaps, an effort that required nearly half his remaining planks of wood, set up his bed, mattress now even stiffer with salt, and fell onto it, groaning at the pain in his hands. He was asleep almost instantly, and lay there without dreaming or even moving until he was awakened by shafts of light passing through the slats in the door he'd built.

Stax got out of bed and walked along the beach, which was little more than a rocky shore beneath brooding cliffs, wincing at the stiffness in his back and arms. After so many hours gripping the oars, his hands felt like they wanted to curl up into claws, and all he wanted to do was rest.

"Not here, though," Stax told himself. This beach was even more bleak and uninviting than the one he'd called home for the last several days. "You can rest all you want back home."

The thought cheered him up a little, and he broke down his bed and sat on the shore next to his boat, eating dried kelp and thinking about his cats. He tried to tell himself that they were all right; Emerald, Lapis, and Coal were clever animals, if a bit spoiled and lazy, and surely an hour of fire and chaos hadn't made them forget how to be cats. Maybe they were snoozing in the morning sun atop chunks of the house's foundation, wondering when Stax was going to return and feed them.

It was a nice idea, one he tried to keep in his mind as he shoved the boat down the beach and took up the oars again.

The day was cooler than yesterday, with lines of clouds scudding across the sky, driven by a steady wind.

But despite the cool weather, Stax was far more tired than he'd been the previous morning. The journey from his house to the lonely shore of his exile had been a long one, and that had been in a boat rowed by a veteran raider. And there was the question of whether he'd be able to find his way home, once he reached waters he didn't remember. He'd hoped the compass needle would be pointing in a different direction by now, but it remained fixed in the opposite direction from where he was going.

Stax rowed for hours, until the bluffs became islands and he spotted bits of land to the north as well as to the south. That was another good sign; he remembered coming this way. But he also remembered that if he stayed on course, he would soon enter what Kivak had called the Sea of Sorrows, where there was no land to be seen in any direction.

Stax stopped rowing and the boat glided to a halt, bobbing gently. The only sound was the faint whistle of the wind. The compass gleamed in the sun, its needle pointed in the same direction as when Stax left the tower.

He wanted to get home desperately, and over the last two days, he'd made a lot of progress toward that goal. But he knew the most dangerous part of the journey lay ahead. And it wouldn't do to plunge into the Sea of Sorrows with night coming and no idea where he might rest.

Stax turned his boat toward a low, rocky island to the south of him, one of the line he'd followed from the bluffs. He dragged the boat up the beach and dug into the side of a hill, hacking out a space just large enough for his bed, then blocking it off with cobblestones and planks to form a rough-hewn, rude little cabin. It was a couple of hours before sunset, so he explored the island, gnawing on dried kelp for dinner. He found nothing of any interest—a few stunted, long-dead trees and more rocks than any human being could count in a lifetime.

That night, Stax had a strange dream. He was in a great library, a soaring hall built out of rare woods, all of them gleaming and polished, lit by flickering torches. The library's shelves seemed to stretch for hundreds of blocks in every direction, filled with everything from heavy tomes bound in leather to rolled-up scrolls. The librarians were a strange folk: squat, gray bipeds with featureless white eyes, clad in rich, heavy robes that came in a rainbow of colors. If you spoke any louder than a whisper, they would turn and wave a bony finger at you disapprovingly.

Through hand gestures and whispers, Stax finally got one of the librarians to understand that he was trying to go home. The librarian pointed to a door Stax somehow hadn't noticed before, one whose door was emblazoned with gilded letters that said MAP ROOM.

The Map Room had its own shelves of rare books, but at its center were large tables covered with piles of charts and maps. Stax started to explain to one of the strange librarians what he wanted, but the gray-skinned being held up a hand to stop him and reached into the center of the pile on the table in front of them, extracting an old map in a wooden frame.

Stax goggled at the map in disbelief. It was the Overworld, rendered in beautiful detail—gray mountain ranges and dark green forests and blue curlicues of rivers and broad yellow deserts. There, marked with an X, was the lonely shore and his tower.

Stax followed the shoreline to the west, watching as it decayed into a series of islands, until he stopped at the little speck of land where he knew he was at that moment tossing and turning in bed. Beyond that lay the Sea of Sorrows, marked by fanciful clouds with baleful eyes and downturned mouths spewing out winds. Excited now, Stax looked farther west. There was the pale blue of an ice field. And there, beyond it, a green triangle of land sticking out into the ocean: the Stonecutter peninsula.

Stax couldn't help himself and let out a cry of triumph, earning stern looks and shushes from several librarians. He snatched up the framed map to take with him, as it would be invaluable for crossing the Sea of Sorrows. But as he lifted it, the map disintegrated, worn away to nothing by age. As Stax watched in horror, it crumbled into flakes of colorful paper that fluttered to the rich green carpet.

Stax put the empty frame back on the table. Only bits and pieces of the map remained at the corners: mere fragments of mountain ranges and savannas. Stax got down on his knees, sifting through the colored scraps, but he knew it was hopeless.

Stax awoke in his cabin to discover the morning was cloudy and slightly chilly. He shook his head at the disquieting dream, but decided he wasn't surprised it had happened. Of course he'd dream of maps; he was trying to get home, and it would have been handy to have a map like the ones that had been stolen from him.

If anything, he was surprised that his sleeping brain hadn't also filled the dream with compasses.

"Well, maybe that will be tomorrow night's dream," Stax muttered to himself as he munched on his familiar breakfast of dried kelp.

He pushed the boat down the beach and got in, surprised at how familiar this morning routine had come to feel. His back and arms even hurt a little less than they had yesterday.

"If I can't get home, I can take a job as a rower," Stax said, laughing at the thought. His laughter suddenly seemed very loud, out in the middle of the sea with only a little dot of a rocky island nearby. But instead of being ashamed of disturbing the silence, Stax decided to disturb it a little more.

"Oh yes," he told the world in a loud voice as the island shrank behind him. "Stax Stonecutter is a very fine rower, yes, sir! Makes his own oars, can row from sunrise until sunset, and only asks for a little dried kelp for his meals. Bit of a loner and talks to himself all day, mostly about cats. And sometimes he can't stop laughing. But everybody's got a few eccentricities, don't they?"

And he kept on talking as the morning stretched on and the islands became fewer and fewer to the south of him. He talked about his new science of rowing, which he called the Stonecutter method. ("The secret is to row all day, and then row some more!") He named each island as he passed it, alternating between "Stax Island" and "Stonecutter Island," and inventing arguments with mapmakers about whether it was appropriate to use only two names for an entire archipelago. He told stories about his cats. He extolled the virtues of dried kelp and invented elaborate recipes using it as an ingredient.

If you're thinking that all this suggests Stax was going a bit crazy, well, Stax thought the same thing. But it made the day feel like it was going by more quickly, and it mostly prevented him from thinking about the dangers of the journey, or becoming anxious about how to get home, or worrying about whether his cats were hungry or frightened. And that made him feel better.

Or at least it did until he passed into the Sea of Sorrows.

Stax was pretty sure that's where he was. It had been at least an hour since he'd seen an island either to the north or to the south. The wind was blowing chaotically, seeming to switch directions almost at will. Stax was over feeling seasick, but still gritted his teeth, hating being alone in the middle of a seemingly endless sea.

And there was another problem. The raiders had sailed across the Sea of Sorrows, but Stax had been asleep or too numb to notice how many times they'd changed direction. He did remember that Fouge's flotilla of boats had spent several hours heading south, judging by the sun's path across the sky, but he had no idea exactly when they'd turned in that direction.

Stax stopped rowing and sat in the boat for a while, turning this problem over and over in his mind and not finding a solution. He'd have to guess. He decided to row in the direction he thought was west for another hour, turn north, and hope he recognized something, or at least found a place he could make his next camp.

It was a relief to turn when the hour was up, or at least when Stax judged it was up by the position of the sun. Stax glanced down at the compass, thinking to himself that it was strange to see it no longer pointing directly behind him.

He rowed throughout the afternoon, seeing nothing but the blue-gray sea around him and hearing nothing but the wind and his own voice. But unlike the morning, Stax found it impossible to keep distracting himself with a stream of cheerful chatter. There was no island nearby if something went wrong. No refuge he could flee to.

With the sun lower in the sky, he scanned the horizon for any sign of land, thinking what a relief it would be to find an island big enough for a little cabin, or with a single hill he could dig into for shelter. But there was nothing. He rubbed the salt out of his eyes as best he could and kept rowing, hoping the sunset might reveal a safe haven. But the sun kept sinking, inevitably and pitilessly, and still Stax saw nothing.

"Miggs rowed all night," he told himself. "I guess I'll have to do the same. But that's no hardship for a seasoned veteran rower like Stax Stonecutter!"

That had sounded good in his head, simultaneously defiant and cheerful, but when Stax actually said it he was struck by how small his voice seemed. Worried now, he kept rowing, peering at the compass and trying to make sure he kept heading north, as best he could judge it. The first stars appeared in the east and the sun became an orange line on the horizon, then a mere smear of color left behind in the sky, until finally it was dark except for the pale globe of the moon.

"Keep going," Stax whispered to himself. "Just keep going."

And he did. But he was frightened now. It was hard to keep the boat on course; every time he looked at the compass the needle indicated he had drifted away from where he thought north was. And he was tired, more tired than he'd been on the previous two days when he'd been able to tell himself that soon he'd be able to sleep.

Stax completed a stroke with the oars and stayed in position, his head back. He shook himself and started rowing again, but the pauses between strokes became longer and longer, until finally he sat slumped over the oars, motionless and half-asleep.

It was a long, miserable night, but finally there was a bit of color on the horizon: sunrise. Stax got the boat turned so that the rising sun was on his right, indicating he was heading north again, and began to row, but he was already exhausted.

And worse than that, he was hopelessly lost. There was no point pretending he wasn't. With no reliable memory of the route Fouge's raiders had taken, Stax had just been guessing when to turn north. He remembered that before turning south and crossing the Sea of Sorrows, Fouge's boats had passed beneath gray mountainous shores and camped on a little island. But there was no sign of any land to the north, and Stax might well have slept through several changes of course by the raiders.

If Stax could find the ice floes, he might have a chance of making his way home, since the frozen spires were visible from his estate. But he had no idea how to get there. He'd thought of his journey home like a jigsaw puzzle, similar to the ones he used to do with his grandparents, but now he realized that he was missing the critical pieces.

Stax decided there was nothing to be done except keep rowing north, in hope that he would spot the mountainous land he remembered. And so that's what he did—he rowed numbly all day, ignoring the wind and the rings of salt that built up around his eyes, stopping only to eat a little dried kelp and stretch out his aching, cramped legs.

But no land appeared—no mountains and no islands. There was just the sea, which he had grown to despise. On the one hand, it was always changing, the color of the water shifting to reflect the sun and the sky above. But despite all that, his situation remained the same: He was in the middle of nowhere, in a huge place that was hostile to him, and he couldn't find his way out of it. Stax rowed more and more slowly, until night came, and then he rowed glumly on through the night for a while, and then he stopped.

Stax was drifting himself by then, his brain wandering in and out of sleep. So when he saw the light, at first he thought he was dreaming. He'd soon wish that had been the case.

CHAPTER 12

GUARDIANS OF THE LIGHT

Things that go thump in the light * Strange fish *
A familiar destination

One reason Stax thought he was dreaming was that the light wasn't a sharp, clear light like you'd expect from a lighthouse or a lantern mounted on a boat. And it was the wrong color. Rather than being the orangey-red of fire, it was a pale, blue-green light that seemed to shimmer and wobble.

Stax reached over the side of the boat and splashed water on his face, to make sure he was awake; he had troubles enough without chasing a figment of his imagination across the dark, seemingly endless water. He accidentally swallowed some of the water and gasped and coughed, the noise sounding dangerously loud amid the ocean's vast, still darkness.

The light was still there, ahead of him and a little to the right. *That should be east*, Stax thought, except when he looked at the compass the needle indicated the light was to the northwest. Either the compass had started pointing somewhere else, or the boat had drifted again while he slept over the oars.

"We'll worry about that later," Stax told himself in a croaking whisper, his voice rough and raw from salt.

He began to row toward the light, half-expecting it to disappear as he did so, revealed as another trick played by the cruel sea. But it was still there, shimmering in the night. It wasn't until he was much closer that Stax realized that the light wasn't coming from a structure on land or from a boat, but from under the sea.

Mesmerized, he drew closer, rowing slowly and straining his eyes to see through the water.

Below him, he saw a strange, eldritch land: pale hills and valleys beneath the surface of the sea. There was a forest down there, but one made of strands of kelp, waving in the currents. And atop a white hill was a sprawling castle made of ghostly green stone, surrounded by a scattering of towers. The mysterious light that had drawn Stax seemed to emanate from the castle.

Stax let the boat drift, enchanted by the strange sight. He was so focused on what he saw that when the thump came against the bottom of his boat he was nearly knocked overboard.

"Wh-what?" he yelped, swiveling his head and trying to find his attacker. The boat jumped again, and he heard a deep, gurgling growl from somewhere in the water nearby.

Stax knew that sound all too well, and pulled frantically on the oars. The boat leapt forward, toward the castle, as Stax rowed as hard as he could.

Something flashed in the darkness, glowing purple. A trident, Stax thought, but this light was a continuous beam, from ahead of him. As he rowed, the beam swiveled and landed on his chest. He stared down at it, puzzled.

The beam turned yellow and Stax cried out in pain. He felt like his flesh was burning. He ducked, pulling at the oars, and turned the boat away from the burning light.

He was above the green buildings now, awash in their spooky radiance. Below him, the scene that had seemed so enchanting had turned terrifying. Spiked creatures like giant fish swam below him, gazing up at him from pitiless single eyes, and he could see the gray-fleshed shapes of drowned swimming toward the surface, their mouths black Os.

Another purple beam flashed past the boat, lancing out into the night. Stax rowed hard, trying to put distance between himself and the undersea castle and its defenders. Something thumped at the bottom of the boat again, knocking Stax sideways and causing him to lose his grip on one of the oars. That sent the boat into a spin, and water washed over the side.

Stax fumbled for his wooden sword, yelling defiantly. A glowing purple shaft flashed by his ear, and this time it really was a trident. He dropped his sword and pulled hard on the oars, grunting with the effort. The glowing castle was behind him, but not far enough, and he waited for the trident to strike him between the shoulder blades, or for the burning light to find him again.

Keep going, he told himself. *Keep going, keep going, keep going!*

He rowed until he couldn't anymore, his arms falling to his sides. He was panting now, desperately gulping for air. His chest hurt where the strange yellow light had touched him.

But he was alive.

Stax risked a look back over his shoulder. He'd rowed farther than he'd thought; the greenish light was a dot far behind him.

Far enough, perhaps, that the guardians no longer considered him a threat, or had given up the pursuit.

Stax wanted desperately to rest, but he forced himself to keep rowing. If the wind or the currents pushed him back over the strange castle, he would be attacked again, and this time he doubted he'd escape.

Stax rowed until he couldn't see the light behind him, and then rowed until he was exhausted again. And then—not because he thought it was a good idea, but because he couldn't help it— he fell asleep at the oars. When he woke up, it was day. The sun had climbed a fair distance above the horizon.

There's not a lot I can tell you about the next two days, be- cause they were pretty much the same as the days I've told you about already. Stax rowed until he was too tired to row any longer and had to slump over his oars, apparently dead to the world, and then he woke up with a start and rowed some more. He no longer talked to himself—he was too weary to do that—and he barely looked at the compass. He simply rowed. At this point, he could barely remember a time when he'd done anything else.

It wasn't until he saw the islands that his exhausted brain started to work again. He saw two at once, one to his left and one to his right, and they looked much the same, dots of dirt and rock.

But Stax's brain didn't work right away. He was so overwhelmed by his ordeal that he assumed his mind was playing tricks on him. So instead of landing on the closest island to rest, he simply rowed past it. But then he passed more islands, some to the north and some to the south, and finally something about them struck him as familiar.

A couple of hours later, there was no doubt at all: There were the gray bluffs, and the shipwrecks in the surf. This was the broad bay into which the raiders had sailed after leaving the perilous Sea of Sorrows.

Stax didn't know whether he'd found his way back there by pure luck or some dimly perceived memory, but now he rowed with grim determination, and even found himself thinking of the sad, ruined tower he'd been so desperate to leave. He rowed until his arms were shaking and nearly limp, staring at the water ahead of him with wide eyes. He was racing the sun again; it was starting to set behind him, and the sky ahead of him was already darkening. Some instinct told Stax that he had used up all his reserves of strength and courage, and wouldn't survive another night exposed to the Overworld's dangers. So he rowed and rowed and rowed.

The first stars were emerging when he saw a familiar low swampy place ahead of him, with pale sandy hills behind it and a spike of stone rising from the beach. Stax cried out and turned for the beach, rowing until the boat crunched into the sand and pebbles beneath it. He tried to stand, couldn't, and fell over the side, landing on his hands and knees in the shallow water. Gasping, he made himself stand, gritting his teeth as his brain insisted the world was bobbing up and down around him. Step by step, he forced his legs to work, carrying him through sand and mud to the familiar patched door in the tower.

Hands shaking, Stax assembled his bed and then collapsed onto it.

"Well, I made it," he muttered.

He tried to laugh, but nothing came out but a dry, awful-sounding croak.

CHAPTER 13

A NEW DIRECTION

A decision made * An unexpected green country *
A cabin and a riddle

It probably won't surprise you to learn that Stax was too tired to do much of anything for several days except eat dried kelp. But little by little, he recovered from his ordeal. He rebuilt his furnace and crafting table inside the tower, gathered more kelp from the shallow waters offshore, and repaired the cracked boards on the bottom of his boat.

While doing these chores Stax found, somewhat to his surprise, that he wasn't as depressed about everything that had gone wrong as he'd feared he'd be. He had built a boat, survived a dangerous journey, and returned to safety. Not so long ago, he'd doubted he'd be able to make it through a single night on his own, but he was still alive, having relied on no one but himself.

"But that's not the way we're going to get home," Stax said.

He'd started talking to himself again, just to hear a human voice. "No, that plan isn't going to work."

Almost without realizing it, he was beginning to make a new plan, turning bits and pieces of it over and over in his mind while gathering dry branches and arranging kelp in his furnace.

Fouge was his best way home—maybe his only way home. He knew the way to the Stonecutter estate, and had stolen the maps created by Stax's father. And Fouge was the one who had destroyed Stax's life. Shouldn't he be made to answer for that?

But the thought of confronting Fouge and his minions made Stax shiver. They were veteran warriors, hardened by combat, and he had only a wooden sword that he'd never used in battle. But facing them was the only way Stax could think of that might get him back to his cats, and give him the chance to rebuild the house and life that had been taken from him.

And if he was right about that, he needed to be heading east, not west. That was the direction the raiders had gone, after marooning Stax on this lonesome shore.

After a few days, this was all Stax thought about; every evening, he'd sit on a rock on the beach next to his boat, staring down at the compass in his hand. The needle pointed east, and though east wasn't the way home, it was the direction he needed to go.

Stax was staring at the compass on a particularly beautiful evening when he heard the first gurgle from down the beach. The sound no longer made him jump in fright; by now he was used to it. It was the drowned, beginning their nightly rounds, and that meant it was time to go inside.

"But not tomorrow," Stax said as he stood up and brushed the sand from his ragged pants. "Tomorrow we're going to be far away from here."

And that was how he realized he'd made up his mind.

The next morning, Stax loaded his boat just as he had not so long before. This time, he didn't call the tower a horrible place as he rowed away from it. Nor did he vow that he'd never see it again. That hadn't gone too well the last time.

He rowed east, cheered slightly by the fact that the shoreline was new to him. New, but no less bleak than what he'd left behind—beaches below desert hills dotted with green cacti. Only one thing was different: Stax no longer saw ruins on the shore or shipwrecks in the water. Why? He had no idea. Perhaps his tower was as far as long-ago explorers had bothered to come, before giving up on this land as a barren waste.

Stax had prepared himself for another long journey, and vowed that this time he would stop well before dark instead of plunging on at night. While he rowed, he scanned the southern shore, looking for any sign of camps used by Fouge's raiders. Any food they'd abandoned would probably be long gone, snapped up by hungry scavengers, but they might have discarded gear that he could use.

It was midafternoon when Stax thought he saw something green ahead of him in the distance. He peered through the haze, curious and ready to head for shore if it was another of the ghostly underwater castles that had been so zealously guarded in the Sea of Sorrows.

But this greenery was above the surface of the water. Stax kept rowing, and a few minutes later his mouth was hanging open. Ahead of him, unmistakably, were green hills, covered with grass and dotted with trees.

Stax rowed harder, but this time he was driven by joy, not fear. A river marked the dividing line between the desert and this startling new green country. Stax brought the boat in to the shore, warily scanning it for monsters, and stepped wonderingly out into the grass.

"I had forgotten what green looked like," he murmured, getting down on his knees. Instead of sand, he was on soft soil, warm in the sun. And ahead of him he saw trees—birches and oaks, like at home—and orange tulips. Bees darted back and forth among the trees, intent on their ancient work of turning pollen into honey. The wind was fresh and clean, with none of the salty tang of the sea.

After his days marooned in the desert, Stax felt like he'd been set free in paradise. He gulped down fresh water from the river, staring longingly at the fish wriggling below him, and wandered through the meadow he'd discovered, lifting up his hands so his fingers trailed through the trees' leaves. And then he lay down in the grass, arms and legs stretched out as far as they would go, and let himself get reacquainted with sights and sounds he'd nearly forgotten: the springy feel of grass between his fingers, the murmuring of the wind through oak leaves, the buzz of bees going about their business.

Stax lay there until he heard another sound he'd wondered if he'd ever hear again: the bleating of a sheep.

He scrambled to his feet and peered through the trees, wondering if his mind was playing tricks on him—and, for one wild moment, afraid that everything around him was some delusion brought on by exhaustion and stress. But no, two sheep were grazing on a hillside nearby, regarding him with dim interest as they chewed.

Stax walked toward them slowly, trying not to scare them off. They paid him no mind, even when he reached out and felt the fleece on their backs, which was soft, unlike his salt-encrusted mattress.

The moment Stax felt the wool beneath his fingers, his belly began to growl. Stax looked down at the plump sheep, thought of eating another meal of dried kelp, and shook his head.

"I'm really sorry about this," he told the sheep.

Three hours later, Stax sat on the stump of an oak tree, licking his fingers and feeling far more human than he had in a long time. He'd eaten several slabs of mutton, which was a nice way of saying he'd devoured them with ferocious speed, burning his fingers and tongue because they were still hot. Then, with his hunger momentarily sated, he'd cooked the rest of the mutton, giving him enough food to get through the next week or so. He'd cut new oak planks to replace the weather-beaten, warped boards he'd salvaged from the shipwreck near his tower. He'd made a new, clean white bed using the new wool. And he'd built himself a little cabin with a roof of pressed dirt, just big enough to hold a bed, crafting table, and furnace.

Stax wanted to hurl his remaining pieces of dried kelp into the ocean, but reluctantly decided not to. However much he hated the salty, chewy seaweed, it had kept him alive during desperate times, and if things went wrong he might need it again. No, he'd keep the kelp; it would be a useful reminder not to let his stores get so low that he'd be forced to eat it.

The spot Stax had chosen for his cabin was a pleasant one. There was even a scattering of tulips and cornflowers in front of it, and for a little while Stax let himself fantasize about finding some bone meal and cultivating those flowers, so that with a little time and effort he could create a garden, maybe one with lines of flowers in blue and orange.

"Not going to stay that long, though, are we?" he said to himself, as the sun began to dip toward the sea to the west. "Still, we'll leave the cabin so someone else has a head start. That's the neighborly thing to do."

He had walked around the area a bit, hoping he'd find something useful, like a cave with exposed iron deposits, and fearing he'd find something dangerous, like a nest of creepers. But he hadn't found either, just trees and flowers and tall grass. The only oddity was a kind of groove in the grass behind his cabin, one that ran from south to north. Stax couldn't decide if it was an animal track, like the ones sheep create while going back and forth between favored grazing spots, or a little-traveled road made by people.

Stax decided he would solve this mystery in the morning, as it was nearly dark and he'd been yawning for the better part of an hour. He rose from the tree stump he'd been using as a seat, gave a last grateful look around him at the green meadow, and entered his cabin.

CHAPTER 14

THE CARAVAN

Meeting Ramoa * Stax must choose *
A disagreement in the night

Stax slept better than he had in a very long time. His new woolen mattress was soft and clean, his belly was filled with something that wasn't dried kelp, and no drowned squelched by his front door making hideous gurgling noises.

In fact, Stax woke up only because he heard bells.

He rubbed the sleep out of his eyes, opened the door to his cabin—completely forgetting to check for monsters that might have survived the morning sun by staying in the shade under the trees—and looked around.

He still heard bells, and not just bells, but also the whinnying of horses, the lowing of cattle, and the braying of donkeys, along with human voices, calling out orders to animals, laughing, and even singing. They were coming from behind his cabin, not the direction of the seashore.

It had been a long time since Stax had heard another person's voice, and his first impulse was to run in that direction. But after an eager first step, he stopped. The last voice he'd heard was that of Fouge Tempro, as he and his raiders left Stax to die. What if these were more raiders and he blundered right into them as if he'd been invited to a picnic?

Stax hurried back into his cabin, disassembled his bed, and strapped on his wooden sword. He felt a flush of shame at how pitiful a weapon it was, but it was better than nothing. He carefully shut the door of his little cabin, gave it a pat of thanks for keeping him safe, and headed across the meadow.

As he'd expected, the sounds were coming from that groove in the grass that he thought might have been a road. Stax approached slowly, eyeing the animals and people going past. There were donkeys weighed down with chests, cattle accompanied by drovers yelling "hi-hi" and "chk-chk-chk," sheep hurried along by barking dogs, and traders in sumptuous robes, looking down their noses from atop sleek, muscled horses.

Stax stood and watched this parade in amazement. For one thing, he'd never seen such a caravan—there weren't any in the part of the Overworld he'd called home. For another, he was a little stunned to be near people and animals again. After the near-silence and solitude of ocean and desert, the caravan seemed incredibly busy, a live thing pulsing with noise and color and eternally in motion.

"Hi," Stax called out, his voice sounding rough and strange to his ears. "Hi! Hello there! Hello!"

At first nobody noticed him, except for a tamed wolf who quickly determined he was neither a sheep nor a threat and therefore unimportant. But then two bearded men saw him standing among the trees. Their backs stiffened in alarm, and one of them reached for the sword at his waist. Then he seemed to think better of it, elbowing his companion and pointing in Stax's direction.

The two swaggered over while the caravan passed by behind them.

"What're you, then?" the taller one asked. "Beggar? Hermit? Madman?"

"I'm not any of those things," Stax said, the words spilling out of his brain faster than his mouth could give them form and threatening to tumble over one another. "My home was destroyed and I was marooned on a desert shore—"

"What's that? Quit mumbling, you shaggy ruffian. Whatever you are, stay out of our way and off the road, or you'll pay the consequences."

"This one ain't no threat, Chigam," his shorter companion said. "Why, look at that, his sword's made of wood. Hand-carved, by the look of it."

Chigam peered at the sword at Stax's waist and grinned, showing his yellow teeth. "Haw haw! You planning on fighting an apple, friend? Or dueling an envelope? Haw haw haw!"

"My home was destroyed and my possessions . . ." Stax began, but trailed off. It was obvious the two men weren't listening.

"Ritzo? Chigam? What's going on here?"

The newcomer was a slim young woman wearing a green tunic above pale blue trousers. She had a bow over her shoulder, and a quiver filled with arrows tipped with bright yellow feathers. Her hair was curly and black, spilling over her shoulders, and her eyes were gray in a pale face. She had spots of red in her cheeks as she frowned at the two guards.

"Nothing, Ramoa, just keeping this vagrant off the road," Ritzo muttered.

"Vagrant?" asked Ramoa, peering at Stax. "Is that how you describe yourself, sir?"

"What? No. My home was destroyed and I was marooned by pirates. I tried to get home across the Sea of Sorrows, but I couldn't find my way and came this way instead. From the desert. That's where I was marooned. In the desert."

Ramoa had listened to this explanation with her lips pursed and her head cocked to one side. Stax was aware that he was rambling, but couldn't seem to stop—talking with someone else again felt so strange.

"You rowed here from the Sea of Sorrows?" Ramoa asked. "That would mean you were marooned in Desolation Bay. You're a brave man, Mister . . ."

"Stonecutter," Stax said. "Stax Stonecutter. For a while there I was afraid I'd never see another living soul ever again."

"Sea of Sorrows, bah," said Chigam. "This one's lying or crazy or both. Leave him, Ramoa. We've got a job to do, remember?"

"Yes, we do," Ramoa said. "We're a caravan, Chigam. A caravan is made up of travelers banding together for protection. And Mr. Stonecutter here is a traveler. That means he's welcome to travel with us, if he wants to, and lend his skills for the greater good."

"Greater good?" scoffed Ritzo. "His weapon's a sharpened stick. His weapon's *flammable*."

"And some of us have no weapons at all," Ramoa said. "Are you good with animals, Mr. Stonecutter?"

"Yes," said Stax. "I raised sheep and cows and pigs and chickens at home. And cats."

"I don't think we're driving any chickens or cats on this trip," Ramoa said with a small smile. "But we've got plenty of the rest. Why don't you walk with me? I want to know more about how you survived Desolation Bay."

"A crazy woman and a cat-herder with a pretend sword," Ritzo said. "You two are perfect for each other."

Ramoa scowled as Ritzo and Chigam departed.

"People need people," she said, and for a moment she looked sad. "Even fleabitten louts like those two. One day they'll figure that out. Well. Anyway. Come walk with me, Mr. Stonecutter."

"Okay," Stax said. "But can I ask where you're going?"

Ramoa laughed. "Knowing where you're going is always a good idea. We're bound for Tumbles Harbor. It's a big town to the north, a couple of days' walk up the coast. They have a big fair every month. That's where all these animals are heading. There's a mining company, and a lot else besides."

"A mining company?" Stax asked, his spirits lifting.

"Tumbles Extracting, or something like that," Ramoa said. "I don't know, I'm not really a miner. I don't feel right if I can't look up and see the sky. Well, Mr. Stonecutter? Would you like to join our caravan? You're welcome to, and frankly I'd recommend it. These lands are unforgiving for a traveler without proper gear."

Stax considered. The compass dropped by the raiders was pointing east, and heading off course for a couple of days didn't seem right. On the other hand, was he really going to face Fouge and his warriors with no armor and a wooden sword? And perhaps there was another way home: If Tumbles Harbor really had a mining company, someone there might know of his family, and be able to tell him how to get back to the Stonecutter estate. His father might even have set up one of his outposts there. Tumbles

Harbor sounded like the kind of place he was likely to have visited.

"Mr. Stonecutter, I hate to rush you, but I have duties to attend to," Ramoa said, hands on her hips. "Are you coming with us, or is this where we say farewell?"

Stax looked behind him, to where he could just see the walls of his little cabin amid the trees. He reached into his pocket and felt the compass that might lead him to Fouge. And he looked at the animals and their drovers, heading north.

"I'll come with you," he told Ramoa, who smiled at him and inclined her chin for him to follow.

Ramoa led him toward the back of the caravan. The drovers waved to her or tugged at the bills of their caps, but they seemed to regard Stax uneasily, muttering to themselves or averting their eyes.

"Nobody here seems to like me," Stax finally told Ramoa, who shrugged.

"You look like a wild man, Mr. Stonecutter," she said. "Your clothes are covered with salt and torn, your shirt's burned through in the center, your boots are falling apart, and you've got a ragged beard."

Stax ran his hand over his chin and discovered his stubble had indeed grown into a patchy beard.

"I hadn't realized," he said. "I must look a fright."

"You're certainly a striking figure," Ramoa said with a little laugh. "It's obvious you've been through quite the adventure. But the people in our caravan don't want adventure, Mr. Stonecutter. Or can I call you Stax?"

"I suppose," said Stax, looking in the direction of his cabin.

"Would you prefer Mr. Stonecutter?" Ramoa asked, raising an eyebrow.

"What? No, Stax is fine."

Stax was aware he wasn't making the best first impression—or second impression, maybe—but it was faintly shocking being among people again, and he still wasn't sure he'd made the right decision by joining the caravan.

"If you're feeling formal, my name is Ramoa Peranze. But don't be, it's just us. Anyway, Stax, these people just want to get their animals and goods to Tumbles Harbor, and they want the journey to be as unexciting as possible. Thing is, the Overworld doesn't always cooperate. But I don't need to tell you that, seeing how you survived Desolation Bay."

"I didn't know that was its name," Stax said. "But *you* know it. And the Sea of Sorrows too."

"Yes," Ramoa said. "Dangerous places, particularly the Sea of Sorrows. It's crawling with drowned, and the Old Ones have several monuments there. Difficult to find a safe route through there, even in good weather."

"The Old Ones," Stax said, rubbing at his chest. "So that's what they're called. One of them gave me this burn."

"That's what they're called in this part of the Overworld," Ramoa said. "Other people have different names for them. I've heard them called elder guardians, fire-eyes, and sea lords. Even met a wayfarer who claimed he'd built a house out of prismarine taken from one of their monuments, down around Porto Reynes. But I never saw the house with my own eyes, so I won't swear that one's true."

"Desolation Bay, the Sea of Sorrows, Porto Reynes," Stax repeated to himself. "So do you know what's beyond the Sea of Sorrows? To the west, I mean? Somewhere out that way there are ice floes, and then a green country of forests and meadows, kind of like this one. That's where I need to get back to."

Stax looked at Ramoa hopefully, but she shook her head.

"I've only traveled in the eastern end of the Sea," she said. "My country's to the south of it, and it's far safer to travel by staying east of the Shining Desert, even though it's the long way around. But one day I'll get there, Stax. I won't be happy until I've seen the entire Overworld, from pole to pole and end to end."

"The entire Overworld?" Stax asked. "Is that even possible?"

"No, it's not," Ramoa said. "But I'm going to do the best I can. It drives me crazy to think that when I breathe my last there will be places—so many places—I never got to. Don't you ever think that way?"

"No," Stax said. "If I'm lucky enough to get back home, I'm never leaving again."

"Really? How can you say that? I mean, I'm sure your own country is lovely, Stax, but oh, the places I've seen. Lava falls in the moonlight. Mountains with roots in the seafloor and tops that lie beyond the clouds. Great rifts in the earth, with diamonds and emeralds sparkling in the walls. Islands in a blue sea, carpeted with flowers whose colors I hadn't known existed."

Stax shook his head, but Ramoa was looking off into the forest, her mind far away.

"Sometimes I wish I were a painter, so I could capture these things and share them with everyone," she said. "But sometimes I'm glad that I'm not. There are too many beautiful things in this world that people want to keep for themselves. I like seeing things that are too big for that, and that no painting could do justice. Places where the only thing you can do is look, and promise yourself that you'll remember."

———

An hour or so before dusk, the caravan's leaders passed down word that the procession would stop for the night in a broad meadow between two rivers. Ramoa and Stax dropped back to the end of the line and helped herd the cattle into pens that had been hastily constructed. Campfires were blazing, and Stax smelled beef cooking and heard songs and laughter.

"These are my favorite moments on the trail," Ramoa said. "All the people are together, and we can look back on another day when we've kept each other safe."

Stax nodded. The last campfire he'd seen had been the raiders', but this felt different—a group banding together for mutual protection, as opposed to a band of rogues seeking to do harm.

The caravan's guards, including Stax and Ramoa, were assigned to the outer perimeter, and would sleep in shifts. Before first watch, Stax excused himself and washed the salt from his hair in the river, then returned to the campfire with his hair cut short and his beard gone. His smooth chin felt strange to the touch.

"Why, Stax, you look positively reborn," Ramoa said.

"Except for these rags," Stax mumbled, suddenly embarrassed by his worn, salt-stiffened clothes and his wooden sword.

"You can fix that when we get to Tumbles Harbor," Ramoa said. "Everyone who does guard duty gets credit at the general store, and I'll make sure you're on the roster."

"Thanks, Ramoa," Stax said, sitting by the fire. Beef was sizzling on spits, and he hoped he wasn't actually drooling with anticipation.

He looked over at Ramoa, figuring he should say something and then realizing he was badly out of practice at figuring out what that something should be.

"So . . . will you be going back south after the fair?"

"No. I'm meeting my good friend Hejira Tenboots in Tumbles Harbor. Heji's been exploring the northern jungles, and said he wants me to see them. Hey! You should come with us, Stax."

Stax shook his head. "I have to get home. Or find Fouge Tempro."

"That's the leader of the pirates who destroyed your house?" Ramoa asked.

"Yes," said Stax, and fished the compass out of his pocket. "He left this behind, or maybe one of his raiders did. I thought I could use it to get home. My father always took a compass on his journeys. But I was wrong. Now I'm thinking I can follow it to find Fouge."

Ramoa took the compass and examined it with what looked to Stax like a practiced eye.

"That's a costly thing to leave behind. You need both iron and redstone to make a compass," she said. "What makes you think you can use it to find this Fouge?"

"Well, it's his, isn't it?"

Ramoa looked at him questioningly.

"I've never used a compass before," he admitted, knowing he sounded defensive. "I never had to. This one's always pointing east. I figured that's because it's where Fouge is."

Ramoa shook her head. "I don't use compasses. I prefer to navigate by the sun. But I could explain how they work, if you like."

"Okay."

"They're oriented toward the origin point of the Overworld," Ramoa explained. "To the place where the priests say people first came into existence. So if you're using one to find a place, you have to know where that place is in relation to the origin point."

Ramoa handed the compass back to Stax, who stared down at it for a moment. So that was what his father had been telling him: the relationship between the Stonecutter estate and the origin point. It had probably been a simple formula, one his father had committed to memory. But Stax hadn't been listening, and now the secret was lost. His father would have written it down, somewhere in his library, but those books had been burned or carried away.

"So using one to find a person . . ."

Ramoa said nothing, allowing Stax to reach the answer on his own. Stax tucked the compass back into his pocket and kicked at the ground angrily. The compass couldn't get him home or help him reach Fouge, making it all but useless. He thought briefly about throwing it into the fire, but stopped himself. Perhaps he could trade it for something in Tumbles Harbor—new clothes, or a sword that hadn't begun life as a tree.

A drover brought them chunks of beef spitted on sticks. Stax took a skewer with a grateful nod and gnawed at the meat greedily, wiping at the juices running down his chin.

"First guard shift is about to begin," Ramoa said, after they tossed their sticks into the fire. "Come keep watch with me?"

"All right," Stax said, but after a moment's hesitation—which Ramoa noticed.

"I try to help people," she told him, getting to her feet, and once again Stax saw a trace of some old sadness in her face. "I'd like to help you. If you'll let me."

"I . . . sure," Stax said. "Sorry. It's just . . . well, it's been a lot."

"I get it," Ramoa said. "You probably trusted Fouge Tempro, and look how that turned out. But you'll see I'm okay. Or at least, I think I am. Come on, Stax."

Stax followed her to the edge of the firelight. The sun was down and the moon was rising. Stax could see its light glittering on the waters of Desolation Bay, to the west beyond the trees. In the other direction he could see rolling hills, with mountains rising beyond them.

"The biggest threats around here are skeletons and spiders," Ramoa said, taking her bow off her shoulder and inspecting its length. "Anything I see, I'll take down long before it gets to us. Your job is to make sure I see everything. And if I should miss, whack 'em with that sword of yours."

"With my fearsome wooden sword?" Stax asked. "What good will that do?"

"More good than fists or harsh language," Ramoa said. "But don't worry. I won't miss."

"So why am I here?"

"To keep me company, for one," Ramoa said. "So, tell me about this Fouge Tempro. But only if you want to, of course."

Stax found that he did want to. Standing at the edge of the firelight, he let the story spill out of him, from Fouge's arrival to the raiders destroying his house to the harrowing ocean voyage and all he'd endured while marooned. Ramoa listened gravely, only interrupting to ask more about the drowned and Stax's dangerous encounter with the undersea monument and its guardians.

"Hold on a minute, Stax," Ramoa said, as Stax was telling her about his decision to head east instead of west. "Things are going bump in the night."

Stax followed her gaze and spotted a slim white figure under the trees: a skeleton, holding a bow. Its head swiveled madly and Stax wondered what it was seeing and thinking. Did it know the firelight meant people? Did it hate them for being alive and walking under the sun unharmed? Or did it simply follow some ancient instinct, without thinking at all?

"Strange creatures," Ramoa mused, selecting an arrow from her quiver and smoothing the feathers. "If you ever get into a shoot-out with one, hold still. It feels like the wrong thing to do, particularly once the arrows start flying, but they're excellent at tracking movement and lousy at hitting a stationary target."

Stax nodded, his eyes riveted on the skeleton. Ramoa nocked an arrow to her bow, sighted along the shaft, and let the arrow fly. It thudded into the skull and the skeleton froze, trying to get a fix on its attacker. Ramoa had already drawn another arrow, the motion practiced and smooth. The second shaft buried itself between the skeleton's ribs.

The monster saw them now and its mouth opened, though Stax heard no sound. It nocked an arrow to its own bow. Ramoa, third arrow against her chin, flicked her eyes to Stax and smiled.

"Remember, don't move," she said.

The skeleton fired its bow. Stax flinched, but the arrow went wide by a considerable margin. Before the skeleton could draw another, Ramoa fired her own arrow and the creature collapsed.

"Any more of them out there?" she asked Stax, who was still staring at the spot where the skeleton had fallen, awed by Ramoa's skill with a bow. At some point during the archers' duel he'd drawn his wooden sword; he put it back in his belt, hoping Ramoa hadn't noticed.

"I don't see anything," Stax said, scanning the darkness.

"Good," Ramoa said. She had returned her bow to her shoulder and was walking through the grass, eyes searching ahead of her. She returned with the arrow that the skeleton had fired, brushing the dirt away from its tip. She handed it to Stax.

"I've never even fired a bow," Stax said.

"Oh, I can teach you. The best way to keep an enemy from hurting you is to take him out from a distance. Now, you were telling me about Desolation Bay?"

So Stax told her the rest of the story, ending with his building the little cabin and hearing the bells.

"You should be proud of yourself," Ramoa said. "Most people would have given up, but you never did. So what are you going to do now?"

Stax had been thinking about that, and had his answer. "Go with the caravan to Tumbles Harbor. If it's a big mining town, someone there may have heard of my family. Maybe even be able to help me get home."

Ramoa frowned. "I've wandered a big chunk of the Overworld, and I've never heard of the Stonecutters, or anything like the place you call home. So what if that doesn't work? What then?"

"Then I need to go after Fouge," Stax said. "And to do that, I'll need better equipment and supplies. I learned how to mine as a kid. Someone in Tumbles Harbor will be able to make use of me."

"I've never heard of Fouge either," Ramoa said.

They stood in silence for a minute, with the stars spilled out over their heads.

"You don't think my plan's a good one," Stax said, sensing Ramoa thought that but was reluctant to say it.

"It's not that, Stax," Ramoa said. "It's just that the Overworld is huge. Infinite, some say. You could spend your entire life searching for this Fouge and never find him. I don't want you to spend years and years on a quest that will probably fail—through no fault of your own—and leave you bitter and angry."

"So I should just accept what this man did to me? I should just let him get away with it?"

"He took your life away, Stax. I get that. Don't let him take your future too."

Stax felt himself getting angry. Ramoa said she was trying to help, but what did she know of what he'd been through, of everything that Fouge had done to him?

"Sounds like you've got it all figured out. So what should I do instead?"

"Come with me and Heji. It's a big world. It's got terrible things in it—I don't need to tell you that. But there's so much beauty too. Let me show it to you."

"So I should just run away?"

"That's not what I said."

"Well, it sure sounds like it to me. Maybe running away is your answer to a problem, but I don't think it's mine."

Now Ramoa sounded angry too. "You don't know anything about me, Stax Stonecutter. You don't know what I've been through, or how I've dealt with it."

"You're right, I don't," Stax said stiffly. "And you don't know as much as you think you do about me. So I think it's better if we just keep watch."

He could feel Ramoa's eyes on him, and wondered if she would say something else, and if he wanted her to. But after a moment Ramoa turned away, and they spent the rest of their guard duty in silence.

CHAPTER 15

TUMBLES HARBOR

A peace offering * Introduction to a busy town *
An unwelcome reunion * The sights and sounds
of the fair * Tumbles Harbor, considered *
A visit to the mine, with free advice

In the morning, while everyone was eating a quick breakfast, Stax left the campfire and climbed over the hill to the meadow where Ramoa had shot the skeleton. He pushed his way through the tall grass, dew soaking his pants, until he found a length of bone and a solitary arrow—all that remained of the unfortunate creature. He brought them back and silently handed them over to Ramoa in what he supposed was a peace offering.

Ramoa smiled and took the bone, saying it would be an excellent source of bone meal for her garden back home. She suggested he keep the arrow for his own collection. But the angry words of the previous night seemed to hang between them, and they weren't able to fall back into the easy rapport they'd had when they first met.

The caravan traveled all day. After a heated debate, its leaders decided to stop and camp again at dusk rather than push on through the night to reach Tumbles Harbor. That night Ramoa shot a pair of spiders, their red eyes winking out after her arrows found their marks. The next morning she was the one who fetched what remained: two long, curled strands of tough silk.

"If you ever find yourself stuck on the Sea of Sorrows again, a fishing pole would be good to have," she said, handing them to Stax.

She was right; the idea of eating dried kelp again, ever, made Stax want to gag. He coiled the silk up and added it to his bundle of supplies.

Soon after the caravan moved out, the road changed from an animal track to a well-traveled thoroughfare, with the grass worn away to dirt. The caravan began to encounter other travelers—hunters carrying animal skins, and stern-faced men and women thundering by on horseback. The occasional traveler became a steady stream and the road grew rutted and pitted, with the conversation among the drovers and traders and guards turning to when they would reach Tumbles Harbor and what would happen if they were late.

It was midmorning when the caravan came over a ridge and Stax saw the town below them. Tumbles Harbor was well-named: a crescent-shaped bay ringed with steep, irregular hills that seemed like they were about to fall into the water. The bay was filled with tall-masted ships and little boats, while houses and shops clung to the sides of the hills above them.

Stax had never been in a town so large—the little town where the Stonecutter office was located had barely a dozen houses—and he gawped at the buildings pressing in on all sides. For their part, the townspeople seemed pleased to see the caravan, leaning out of their windows to hail old friends, offer good-natured jeers that they were late, or just wave. The line of people and animals wended its way down the hillsides, with only one spooked cow breaking away and needing to be retrieved, and the drovers cried out theatrically, showing off for the gathering crowd as they led the animals to pens in the central square. The fair was clearly about to begin; workers were straightening colorful banners, while traders were setting up their stalls.

"That's the caravanserai," Ramoa said, pointing to a sprawling inn on one side of the square. "It's where you get your wages from the caravan agent. They'll have a bed for you tonight, and in the morning you'll be on your own. Unless you've changed your mind about going with me and Heji?"

"I don't think so," Stax said, though he was relieved that Ramoa had decided her earlier invitation was still good. But he sensed something else behind her words. "You're not staying for the fair, then?"

Ramoa shook her head. "I'm moving on. Towns aren't really my thing, and buying a bunch of stuff would just slow me down. But I pass through town every month or two. Leave word of where you are with Brubbs, at the general store. Brubbs knows everybody. That way I'll be able to find you."

Stax agreed that he would, and Ramoa smiled. They looked at each other for a moment and then shook hands, a little awkwardly. Then Ramoa turned away and threaded her way through the marketplace crowd. Stax saw a flash of her curly black hair, then a bit of her green tunic, and then she was gone.

Stax sighed, wondering if Ramoa would really try to find him next time she was in town. He'd lost his temper with her for no good reason, and with it, he feared, his chance to have at least one friend in this strange new town.

Now he wasn't sure what to do. After days in the wilderness, Tumbles Harbor seemed impossibly busy, with too many sights, sounds, and smells for him to take in. Stax made his way through the crowded square, apologizing profusely to everyone he bumped or elbowed or who bumped or elbowed him (which was more or less everyone) until he reached the marketplace's perimeter and was able to lean against the wall of a cooper's shop, the nature of its business clearly indicated by a large birch-wood barrel hanging above the door.

"It was quiet by the tower, if you don't count dead things gurgling in the night," Stax muttered to himself. "Would you like that better?"

"Don't think I would, stranger," said a man bent under a heavy stack of cowhides. He offered Stax a lopsided grin before shouldering his way deeper into the crowd.

"Okay, the first thing I need to do is stop talking to myself," said an embarrassed Stax, except he also said that out loud, which led to a testy conversation with a confused flower seller. After that Stax simply watched the crowd for a while, bewildered by the ceaseless thrum of activity. He wondered if his father had been to Tumbles Harbor and tried to picture him in the middle of this throng, weighed down by chests containing precious stones and ore samples that he'd brought over the sea. Would he have greeted old acquaintances? Traded gossip about doings in far-off lands? Stopped off at the inn for a bowl of soup?

While Stax couldn't know if his father had visited Tumbles Harbor, he must have seen towns like it. Stax wondered what it had been like for him to come home after that, to step off the boat at the Stonecutters' dock and hear nothing but the sounds of farm animals and the wind ruffling the birch leaves. Had his father sighed with relief to return to a place that was quiet and still? Or had he found the tranquility of home boring, and counted the days until he could depart again? Stax didn't know. He wished he'd asked his father, before he vanished, but now of course it was far too late.

A crier announced the fair's official opening and the crowd cheered. Eager buyers rushed forward for a first chance at the best material, while wandering traders circulated through the crowd hawking food. From his vantage point, Stax saw people selling melons, pumpkins, loaves of bread, cocoa pods, skewers of meat, fried fish, and slices of cake. His stomach rumbled and he patted it.

"Sorry, but I don't think anyone will have dried kelp for sale," Stax said to himself, forgetting he'd just vowed to stop doing that. "Guess I better see about getting paid."

He made his way through the crowd, passing a fishmonger who was indeed offering dried kelp, to his amusement, and pushed open the caravanserai's front door. The inn was crowded with the drovers and laborers from the caravan, celebrating their safe arrival by talking and laughing and clinking mugs.

A drover he vaguely recognized pointed him to the caravan agent's office. To his annoyance, Stax found himself in line behind Ritzo and Chigam. He said nothing to the two disagreeable men, hoping they wouldn't recognize him now that he'd cut his hair, but after a moment Ritzo elbowed Chigam and they both fixed Stax with broad grins.

"Well, if it isn't Ramoa's pet beggar from the road," Ritzo said with a cackle. "Stax Shipwreck, or something like that."

"Not a beggar, but a hermit," Chigam said. "Spent years meditating on the mysteries of sand and salt."

"I say beggar, you say hermit," Ritzo shrugged. "We could just say 'useless layabout' and be done with it."

Stax turned away, determined to ignore them, but Chigam refused to let it go.

"Careful now," he told Ritzo. "Stax Shipwreck's still got his wooden sword. Better call him Sir Stax, unless you want to get splinters."

"He's got more than that," Ritzo said. "Now he's got two arrows. Two arrows but no bow! Walking arsenal, this one! What a fine guard you'll make for the next lucky caravan, Sir Stax Shipwreck!"

"I had a diamond sword at home," Stax said a bit stiffly.

"Sure you did," Chigam said. "Bet you was clad head to toe in diamond, Sir Stax."

Stax endured their gibes in disgusted silence until Ritzo and Chigam had collected their pay and departed with a flurry of mocking bows.

The caravan agent was a little man sitting in a little office, scratching with an ink quill in a big leatherbound book. He didn't even look up as Stax approached.

"Emeralds or credit chit?" he asked in a flat monotone.

"Excuse me?" asked Stax, baffled.

"*Emeralds or credit chit?*" the agent repeated. "How do you want your pay?"

"What's a credit chit?" Stax asked.

The agent sighed. "Did you just fall off the beetroot donkey? A credit chit is money that's good at the Tumbles Harbor general store, here at the caravanserai, and with the better vendors at the fair. Anyway, what's your name? I assume you know *that*."

"Stax Stonecutter."

The agent started flipping through the pages of his book, brows creased in consternation.

"I'm probably at the end," Stax said. "I signed on just a couple of days before Tumbles Harbor."

The agent peered dubiously at him, his beady eyes lingering on Stax's ragged clothes, then shook his head and flipped to the back of the book.

"I found you," he said, sounding disappointed. "Well, the decision's made for you. You didn't do enough work for us to earn an emerald. Enjoy your credit chit."

Stax took the sheet of paper the agent handed over, which contained his name and a scrawled number. He turned to go, then looked back. "My friend said I was entitled to a bed here tonight?"

"That would logically be a question for the innkeeper," the agent said, not looking up from his book.

Stax was beginning to think he didn't like Tumbles Harbor, but fortunately the innkeeper was both kind and helpful, showing him the neat, clean little room that had been reserved for him and pointing the way to the general store, though she warned him that like most everything in town, it was closed for the day because of the fair.

Now that he had his room sorted out, Stax took a deep breath and headed back out into the crowd, peering over the shoulders of the fairgoers to see what each stall had for sale. There was every imaginable kind of food, and plenty of offerings Stax had never imagined eating. But there was a lot more than food. Lumber merchants offered planks of exactly cut wood, including rich, dark woods Stax had never seen before. Metalsmiths showed off iron swords, including some that glowed with the eerie magenta of enchantment. Chests overflowed with carefully cleaned and combed wool in every hue. Leatherworkers and carpetmakers made lavish promises about the quality of their wares. There were smiths holding up armor made of leather and iron and chain links, and weavers promising to make banners in any color or design you could imagine, and booksellers showing off the clean white pages of librams and tomes. And there were stranger things too: paintings of strange vistas, exotic flowers in pots, brilliantly colored fish in buckets, and the polished shells of turtles and mollusks.

Just a couple of weeks earlier, when money had been no object, Stax would have gleefully filled chests with knickknacks and new curiosities to adorn the walls of the Stonecutter estate. He would have tried all the strange foods—or some of them, at least—and bought rare fish as treats for Lapis, Emerald, and Coal. But now most everything that caught his eye cost more than he could afford, and Ramoa's warning about saving his money was uppermost in his mind. He limited himself to a skewer of mutton and a cookie, deciding to get what he needed at the general store tomorrow.

For now, he'd explore the town. He left the fair behind him and strolled along the docks, where men and women were unloading ships, singing and laughing as they passed chests, barrels, blocks, and bales from the decks of the ships and rearranged them in neat stacks on the docks. The ships' sails were furled, but many bore colorful banners festooned with stripes, circles, and diamonds.

Stax made his way through the dockyards, waving off fishmongers crying out that their catches were so fresh they were still flopping, and followed a narrow road between a line of buildings made of wood and stone. The road was paved with cobblestone, and Stax found himself instinctively studying the quality of the stonework and its composition.

The road led up and away from the marketplace, and within a few minutes the crowds had dwindled and then vanished, so that Stax was sharing the street with just a few locals busy with errands or simply out for a stroll. He stopped to look down at the town, trying to imagine what it had looked like before the first explorer decided it would make an ideal harbor.

If he closed his eyes, Stax could almost see it: a half-circle of sand bordered by a lush meadow, ringed by hills. He imagined a single house on the shore: a simple dwelling of sod, constructed as a refuge from the dangers of the night. And then a few more, and more still, until eventually whoever lived there would have to get together and talk about organizing things, creating docks to handle the boats, and clearing a town common, and maintaining the roads, and all the rest.

Making decisions like that had never been an issue for Stax, who could do whatever he wanted on the Stonecutter estate without having to consult with anyone else. On the other hand, no individual house or estate could ever create a riot of creativity and controlled chaos like Tumbles Harbor. You needed more people for that—lots more people, building houses and tearing them down, imagining businesses and making them work, and bringing in goods and art and food and stories and everything else that other people would want.

Looking down at the town, Stax smiled. He could see the bay as it existed before all that happened, pristine and beautiful, but he could also appreciate everything that generations of people's creativity had brought to it, and how their efforts had remade a beautiful place as a thriving port.

As Stax kept going up the hill, the houses grew smaller, gaps appeared between them, and eventually most sat apart from their neighbors, in little fenced yards. After walking for a few more minutes, Stax found himself in a dusty saddle of land where five roads converged. A cluster of signs pointed the way to four places Stax had never heard of and a fifth place that he had, though by a slightly different name: The Tumbles Extraction Company.

"Now, that's a good omen if ever I saw one," Stax said.

He followed the road up a series of low hills, until he found himself below what had once been a mountain, its top now squared off with a precision never found in nature. A black tunnel yawned in the side of the mountain, behind a fence, and next to the fence was a low-slung, windowless building made of gray stone, which Stax recognized as andesite. It had an oaken door and a sign next to it out front:

MINE OFFICE

EXPERIENCED WORKERS WANTED

CRIMINALS, LAYABOUTS, THE ACCIDENT-PRONE, AND NEWCOMERS

NEED NOT APPLY

MUST FURNISH OWN TOOLS

Stax was about to knock on the door when someone called out that the office was closed.

"On account of it being a holiday, what with the fair and all," said a shuffling, bent-backed man with a gray beard and a rusty sword on his belt. "You a miner? Manager's a bit particular about who she takes on."

"No," Stax said. "Well, yes."

"Eh?" the man peered at Stax. "Which is it, friend? Yes or no?"

"I am a miner, but that's not why I'm here. I'm trying to get back home."

"Unless you live in the Tumbles quarry, I'd say you're in the wrong place."

"It's a little more complicated than that," Stax said. "Will the owner be here tomorrow?"

"The owner? Wouldn't think so. He lives in a big house a few hills over yonder, overlooking the backcountry," the man said, waving in a vague direction. "But the manager will be in. She's Mrs. Taney. That's pronounced TAW-nee but spelled TAY-nee, and don't mix up the two if you know what's good for you. All mine business goes through her."

"Right," Stax said. "I'll be back tomorrow, then."

"You want my advice, friend? Before you come, get yourself some tools. She won't see you if you don't have tools. And get some new clothes. Like I said, Mrs. Taney's particular about who she hires, and you look like a beggar or someone who's crawled away from a shipwreck."

"You're more right than you know," Stax said, offering the man a low bow. "Until tomorrow."

CHAPTER 16

THREE CURIOUS CHARACTERS

Brubbs and Xinzi * The right tool for the job *
Mrs. Taney has questions

By the time Stax returned to town, the crowd at the fair had thinned, stalls were closing up, and drovers were emerging from the caravanserai to round up the cattle, sheep, and pigs that hadn't been sold. Stax used a bit of his credit on a bowl of stew and sat in the inn's common room, surrounded by traders comparing notes on how the fair had gone and tired customers doing the same.

Stax found himself yawning repeatedly and went to bed. He woke up baffled, confused by the oak planks of the ceiling and the light coming through his room's little square window, until he remembered where he was.

After a breakfast of bread with honey, Stax headed across the town common, now strangely empty after yesterday's hustle and bustle, and climbed the stairs to the low porch that surrounded the general store. A couple of aged townspeople exchanging gossip bade him a good morning; Stax nodded politely and headed inside.

The general store was like a scaled-down version of the fair, its shelves piled high with gear, supplies, and stores of every conceivable variety, though Stax noticed it didn't stock any of the more eccentric items that had been for sale yesterday; there were no chests full of cocoa pods or buckets of tropical fish.

"Well, good morning, young sir, and how can we help you?" called out a squat, cheerful man from behind the counter.

Stax had half-expected his ragged clothes to be met with snide comments or at least raised eyebrows, and felt himself relax at being greeted so respectfully. A second man, this one extremely tall and thin, was at the other end of the counter, polishing a metal bucket.

"I need some new clothes," Stax said, fingering his shirt, which was indeed dirty and disreputable. "Will this credit chit do?"

"Certainly, sir," said the man, after a glance at the paper Stax passed over. "Don't think I've seen you in here before. Came in with the caravan, did you?"

Stax started to mutter something vague, then stopped himself. He needed help getting home, and anyway the man seemed kind.

"That's right," Stax said. "I was . . . well, it's a long story. I was marooned."

"That sounds like quite the ordeal! Glad it's behind you," the shopkeeper said. "I'm Brubbs, and the silent statue over there is Xinzi."

"Stax Stonecutter."

Brubbs gave Stax's hand a warm shake, while Xinzi looked over and nodded minutely.

"Good to meet you, Stax! But I'm afraid to say we don't have anything as fancy as this shirt. I can tell it was a fine garment, before everything that happened to you."

"That's all right," Stax said. "I don't need fancy, just some work clothes. And some information, maybe. Do either of you know the lands on the other side of the Sea of Sorrows?"

"Can't say I do," Brubbs said. "Never been more than a day's ride out of Tumbles Harbor, in fact. Xinzi, how about you?"

The tall, thin man shook his head.

"You might try down at the docks. I swear there were more ships in port yesterday than I'd seen in four or five months, what with the fair and all," Brubbs said. "Of course most of them have pulled up anchor and left, now that it's done."

Stax could have kicked himself. He'd been too overwhelmed by the sights and sounds of the town and the fair to think of asking the ship captains.

"Is that where you're from, Stax?" asked Brubbs. "The other side of the Sea of Sorrows?"

Stax decided he liked the man's gentle eyes and nodded. "Unfortunately, I don't know my way back."

"Well, Xinzi and me will keep an ear open," Brubbs said. "In the meantime, let's get you dressed."

With Brubbs's cheerful help, Stax picked a plain brown shirt and blue pants, changing into them in the back of the general store.

"Much better," Brubbs said, holding up Stax's salt-encrusted, threadbare old clothes. "And what shall I do with these?"

"Burn them," Stax said, disgusted.

"Off to the furnace they go. And now, new clothes for a new home."

Stax knew Brubbs was trying to be friendly, but the suggestion that he needed to forget his old home left Stax feeling morose. The shopkeeper seemed to sense that, and clapped a hand on Stax's back, his other arm waving at the store's many offerings.

"Anything else you need today?"

Stax remembered the mining company guard's warning about Mrs. Taney and her suspicions about potential employees.

"A pickaxe," he said.

"Certainly! Let me see what we have."

Brubbs vanished into the back room, calling out the selling points of various pickaxes he had in stock. Stax glanced at his credit chit, wondering if he could afford a decent piece of equipment and if that was how he should spend the rest of his funds. He imagined visiting Mrs. Taney, shiny new pickaxe in hand, and discovering she was an old friend of his father's and would be happy to help him get home, except because he'd bought a pickaxe, he didn't have enough money to pay for passage back across the Sea of Sorrows.

"That would be a really stupid way to wind up working in the mines," Stax said out loud. That habit was proving hard to break.

"What was that, Stax?" asked Brubbs, poking his head out of the back room.

"He was talking to himself," Xinzi grumbled.

"So? Let him talk to himself! There's certainly no point talking to you. That's the most you've said in six weeks."

Xinzi mumbled something—or at least his lips moved—and he returned to his polishing.

"Now, Stax, here's what we have in stock," Brubbs said, returning weighed down with pickaxes of wood, stone, and iron.

Stax decided to get the iron pickaxe; it was a well-made tool, and if he did get home, he'd need to replace everything that

Fouge and his raiders had stolen. So what if he had to work for a couple of weeks to afford a berth on a ship? Wouldn't he have done anything for such a chance while stuck on the desert shore in his ruined tower?

But there was one more thing.

"Could you mount the pick head on a slightly longer stick?" Stax asked. "I want one that's exactly a block long, and this looks a little short."

Brubbs looked over at Xinzi, who shrugged.

"I don't see why not," Brubbs said. "But can I ask why?"

"It's what my father always used, and so it's what I've always used," Stax said.

Stax bought the pickaxe, modified as he'd requested. With nearly all of his credit depleted, he said farewell to Brubbs and Xinzi. He slung his new pickaxe over one shoulder and strolled up the hill to The Tumbles Extraction Company, finding the mine office's door open. The gray-bearded guard peered at him with no apparent sign of recognition, which Stax decided was a good thing. Stax nodded politely at him and entered the office, where a white-haired, hatchet-faced woman was sitting behind a table piled with ledgers and adorned with a sign that read:

MRS. GUINEVERE TANEY,

MANAGER

She looked a little like Stax's grandmother, whom he remembered as thin, wiry, and tough, and Stax felt hope blossom somewhere inside him.

Mrs. Taney's dark-eyed gaze flitted from his clothes to his pickaxe and then settled on his face.

"That pickaxe's never been used," she said, making it sound like an accusation. "There's nary a scratch or scuff on it."

Stax had been so worried that Mrs. Taney would think poorly of him if he showed up without a pickaxe that he'd never considered she might think poorly of him if he showed up *with* one. This suddenly struck him as unfair, and he didn't know what to do, so he stood there with his mouth hanging open, which was basically the opposite of doing something.

"I lost my old one," he said finally.

"Careless," Mrs. Taney snapped, in a voice that wasn't very grandmotherly at all. "We don't like that here."

Stax thought of explaining what had happened to him, but decided not to. Mrs. Taney might consider having his house destroyed and being marooned on a barren coast careless too.

I feel like it's my job to remind you that Stax didn't know very many people, having spent much of his youth alone with his cats and with trees and flowers—which, while lovely, don't offer a lot of conversation. And he'd become quite the loner, living by himself on his estate. A little too much of a loner, Stax was beginning to suspect.

Now that he was out in the Overworld, he was discovering something about people that all of us discover eventually: namely, that they're funny. Not "funny" as in "they make you laugh," though that's an excellent quality in a person, but "funny" in the other sense of the word, as in "peculiar." All of us are peculiar in a lot of ways, most of which are harmless and worry us a lot even though no one else knows about them, or wouldn't care if they did. But a few of us, unfortunately, are peculiar in ways that are difficult or unpleasant to deal with. Stax wasn't sure which was the case with Mrs. Taney; all he knew was that his interview, if that's what it was, didn't seem to be going well.

"Did you ever use the pickaxe you lost?" Mrs. Taney asked after a moment.

"Yes," Stax said, and decided to try being charming. "Why, I've been a miner all my life, in fact. I'm Stax—Stax Stonecutter. 'Stonecutter by name and stonecutter by trade,' that's what my father used to say."

Stax had hoped the Stonecutter name would cause Mrs. Taney to look up in surprised recognition, but she just made an odd noise, something between "huh" and "hmm" and a grunt.

"Any chance you knew my father?" Stax asked. "He traveled a lot, working for our family mining company. I'd hoped maybe he'd visited Tumbles Harbor."

"Never heard of anyone named Stonecutter," Mrs. Taney said, and Stax hung his head as she worked a ledger free of its pile and opened it. "Now, as to your qualifications. Are you afraid of heights?"

"No," Stax said, remembering Fouge Tempro shrinking back from the edge of the stairs in the Stonecutter mine, the one he'd left flooded and ruined.

"Any history of claustrophobia? That's a fear of tight spaces."

"I know what it is."

"Good. And do you have a history of it?"

"No history of claustrophobia."

"Are you afraid of the dark?"

"No."

"Are you afraid of falling into lava and burning to death?"

"What?"

"Are you afraid of falling—"

"Of course I'm afraid of that. Anyone with any sense at all would be afraid of that."

"Hmm," said Mrs. Taney, making a checkmark in a different row.

"The trick is not to fall into lava in the first place, isn't it?" Stax asked. "My grandmother taught my father how to avoid that, and he taught me. He also showed me how to make sure you're not digging beneath a pool of it. That's the real danger, down in a mine."

"I'm not hiring your father or grandmother," said Mrs. Taney. "How about being hacked apart by zombies, shot full of arrows by skeletons, or blown to smithereens by creepers? Do any of those things concern you?"

"Very much so."

"And yet you want to be a miner," Mrs. Taney said, leaning back and folding her arms over her chest.

"Those things you mention are bad, but they only happen if you make mistakes down in the mine," Stax said. "Properly placed light sources keep monsters out. If you break into a cavern or rift, you block it off and look for a way around it, or move slowly into it with enough personnel and clear it of hazards. These are all things I learned, working in my family's mine."

Mrs. Taney stared at Stax for what felt like quite a while. Then, to his surprise, she smiled.

"It's good to have someone come in who has a little common sense," she said. "Most of the applicants we get barely know which end of the pickaxe goes into the rock. When can you start?"

Stax hadn't necessarily been looking for a job, but with no leads on Fouge or on how to get home, and with his rapidly dwindling resources . . .

"Now?" Stax asked.

"A young man in a hurry, that's also good," Mrs. Taney said. "Since you're not obviously an idiot or otherwise unfit for duty, let me explain how we do business. We work in three-person crews: two miners digging, one supervising. Everyone switches roles.

Ore and gems are collected and brought to the surface. You get paid for every day you work, plus a bonus for anything your crew finds. Low bonuses for diorite and granite, higher for coal, iron, and redstone, premium for gold, lapis lazuli, and diamonds."

"How about emeralds?"

"If you find any below the Tumbles, you'll be the first," Mrs. Taney said. "You'll start working in the upper levels, on an ore crew. This is Mr. Barnacle's month running the ore crews and he has an opening, so I'll place you with him. You'll find him an interesting character, I think."

Stax wasn't sure what that meant, and he really wasn't sure he liked the way that sounded, but Mrs. Taney wasn't finished.

"Mr. Barnacle can be a handful, but be patient and put up with him and in a couple of weeks you'll move to a gem crew. Do poorly, on the other hand, and I'll get rid of you—and there won't be any warnings. Any questions?"

"Is there a place I can sleep?" Stax asked.

"Miners' dormitory. If you sleep or eat there when you're not on a shift, it comes out of your wages. If you're below ground working, no charge. Anything else?"

Stax shook his head, feeling a little dazed at how quickly the situation had changed. "I don't think so."

"Then welcome aboard," Mrs. Taney said. "Go see Ms. Lea at the headhouse. She'll assign you a bed and a chest for your personal items and outfit you with torches and rations. If she gives you the okay, you'll go down with Barnacle's next crew. Good luck, Mr. Stonecutter."

Stax shook hands with Mrs. Taney, took his pickaxe, and headed for the quarry entrance.

"Come to think of it, Grandmother was a pretty tough old bird too," he said to himself, and the memory made him smile.

CHAPTER 17

DOWN IN THE HOLE

The troublesome Mr. Barnacle * Extraction methods
explained, and complained about * The tale of the
Brandywine Hill Mine

And so Stax became a miner with The Tumbles Extraction Company.

The other miners on Mr. Barnacle's crews were familiar to him from his long-ago memories of being an apprentice down in the Stonecutter mine; they weren't the same people, of course, but they reminded Stax of the miners who'd been employed by his family back then.

Cresop liked to work in silence, disliking any sound other than his powerfully muscled arms reducing block after block of rock to loose debris. Hodey was little more than a kid, and loved to talk, telling everyone about the great things he was going to do after he struck it rich as a miner. Billups was what Stax's father had called a mineshaft lawyer, full of complaints about how things were run and opinions about what should be different. Tanner had a keen eye for changes in the composition of rock, but was careless about safety measures and kept forgetting equipment. Jirwoh, on the other hand, would refuse to dig if he suspected anything wasn't exactly as it should be. Then there were the miners who left no particular impression beyond wanting to do their jobs and go home—Pyx, Gibbons, Ulias, and others whose names he hadn't got straight yet.

The only miner Stax couldn't figure out was a young woman named Osk Fikar.

Osk had pale skin and wild squiggles of red hair. She wasn't a particularly good miner. For one thing, she wasn't very strong, often stopping to slump over her pickaxe while the hardier miners were still carving away at the rock. But she was also frequently distracted, telling anyone who'd listen about fantastic inventions she'd dreamed up and insisted would change the world. The key to these wonderful machines, Osk explained, was redstone.

Stax was familiar with redstone from the Stonecutter mine: It was a gleaming red mineral found deep underground, and an ingredient for making compasses and clocks. But demand for those things had never been enormous, so redstone tended to pile up. Pretty but purposeless, his grandmother had said, and Stax had never had any reason to think differently.

The other miners mostly tolerated Osk because she was amiable and cheerful. Except for Mr. Barnacle, who detested Osk and looked for any opportunity to berate her.

Remember our discussion about people being funny in the sense of peculiar, and the kind of peculiar that unfortunately creates a burden for others? Well, I'm afraid that describes Mr. Barnacle pretty well.

Stax knew within seconds that his relationship with Barnacle wasn't going to be a good one. He was a glowering hulk of a man who shook Stax's hand with a grip that was hard enough to hurt, then said, "So, you're the rich kid from a family business."

Stax opened his mouth to explain that his possessions consisted of his clothes, his pickaxe, a wooden sword, a bed, two arrows (but no bow), a length of spider silk, a compass, and a very small amount of credit at the Tumbles Harbor general store. He was pretty sure that didn't add up to being rich. But he sensed Barnacle wouldn't be interested—and, indeed, the crew boss was already warning him that he was A Man Who Didn't Tolerate Layabouts, that mining was A Very Serious Business, and loudly saying other things that were meant to inform Stax and all the other miners within earshot that he, Mr. Barnacle, was a man who must be respected.

So Stax limited himself to saying "yes, sir" and "no, sir" and hoped that he and Barnacle would get along better once the crew boss saw that Stax really did know about mining.

(The funny thing was that Stax had to admit he *had* been something of a layabout until very recently, doing nothing more vigorous than chopping down the occasional young oak. He tried to remember the last time he'd been down in one of the Stonecutter mines to actually work.)

Stax had the good sense not to share any of that with Barnacle, resolving to work hard and give the crew boss nothing to complain about. To his relief, he found that the days spent hacking timber from the shipwreck and rowing had toughened up his hands and strengthened his arms; a full day of labor in the mines, while not exactly relaxing, was something he could handle.

Stax was more surprised to discover that he actually enjoyed being underground again, after so long. The routines of digging through stone in search of ore soon came back to him—placing torches, feeling the head of the pickaxe bite into the rock, breaking down a block of stone in front of you, clearing it away, and seeing what had been revealed.

He also remembered the precautions his father had taught him, like making sure no one was right behind you when you swung your pickaxe, keeping the mine well lit, inspecting the ceiling and walls and floors for dripping water or excess heat, and listening for the growl of zombies or the music of running water.

All of those things came back to Stax. So did the pleasures of being underground: the cool air, the clean lines of the revealed stone, and the oddly sharp, faintly burnt smell left behind when iron struck rock. It wasn't so bad, working beneath the Tumbles; he didn't want to do it for the rest of his life, or for any longer than he had to, but it wasn't the ordeal Stax had feared it might be.

Or at least that was true when Barnacle left Stax and the other miners alone. Unfortunately, that was rarely the case. Barnacle always found some reason to criticize Stax's crew, with Stax himself attracting his angriest and loudest complaints. Most of these complaints added up to Stax being slow, both as a digger and as a supervisor. In Barnacle's eyes, Stax took extra time to do anything, not because he valued safety but because he was lazy.

Their first real confrontation happened about two weeks after Stax started. It was the last day of the month, meaning tomorrow Barnacle's crews would start working in the deeper sections of the mines, where gems were more common, while the crews working for the other crew boss, the mild-mannered Mr. Koppe, would shift to ore mining. That meant the possibility of larger bonuses for Barnacle's miners, and for Barnacle himself.

It was Stax's turn to supervise, and so he'd ordered his diggers—today they were Hodey and Jirwoh—to mine the way his father had taught him. First they dug a main feeder tunnel that was two blocks wide, meaning the diggers could work side by side, and sixty-four blocks long. Torches were placed on the left-hand side of the tunnel—and only on the left—every eight blocks.

You're probably thinking those measurements sound too exact to be real, but I can tell you that they're correct. So now you're probably wondering how Stax could measure distance so precisely, down there under the ground. The answer is in the modification he'd asked Brubbs to make to the handle of his pickaxe. By making the handle exactly one block long, Stax could use his pickaxe not just for chiseling out rock but also as a precise measuring stick. His diggers had admired that little trick when Stax first showed it to them, and had become so precise in their digging that Stax rarely, if ever, had to correct them.

Not even Jirwoh found anything to complain about, except for being distracted by Hodey's ornate descriptions of the undersea house of glass he was going to build for his sweetheart with the wealth they'd make after they found seams of diamonds for the company. Stax remembered the spiky, scaly guardians of the Sea of Sorrows—the nasty burn on his chest had left a puckered pink scar he suspected he'd have for life—and shivered a little, but decided not to tell Hodey of his brush with death. So long as Hodey did his work, there was no harm in letting him dream of castles beneath the waves.

Digging the main feeder tunnel took up much of the morning, and turned up nothing but a few short veins of diorite and one of granite. On Stax's insistence, he and Hodey and Jirwoh took the loose stone they'd dug out and hauled it back to a junction of tunnels where there was a headhouse, depositing the stone in chests for disposal later. When they returned, Stax surveyed the clean, straight lines of the feeder tunnel with satisfaction.

"Okay, gentlemen, now it's time to make some money," he said, directing them to dig a branch tunnel on either side of the main feeder tunnel. These two branch tunnels, he explained, would be precisely sixteen blocks long, with one torch eight blocks in and another at the end of the tunnel.

Jirwoh was halfway down the right-hand tunnel when he intersected a seam of coal; a few minutes later, Hodey cried out that he'd uncovered iron in the ceiling of his tunnel. Stax calmed the excited Hodey and fetched Jirwoh. The vein of iron ore snaked across the ceiling for several blocks, while the coal vein was long enough to reach where the next branch tunnel would be.

Once the veins were exhausted and the coal and iron-rich ore set aside, Stax told the others to fill in the gaps with cobblestone, restoring the pristine lines of the branch tunnels instead of leaving them honeycombed with gaps. Then he ordered a halt and they sat in the feeder tunnel, eating bread sweetened and softened with some honey Stax had bought on a trip to the general store.

They were just finishing this simple lunch when Barnacle arrived.

"Lazy!" he cried out, striding down the tunnel and stopping so he towered above them, hands on his hips. "Layabouts and do-nothings, wasting the company's money and costing me my bonus!"

Hodey and Jirwoh all but leapt to their feet, blinking nervously, but Stax quietly ate his last bite of bread before he got up.

"Oh, don't bother getting up, *Sir Stax*," Barnacle sneered.

"Why not spend the rest of the day eating and snoozing while other people do the real work?"

Stax was curious how Barnacle had figured out the insulting nickname "Sir Stax"—did he somehow know Chigam and Ritzo from the caravan? He also thought that until just a few weeks ago, he had indeed spent most days eating and snoozing, and would have been perfectly happy returning to that life. But neither point seemed wise to bring up with Barnacle.

"Regarding your bonus, Mr. Barnacle, I'm proud to say we've had a profitable morning," Stax said. "A fair-sized vein of coal located by Mr. Jirwoh, and a seam of iron found by Mr. Hodey."

"'Regarding your bonus,'" Barnacle said loftily, his voice rising in an imitation of Stax's. "*Mr.* This, *Mr.* That. You don't fool me, Sir Stax. Your nice manners are how you get away with doing nothing. What more might you have found if you'd kept working instead of throwing yourselves a carnival feast? Ever think of that?"

Stax started to defend himself, but Barnacle was already striding down the right-hand branch tunnel, his face turning bright red as he became angrier.

"Is this where you found the coal? Why did you seal these walls back up? What a waste of time! And for what? So the walls look pretty? I don't know how they did things in your daddy's mine, Sir Stax, but around here we don't pay for pretty. We pay for ore and gems."

Jirwoh opened his mouth to protest, but Stax shook his head.

"It's not so the walls look pretty," Stax told Barnacle. "It's so—"

"—you always know where you are," said another voice.

It was Mrs. Taney, her expression even more stern than it had been on the day Stax had met her. As Barnacle looked on with dismay, Mrs. Taney walked up and down the length of the feeder tunnel, then inspected the two branch tunnels.

"I see you've excavated the first branch tunnels, Stax," she said. "How far down the main tunnels would the next ones be?"

"Eight blocks," Stax said. "Then you bore tunnels parallel to the main tunnel. One eight blocks in, where the torch is, and another at the end of the corridor. Making a grid."

"A grid where everything's properly lit, with the minimum use of torches to accomplish it," Mrs. Taney said. "Torches on the left, correct?"

Stax nodded.

"That way you can never get lost, even if you keep expanding the grid," Mrs. Taney said, turning to stare at Barnacle. "If you lose track of where you are, you make sure the torches are on your right and walk until you hit a wide tunnel. That's how your family mine operated at home, Stax?"

"Yes," Stax said. "My father worked out the system with my grandmother."

"They were excellent miners, then," Mrs. Taney said. "Mr. Barnacle, this is the system I've tried to explain to you, not just once but several times. Let's make this a demonstration project. Stax, I want you to mine the entire grid, using your system. When you're finished, we'll tally up how much time was required and the amount of ore yielded. The results might prove . . . *instructive* to our other crews."

"Yes, ma'am," said Stax.

"All right then, carry on," said Mrs. Taney, pivoting smoothly on one heel and marching down the tunnel the way she'd come.

Stax decided immediately that it would be wise not to cause Barnacle any more embarrassment.

"Mr. Jirwoh, Mr. Hodey, the three of us need to get back to work," Stax said, clapping his hands for emphasis and pointedly not looking in Barnacle's direction. "Let's do that, please."

Jirwoh and Hodey hefted their pickaxes and followed him farther down the feeder tunnel. But Stax could feel Barnacle's gaze between his shoulder blades, burning almost as fiercely as the guardians' from the Sea of Sorrows, and sensed more trouble ahead.

Jirwoh sensed it too.

"This is bad," he told Stax, after a muttering Barnacle had left the three of them alone. "He'll be after us every day, demanding to know why we aren't delivering the kind of big bonus he deserves. Accusing us of trying to cheat him, or of being lazy."

"We can't worry about that," Stax said. "All we can do is work hard and hope we hit some more rich veins. Which will happen, you'll see. Haven't we already found coal and iron today?"

"It won't be enough for Barnacle," Hodey said. "It hasn't been since the Brandywine Hill Mine went bust."

"Don't say that name," Jirwoh snapped, looking cross. "You know it's bad luck."

"Sorry," Hodey said, and would have dropped the subject, if Stax had let him.

"What's the Brandywine Hill Mine?"

Hodey looked over at Jirwoh, who threw up his hands in disgust.

"It's just the other side of the eastern ridge," Hodey said. "Barnacle promised the Taneys that there was a fortune in gems beneath it, and when they doubted him, he sunk a lot of his own money into it. Well, he was wrong. Ever since then, he's been frantic for a big score to make their money back, and his too."

"And that's bad luck?" asked Stax. He'd known some superstitious miners in his day, and everyone knew mining was capricious—you could miss a vein of diamonds by a single block and it would go undetected for a thousand years. But while he'd heard of unlucky miners, the idea of an unlucky mine was new to him.

"I worked that mine, Stax, and it's true," Jirwoh said. "Day after day, nothing but stone. We must have taken out a hundred chests full of rock, with barely two pieces of coal to rub together. Never seen anything like it. So now we don't discuss it. Besides, if Mr. Barnacle overhears the word 'Brandywine,' he goes insane and your next few days are unbearable."

"Now, *that* I believe," said Stax. "Tell me more about this mine. I want to know everything."

CHAPTER 18

STRANGE CHARACTERS

Who is the Champion? * Stax makes a proposal *
Osk's inventions are found wanting

During his time working for The Tumbles Extraction Company, Stax had made it a habit to visit the general store every three or four days. It was a relief to see something other than the miners' dormitory and hear discussions that weren't about ore and gems, and he enjoyed Brubbs's ready supply of news and gossip.

Every time he visited, Stax asked if Brubbs had heard from a traveler who knew the lands beyond the Sea of Sorrows. Every time, the answer was no. Until finally, standing in the general store and hearing this disappointing news yet again, Stax realized that the answer was always going to be no. If he was going to get home, he couldn't wait for some knowledgeable ship captain to get him there. He would have to find some other way.

And the only answer Stax could think of was the one that

frightened him: He had to find Fouge Tempro. Fouge knew how to get from the eastern end of the Sea of Sorrows to the Stonecutter estate. And, of course, he deserved to answer for what he'd done to Stax.

But while Stax fantasized about having his revenge, brooding over the compass Fouge had dropped, he couldn't imagine confronting the pitiless raider. Over the last few weeks Stax had proved to himself that he could survive difficulties and dangers, and he'd remembered the craft of mining and adjusted to long days of hard work belowground. But those successes hadn't transformed him into a warrior. He still had no weapons except a wooden sword and a pair of scavenged arrows, and he knew it would take more than that to survive against Fouge.

So it felt like a stroke of good fortune when Stax overheard Brubbs chatting with a leather trader about someone they called the champion. Listening to their conversation, Stax sensed that whoever this mysterious entity was, he or she deserved a capital letter—not the champion, but the Champion.

As Brubbs and the leather trader moved on to negotiating the price of a shipment of hides, Stax realized he'd heard the Champion mentioned before a time or two, overhearing that name spoken by miners, customers in the general store, or locals at the caravanserai. When the leather trader left, Stax sidled up to the counter.

"You were just talking about someone called the Champion," Stax said. "Who is that?"

"You don't know about the Champion?" Brubbs looked surprised. "The man who brought Dark Ulric to justice? Who cleared out the creeper nest below the Splinter? Who sent the Mulraven Bandits fleeing into the wilderness?"

Stax had to shake his head.

"Oh, he's quite the local hero," Brubbs said. "Lives a week or so out of town, in the mountains to the east. Though I doubt he's journeyed beyond the Sea of Sorrows, if that's what you're asking."

"No, nothing like that," Stax said. "So he's an experienced warrior, then?"

"Greatest swordsman of the realm, if the stories are true," Brubbs said. "He used to come in here now and again, you know, though I haven't seen him in years. They say he uses his castle as a base to explore strange realms: the Nether, even the End. Anywhere evil threatens good people, he'll be there."

Stax felt his hope rise. He liked to think he was good people, and he'd certainly had a distressing encounter with evil.

"So people ask him for help?" he asked Brubbs.

"They do," Brubbs said. "Though I hear the Champion expects those who seek his help to offer what they can afford. Not for him, but so he can help others in need."

"He's a mercenary, then?" asked Stax.

Brubbs started to object, then stopped and laughed. "It does sound like that, doesn't it? That's a good lesson, Stax: Don't assume your local heroes are everything legend says they are. But no, I don't think that's quite fair. It was a band of poor farmers who asked the Champion to run off the Mulraven Bandits, and I hear he agreed in return for a loaf of fresh bread each week. But when the royal twins of Far Nalur were kidnapped, the Champion retrieved the prince and princess in return for the king and queen agreeing to suspend all taxes until the children's next birthday. That sounds like a fair outcome, doesn't it?"

"I suppose it does," said Stax. He thanked Brubbs and left the general store, deep in thought. He was trying to imagine himself journeying to the Champion's mountain castle, and what this great warrior might say after Stax told him of all he had suffered at the hands of Fouge Tempro.

Stax reluctantly decided his case sounded a lot closer to that of the missing princes than it did to that of farmers plagued by bandits. Which meant the Champion would want a lot more from him than a weekly loaf of bread. He'd made a little money as a miner from his wages and bonuses, enough to build his credit back up at the general store, but nothing approaching a royal ransom.

Then Stax had an idea.

"You want to do what?" asked Mrs. Taney.

"Reopen the Brandywine Hill Mine," Stax said. "I don't believe it's unlucky, or cursed, or whatever your miners think it is. I'd like to see what I can extract from it for you, using my system. Well, my family's system."

Mrs. Taney regarded him for a long moment from the other side of her desk, her gaze even.

"I embarrassed Barnacle in front of you and the others because I'd been trying to get him to listen for a long time," she said. "Now that I've made my point, it wouldn't do to make him look bad all over again. Because that's what this is about, isn't it?"

"No," Stax said.

"Then what *is* it about?"

"Justice," Stax said grimly. "A man destroyed my life. I intend to make him answer for that."

"I think you'd better tell me that story, then," Mrs. Taney said.

So Stax told her about Fouge Tempro's raid on his house, about being marooned, about his inability to find his way home, about the Champion. Mrs. Taney listened gravely, elbows on the desk in front of her and fingers steepled.

"I know about the Champion, though I can't say I've met him myself," she said. "So you want to enlist him to find this Fouge Tempro and defeat him for you. But to do that, you need money."

"Yes."

"Well, you're making money," Mrs. Taney said. "The bonuses from the last round of excavations will be pretty good. And next month you'll be on a gem crew, with the prospect of bigger bonuses."

"I know. But I'm in a bit of a hurry."

"I see. In that case, stop being indecisive or unnecessarily coy, or whatever this is, and tell me what you're proposing."

Stax looked down at his hands. His palms had become rough and calloused from days wielding a pickaxe.

"I'll mine Brandywine Hill on my own time, with any miners who'll volunteer to work with me. You pay their wages, but not mine. I'll work for free. Standard bonuses for the miners, and I get the bonus due a crew boss. You get your owner's cut, of course."

"Even if you can make that mine pay off like you think you can, it won't be enough to hire your Champion."

"I know that," Stax said.

"And?"

"If Brandywine does pay off, you hire more miners and expand operations there."

"With you as crew boss," Mrs. Taney said. "Is that the idea?"

"That's the idea."

Stax waited while Mrs. Taney considered this. He could almost see her brain making the calculations and then double-checking them.

"I have conditions," she said. "First, you work one four-hour shift a night, maximum. I don't need tired miners making mistakes during their regular work hours. Second, it's a three-person shift—you and two other miners. Third, you get the rest of the month to prove you're right. No longer."

Stax reviewed the calendar in his head. That gave him about a week. He winced but nodded.

"Fourth, Barnacle gets a miner's cut of any bonuses out of your share as crew boss."

When Stax started to object, Mrs. Taney put up her hand. "I know Barnacle's a handful, Stax. I know it a lot better than you do, in fact. But he was with me and my husband at the beginning, when we were just two fools scratching in a hole in a hill. He's been loyal to us, and so I'm loyal to him. He gets his cut."

"All right," Stax said, not seeing what choice he had. "Which miners do you want to ask?"

"Cresop and Tanner," Stax said.

"You can't have either," Mrs. Taney said. "They're the first miners every crew boss asks for. I need them where they are."

"Hodey, then."

"You can have Hodey if you take Osk," Mrs. Taney said.

"The little inventor? She can barely swing a pickaxe."

"I know she's not much of a miner, though something tells me she'll work a bit harder for you than she does for Barnacle," Mrs. Taney said. "The thing is, she's smart. Which brings me to my final condition: I want you to visit her laboratory, out on the edge of town. I can't figure out if Osk is a genius, a madwoman, or both, and I need a second opinion."

"So," Stax said. "One shift a night, I get Osk and Hodey, Barnacle gets his cut, I have till the end of the month, and first I need to go look at Osk's crazy machines."

"That's right," Mrs. Taney said.

"Deal," Stax said, and stuck out his hand.

Osk had the day off. All too aware that time was precious, Stax got Mrs. Taney's permission to visit the laboratory that afternoon.

He followed her directions to a little house on the outskirts of Tumbles Harbor, one that struck him as much the same as its neighbors, down to a little square of grass in front of it with carefully arranged flowers. Except instead of a torch or lantern for light by the gate, this house had a curious faceted cube.

"That's odd," said Stax, who hadn't entirely broken the habit of talking to himself, though he'd mostly stopped doing it when other people were around.

He stepped onto the porch and noticed the house's front door was iron, not the oak or birch he usually saw in Tumbles Harbor. Stax knocked on the door, startled by the metallic *bang-bang-bang* this produced, and waited.

Nothing happened. Stax rapped on the door again, and this time he heard a muffled voice from within yelling something.

"What?" he called out.

"The button! Push the button!"

Stax noticed a little nub of wood next to the door. He pushed it, heard a musical chime from inside the house, and then the door snapped open, nearly smacking him in the head. He stumbled backward and noticed the strange cube at the gate was now glowing a warm yellow.

Osk came to the door, wearing a leather apron marred by red blotches and streaks.

"Oh, hullo, Stax," she said. "Didn't you read the sign?"

"There isn't a sign," Stax said.

"There isn't? Oh, you're right, there isn't. I forgot to put it up. That's a nuisance."

Osk returned a moment later with a sign that read RING DOOR-BELL, which she leaned against the outside wall of the house.

"It's a redstone circuit," she explained. "I can rig it to open the door, or to alert me down in my laboratory, so I can decide if I want to see visitors or not. I'm thinking of adding a pit in the porch. You know, for salespeople. Ha-ha, I'm just kidding, I'd get in trouble for that. Anyway, isn't it great? Plus it makes the light come on, so you can see at night."

"The light's back at the gate," Stax pointed out. "If you're already at the front door, that's a little late for the light to come on."

"Huh. You're right. I didn't think of that."

Osk looked so crestfallen that Stax felt sorry for her. "I'm sure that's something you can fix pretty easily," he pointed out.

"It's a little work, yeah. But you're right, easily fixed! In fact, I should make it so the light comes on automatically at dusk. That's a great idea. Thanks, Stax!"

"You're welcome," said a bemused Stax, who hadn't actually thought of anything.

"Anyway, I'm glad to see you. I suggested Mrs. Taney send you over, to look at my inventions, and here you are. So welcome! Come inside!"

"Wait. You asked her to send me?"

"Sure. That trick of yours, with the pickaxe handle? It's a clever innovation. Mining needs a lot more innovation. And, well, innovation's practically my middle name. Well, actually it's Eunice, but never mind that. Come on in, I have a lot to show you!"

The inside of Osk's house was a mess, with gear lying around as if dispersed by a particularly ferocious windstorm. Osk led Stax to a trapdoor in the corner of the house, pushing a button on the wall next to it. Nothing happened.

"That's a nuisance," Osk said after several tries, reaching down to open the trapdoor herself and scuttling down a ladder.

Stax followed her, emerging in a sprawling underground laboratory filled with a bewildering variety of objects: iron rails, squat squares that looked like they were made of cobblestones, and stone blocks with wooden stalks sticking out of them. Tables were covered with books, papers with diagrams scribbled on them, sticky-looking balls that were a sickly green, and mounds of brilliant redstone dust.

"Did you build all this with your wages from mining?" Stax asked, startled.

"What? Oh, no. I've only been working for Mrs. Taney because I thought it would give me ideas for new inventions. And because she gives me a special rate on redstone."

"I see. So what *do* you do, Osk?"

"Why, whatever anybody will pay me to do!" Osk said with a grin. "Isn't that the way these days? I'm an enchanter, for one—best in Tumbles Harbor, or at least the second best. Hmm, there's Grimble, and he's pretty good, so maybe I'm the third best. Anyway, I'm an enchanter, but it bores me, if we're being honest. So I'm also an architect and an engineer. But what I'm going to be is an artificer."

"An artificer?" asked Stax.

By way of an answer, Osk scooped up a handful of the crimson dust.

"You know what this is, right?"

"Of course," Stax said. "Redstone. It's used to make compasses and clocks." And as he said that, Stax's hand strayed to the compass in his pocket, while his mind was filled with fantasies of facing down Fouge Tempro with a diamond sword.

"Compasses and clocks?" Osk said, shaking her head. "Think *big*, Stax! Redstone is used for so much more than that! You can channel it to direct power and make machines. Why, I'll show you something that will transform mining. Now, what did I do with that schematic?"

Osk sorted through her papers, picking up and then discarding diagrams for a variety of baffling devices before thrusting one under Stax's nose: a massive assemblage of blocks and levers, and objects labeled as . . .

"Does this drop TNT?"

"Yes!" Osk said excitedly. "See, and then these mechanisms come along and take away the water. It'll clear a massive quarry in the better part of a day. I thought we could use it to speed things up at Tumbles."

"If we had enough TNT to destroy a city," Stax said. "And a fortune in emeralds to buy all this. And if Mrs. Taney didn't mind us leveling the mountain."

"Well, it's just one idea," said Osk, a bit defensively.

"It's clever," said Stax, though actually he found Osk's proposed machine frightening. "You know our mines, Osk. Do you have anything smaller? And more affordable?"

"Sure. Wait until you see this!"

Osk hurried over to a niche near a set of bookcases and ducked inside. There was a great deal of whirring and clicking, a flurry of motion, and a moment later Osk was decked out in leather armor, with an iron pickaxe in one hand and an iron bucket in the other.

"Ow!" she said, putting the pickaxe down and shaking her hand with a grimace. "That's my fault, I had my hand in the wrong place. I call it the Insta-Miner. You're geared up and ready to go in thirty seconds, tops!"

"It would certainly prevent Tanner from forgetting his equipment," Stax said. "But you know most of us don't wear armor underground. It's too much weight. And I can pick up my own pickaxe, thanks to an enchantment known as the opposable thumb."

"Well, if you want to do things the old-fashioned way," muttered Osk, stripping off her armor. But a moment later she had brightened again. "How about this? See? It can sense when night's come, and switches on redstone lamps throughout the mine."

"Osk. Mines are dark in the daytime too. So you need lights all the time."

"Oh yeah, you're right of course. I always forget that, somehow." Osk looked down at the floor. "You're going to tell Mrs. Taney I'm some kind of loon, aren't you?" she asked sadly.

"I'm going to tell Mrs. Taney there are some great ideas here, and they just need a little more work," Stax said. "My suggestion would be to think about the challenges we face every shift. How about a machine that could detect gems from several blocks away? Or sense water or lava from that distance? Or a machine that could neutralize lava?"

Osk furrowed her brow, her hands plucking at her leather apron and raising little plumes of redstone dust.

"That last one's an interesting idea," she said. "Hmm. You'd need water, of course. Maybe you could use a light sensor. And pistons to block off the area. That might work. Let me think about that some more."

"That would get Mrs. Taney's interest," Stax said. "But remember it needs to be small. And not too expensive."

"Well, that's a nuisance," Osk said. "But I can work with those limitations. Limitations can lead to genius too, though money works a little better. I know you don't believe me, Stax, but redstone really is the future. You can do anything with it. It could change mining, farming, travel, everything."

"I do believe you, Osk," Stax said. "And I've got a proposition for you—one that might give you some new ideas."

"I'm listening," Osk said.

So Stax told her about his plan for the Brandywine Hill Mine, and Mrs. Taney's conditions.

"I'll join your crew if I can have any redstone we find," Osk said with a grin.

"It'll all be yours, Osk," said Stax, who hoped that the Brandywine Hill Mine would indeed turn out to be filled with redstone—and many more ores besides.

CHAPTER 19

THE UNLUCKY MINE

Hodey joins the crew * Beneath Brandywine Hill *
A treasure and its guardians

To Stax's relief, Hodey said yes to his proposal immediately. Now he had his crew.

But the miners loved to gossip, and word soon reached Barnacle about the deal Stax had struck with Mrs. Taney. After the day's shift, Barnacle swaggered into the dormitory where Stax, Osk, and Hodey were gathering their equipment.

"Uh-oh," Hodey said.

Barnacle's face was brilliant red, his beady black eyes intent and searching. He spotted Stax and came to a halt, the corners of his mouth twitching.

And then Barnacle began to laugh.

"So you really think you can make that cursed hole in the ground pay off?" he wheezed. "Think you're that much smarter than everybody else? Well, you're welcome to waste time trying—you and anyone dumb enough to believe in you. That hole's all yours, Sir Stax, and I hope I'll see you buried in it."

Barnacle departed, cackling.

"Well, wasn't that nice?" Stax asked with a smile. "I can't wait to see his face in a week, when we're all rich."

An hour later, they opened the gate securing the entrance to the Brandywine Hill Mine and explored the galleries of tunnels that had been bored through the rock.

Stax tsk-tsked repeatedly. The excavation had all the signs of Barnacle's handiwork, with tunnels dug haphazardly in all directions. Stax could easily imagine the burly crew boss ordering new digs based on nothing but gut instinct, then standing over the miners impatiently as more and more rock was stripped away, and blaming them when their pickaxes failed to uncover the great wealth he'd imagined was below the hill.

But Barnacle's haphazard work practices weren't what interested Stax. Once he'd toured the entire mine—thankfully, no monsters seemed to have taken up residence in the darkness—Stax sat down with Osk and Hodey in the center of the lowest level.

"The biggest problem with this mine is that Mr. Barnacle didn't dig deep enough," Stax explained. "He was unlucky not to hit a fair amount of iron and coal and even some gold, but I'm not surprised he came up empty where gems were concerned."

Osk grinned—she hated Barnacle, who never missed a chance to mock her belief in redstone—while Hodey looked rapt, hanging on Stax's every word. Stax hoped the young miner's faith in him would prove justified.

"Now, my father had a system for finding the most valuable

deposits," he explained. "He worked down from sea level to find the right depth for the most profitable mining. Unfortunately, I can't determine sea level here, and I don't know how my father made his calculations."

"Are you saying you want me to build something that could do that, Stax?" Osk asked. "Because that's quite the puzzle."

"That would be amazing, Osk. Definitely think about it. But in the meantime, we have another way to find the right depth. Instead of working down from sea level, you work up from bedrock."

"Bedrock?" Hodey asked. "Never seen that, Mr. Stonecutter. Isn't that what the center of the Overworld's made out of?"

"Maybe. To be honest, the science was always a little over my head," Stax said. "But lucky for us, you don't have to dig as far down as the center of the Overworld to hit bedrock. Still, we'll be below the lava line. You know what that is, right?"

Osk shook her head, but Hodey was nodding.

"It's the depth where you start finding a lot of lava lakes," he said.

"Exactly," Stax said. "And the ideal depth for gem-hunting is right above it. So the dangerous part is that we'll have to dig all the way down to bedrock to get the right measurement, and then back up to where it's safer. So before you put a pickaxe into rock down there, check to see if it's hot. If you think you see steam, or little blobs of stone on the ceiling or walls, don't keep it to yourself. Same if you think you hear sloshing or bubbling. And you always, always have a water bucket nearby. Don't forget that part. If I'm right, we're going to find wealth somewhere down under our feet—wealth enough, Hodey, to build your girl that undersea dream house of yours. But you can't build anything if you're dead. Remember that."

Osk gave Stax a thumbs-up, while Hodey grinned and applauded.

They started digging a staircase down, narrow enough that you were constantly turning left to descend and wound up faintly dizzy if you hurried. To Stax's relief, they didn't encounter lava as they dug down and down and down; to his disappointment, they also didn't discover any valuable ore or gems. There wasn't even a small vein of coal. At the end of the first night's work, Stax caught himself worrying that the rumors were true, and the Brandywine Hill Mine really was cursed somehow. But he simply smiled and told the others to get some sleep.

Stax was tired the next day, but vowed to push on. After dinner, he joined Osk and Hodey for another night's work. They'd been digging down for the better part of two hours when Hodey's pickaxe struck something with a sharp, high-pitched ping instead of a dull thunk.

"Easy now," Stax said. "Let's clear some of this away and see what we have. Obsidian makes that sound sometimes too."

Hodey was excited by the prospect of seeing bedrock for the first time, so Stax and Osk hung back, a block above him, as the younger miner cleared away the loose rock. What was revealed was definitely bedrock—dull gray and seamed. And impenetrable: The three of them could hammer away at a single chunk of bedrock until they grew old and stooped, wearing hundreds of iron tools down to nubs in the process, and not so much as scratch it.

"So now we can work our way back up?" asked Hodey, sweating and breathing hard but also grinning broadly, pleased that he'd been the first one to reach their goal.

"Not quite yet," Stax said. "Bedrock isn't an evenly distributed layer; it's more of a lumpy line. We need to be confident we've found the lowest point. That will give us a baseline for how far we need to go up."

"I never knew how much science there was to be aware of down here," Osk said. "I thought it was just about putting a pick-axe into rock."

"Well, almost," Stax said. "My grandmother used to say it was about putting a pickaxe into the *right* rock."

The three of them spread out in all directions from the staircase, hollowing out a chamber tall enough to stand up in. Stax had to keep reminding Osk to check for hot spots and make sure the water bucket was close at hand instead of chattering about how to make a depth gauge using redstone. And he had to repeatedly assure Hodey that there was no point hammering away at the bedrock, despite his burning curiosity about what lay below it.

As Stax had predicted, the bedrock was mixed with other varieties of stone, and the boundary formed a wavy line that rose and fell. With their four hours nearly gone, Stax halted the work and the three of them surveyed the room they'd hacked out of the rock, identifying the lowest points.

"I don't think we're going to find anything lower than that," Stax said. "Excellent work, people. Tomorrow, we work our way up and start to really dig."

With the unglamorous task of figuring out the proper depth finally behind them, Stax found himself impatient to get through his next day's work in the mine—a wait that was made far worse because Barnacle insisted on tormenting him. The man alternated between scoffing at him for his after-hours project and demanding to know, with a hint of worry in his voice, if he'd found anything. Stax gave Barnacle little beyond polite nonanswers, and was careful not to give the crew boss any reason to criticize him. Barnacle found things to yell about anyway, and Stax was tired and cross by the time his regular shift finally came to an end.

His spirits rose when he saw that Osk and Hodey were clearly eager to continue the project. They made their way down the tight, winding stair they'd carved out of the rock, until they reached the bedrock chamber. Stax knelt down at one of the lowest points they'd found and set his pickaxe on its end, then used it to measure the distance to the ceiling.

"About three blocks," Stax said. "That's what I figured. So now we dig up nine blocks above the ceiling. And then we can start."

At Stax's insistence they worked slowly to build a new staircase up, always mining to one side instead of directly above their heads. After a few more minutes of work, Stax called a halt and asked Hodey to take a measurement. Twelve blocks above bedrock, the young miner reported, a figure Stax checked for himself and confirmed.

"Very good," Stax said. "This should be the ideal height for gems, then. We've got another hour or so. Let's start on the feeder tunnel. Two blocks wide, sixty-four blocks long. Maybe we'll even find something tonight."

And they quickly did—a vein of iron that snaked its way across the ceiling of the feeder tunnel. They followed it until it petered out a couple of blocks above them, then filled in the rock they'd removed. Stax was pleased about this quick success, but the rest of the hour passed with nothing found. Still, Osk and Hodey seemed optimistic as they packed up their tools, convinced that tomorrow Stax would be proved right about the mine.

But he wasn't. In carving out the length of the feeder tunnel, they found nothing but a few short runs of coal ore. And the day after that was a disappointment too. They excavated six branch tunnels, but found nothing but some scattered deposits of coal and iron—more than Barnacle had found, perhaps; but not enough to justify the time they'd spent, and certainly nothing that would convince Mrs. Taney to hire more miners.

As they trudged back to the surface, Hodey muttered darkly about the gremlins his grandpa had told him could infest mines, working ahead of the crews and cackling as they stole away gems and replaced them with ordinary rock. Osk just hung her head; she'd hoped they'd at least find redstone. Stax assured them the next day would be different, but his words sounded hollow and he was sure his smile looked forced and fake.

They had only two nights left to make Stax's gamble pay off. Stax stumbled through the day, earning savage rebukes from Barnacle that he had to admit he deserved. He was exhausted by the extra work and the lack of sleep, and knew Osk and Hodey were also suffering.

Stax's father had taught him that ideas such as hope and luck didn't belong in mines. There was only trust that your calculations and procedures were correct—and because of that trust, patience and belief that the odds of finding wealth were in your favor.

Still, Stax couldn't help hoping for a little luck; an early discovery that would lift them up and give them the faith to push through these last two nights. He didn't dare hope for diamonds, the most valuable thing under the ground, but even a small seam of gold or lapis would be encouragement enough to keep going. Or a little run of redstone—that would at least cheer up Osk.

But there was nothing except a little more coal and iron. For the first time during the project, Hodey asked if it was time to go to bed when they still had more than an hour left. As Osk and Hodey shuffled off dejectedly, sore and dirty and tired, Stax couldn't muster the strength to think of words that might rally them.

"One more night," he told them. "Things can still change."

He felt numb all the next day, barely hearing Barnacle's taunts and promises that he would work Stax like a rented donkey once Mrs. Taney declared his project was the failure everyone but Stax and two deluded fools had known it would be.

Stax half-expected Osk and Hodey not to show up for the last night of work, but they were there. They were there, but neither one of them said a word as they descended beneath Brandywine Hill.

They had three branch tunnels left to excavate—two to the left of the feeder tunnel and one to the right—and Stax wondered if they had enough time to finish that work, tired as they were. But there was nothing to do except get started.

The first tunnel yielded a seam of redstone, and Stax smiled at Osk's glee. At least the little inventor would wind up getting something out of the whole misadventure. Halfway down the second tunnel, Stax noticed he was sweating more than usual, and yelled for Hodey to stop.

The other miner turned in surprise, having managed to stop his pickaxe in midswing.

"Check if that rock's hot," Stax said.

"It's fine," said Hodey, patting the wall. "See? It's—wait. You're right. It's hot."

"Shh," said Osk, holding up her hand. "I hear something."

Stax heard it too: a bubbling and chuckling noise from behind the rock wall.

"Lava," he said.

"So we stop?" asked Hodey.

"We can take a look," Stax said. "But we do it carefully. Dig out the ceiling and raise up the floor, to ensure we're above it. We'll dig from there."

Osk and Hodey did as he directed. They were all sweating freely now in the hot tunnel.

"All right, Hodey," Stax said. "Osk, have the water bucket ready to pour on any lava that flows in."

Hodey swung his pickaxe against the rock wall, grunting with the effort. On the third blow, the rock wall exploded inward. Fiery light filled the tunnel, forcing the three of them to blink against the sudden brightness. Stax peered over Hodey's shoulder at the lake of bubbling lava beyond the wall. Lava, and something bright beyond it . . .

An arrow zipped above his ear, actually parting his hair, and rattled as it bounced off the walls of the tunnel.

"Skeletons!" Hodey cried out. "Close it up! Close it up! Before they come!"

"No!" Stax yelled, surprising himself. He pushed past Osk and Hodey, scrambling through the gap to stand panting on the stony lip of a pool of lava. Two skeletons stood in front of him, arrows nocked, their skulls swiveling madly on their backbones.

Osk and Hodey were yelling, but Stax barely heard them. He swung his pickaxe at the first skeleton, knocking the monster backward into the lava, its bow bursting into flame before it vanished beneath the surface of the molten rock. A stray gobbet of lava struck Stax on the arm and he heard himself cry out.

The second skeleton fired and Stax grunted with pain. He swung wildly at the skeleton, missing, then connected with the backswing. The skeleton opened its bony jaws, but no sound came out, and Stax brought the pickaxe down again—and kept swinging it.

Someone was yelling his name. It was Osk, he realized.

"Stax! Stop! They're gone! You're all right!"

Stax dropped the pickaxe and put his hands on his knees, panting.

"Check . . . check the rest of the cavern," he managed to say. "Make sure there aren't any others."

"I did," said Osk. "It's just us. But Stax, come see!"

Stax looked where the woman was pointing, at the glittering points in the floor and on the walls. The glint of gold. The crimson gleam of redstone. The blue sparks of lapis. And up near the ceiling, a cooler radiance, almost icy.

"Are those what I think they are?" asked Hodey, sounding awestruck.

"They sure are," said Stax, and he began to laugh. "Diamonds."

CHAPTER 20

THE ACCIDENT

Barnacle's mania * Digging in the wrong place *
Light in the darkness

The lava cavern beneath Brandywine Hill was a nexus of gem-stone seams, and the wealth that came out of the mine over the next several days had even the old-timers whistling in delighted surprise. It also made Stax a hero; he was asked to tell the story of the fight in the cavern innumerable times, and often had to deny exaggerated versions of it that were already making the rounds among the miners and the people of Tumbles Harbor.

Within a few years, he was certain, the tale would have grown so large in the telling that miners who'd swear they'd been there would speak in hushed tones about how Stax Stonecutter fought off a dozen skeletons at once, all of them firing flaming arrows and wearing diamond armor.

Mrs. Taney was pleased, of course, going so far as to give Stax a grandmotherly smooch on the cheek in front of the assembled miners before announcing that The Tumbles Extraction Company would be hiring men and women for further excavations.

Even Barnacle congratulated Stax—as he should have, given the size of the cut coming his way despite having done nothing but laugh at the whole project. As for Stax, he received a sack of emeralds along with that kiss on the cheek. He was pretty sure it wasn't enough wealth to hire the Champion, but it was a start. And once he became a crew boss, he could expect a steady stream of such payments, provided the Tumbles mines kept paying off.

Stax still found himself sitting up at night in the miners' dormitory, staring down at his compass and brooding about Fouge Tempro and all he'd suffered because of him. Sometimes he imagined taking his sack of emeralds to the general store, outfitting himself in armor, and buying a sharp sword. Then he'd stride out of Tumbles Harbor, face grim, and search for Fouge until he had his chance for revenge—or died trying.

But there was no guarantee that he'd ever find Fouge. And finding a fortune in gems didn't make Stax a warrior. The wise thing, Stax told himself, was to be patient. He had a job that was bringing in the wealth he could use to arrange Fouge's downfall, and give him a chance to get home.

But that was a lot easier to think than it was to actually believe. And so night after night, Stax would find the compass in his hand again, as if it were mocking him.

And Stax had another problem. Until Mrs. Taney could find enough miners to handle the new operations beneath Brandywine Hill, Stax was stuck working for Barnacle.

At first Stax thought that might not be so bad. Barnacle stopped addressing Stax as "Sir Stax," and treated him with more respect than he had. But Stax's success beneath Brandywine Hill seemed to increase Barnacle's hunger for money instead of easing it, and now he was determined to prove he could do what Stax had done.

With the calendar having turned to a new month, Barnacle's crews were now working deep in the mines hunting for gems, with Koppe's crews working higher and searching for ore. After watching Barnacle push the miners through a grueling shift in which he ordered them to dig seemingly at random, Stax decided to take the man aside and reiterate the system his father had taught him years ago for maximizing the chance of finding wealth.

Barnacle listened, eyes narrowed, as Stax explained why he'd made sure the handle of his pickaxe was exactly a block long, and how he'd used that to measure distance and ensure they were digging just above the lava line.

Which was when Barnacle turned his back on him.

"Stop lying, Stax," he said. "Spare me that phony story about heroics in that lava cave. You found those veins right at bedrock, and we both know it. So that's where we're going to be digging."

"That lava cave was real, Mr. Barnacle. In a week or so I'll take you there myself. If we'd dug into it from below, skeletons would have been the least of our problems. We all could have died! Mr. Barnacle, you can't do this!"

Barnacle reached out, grabbed Stax by the front of his shirt, and pulled him close. His voice was low and deadly.

"Don't tell me how to mine. I've been down here earning a living since before you were born. You check walls for heat. You watch for strange formations and bright spots. And when your crew boss gives you an order, you follow it."

———

The next day Barnacle supervised the excavation of a staircase all the way down to bedrock—and then, once they reached it, he ordered them to dig out a feeder tunnel two blocks wide.

Mrs. Taney had given Osk permission to take the day off and brainstorm creating a depth gauge, despite Stax's doubts that such a thing could be built. So Tanner had replaced the little artificer on Stax's crew. Which made Stax nervous: Tanner was even more forgetful than Osk, capable of forgetting the water bucket, torches, and even his pickaxe on occasion.

At least he had Hodey, who took Stax aside when they had a spare moment, looking to make sure Barnacle wasn't watching.

"Why are we digging down here?" he asked. "You told us we had to dig up first."

"Those are our crew boss's orders," Stax said, reluctantly, not wanting Hodey to risk a confrontation with the volatile Barnacle.

But Tanner wasn't so restrained. "We're digging down here because our crew boss is a fool," he said.

"Just remember the safety checks for lava," Stax said. "For instance, Tanner, where's the water bucket?"

"Ah, I left it back at the junction. Gimme a minute."

"You can't forget it," Stax said. "*Ever.*"

The mining proceeded slowly, with the crews repeatedly hitting bedrock and having to find paths around it. Stax hoped they wouldn't find anything of value, and that the lack of rewards would convince Barnacle that Stax had been telling the truth. But barely an hour into the shift, Jirwoh's crew hit a seam of gold, and an hour after that Pyx's crew located a small, snaking run of lapis.

During the lunch break Barnacle paced the length of the feeder tunnel, slapping men and women on the back and laughing as he predicted the wealth that would soon be flowing in.

"You thought Brandywine Hill was a good payday, just wait!" he exclaimed, and ordered them back to work twenty minutes early, despite Billups's protest that this was a violation of work rules. The other miners ignored Billups, which was no surprise. The rules-obsessed miner rarely went a day without finding a violation he could talk about at length. And, of course, they were afraid of Barnacle and his temper.

But there wasn't too much grumbling, and Stax knew why: They all wanted to find more wealth, and take home the bonuses that would come with it.

And that was dangerous. In a mine, haste could be deadly.

When Barnacle went back up to the surface to ask Ms. Lea for additional equipment, Stax checked in quickly with all the mining teams, urging them to check for heat and hardened blobs of magma. Barnacle wouldn't like that if he found out, but it was better than the alternative.

The crew boss came back after about half an hour, barking for the miners to hurry up. He found Stax, Tanner, and Hodey working sideways around a knot of bedrock, their pickaxes rising and falling, striking sparks from the gray stone.

"Why are you half a tunnel behind every other crew?" Barnacle demanded. "Slowcarts, the three of you. This wealthy lickspittle has one bit of luck, in a mine started by someone else, and now you three think you can swing pickaxes while sitting in comfy chairs on a porch. Well, not on my shift. Hurry it up!"

He stormed off to yell at someone else and Stax shook his head, exasperated.

"He has some nerve, calling us slowcarts," muttered Tanner. "I'll show him. Hey, Hodey, I bet we can finish this branch tunnel in half an hour. Are we on?"

"None of that," Stax said. "We mine what we mine and we find what we find. My father taught me that one too."

But Tanner and Hodey were determined, and swung their pickaxes as hard as they could, making rock fly as they dug out the tunnel. It was Stax's turn to follow behind them, clearing away the loose rock, and he was constantly hurrying up and down the tunnel, taking rock away for removal to the surface and returning to find more waiting for him.

He was walking back when he heard the sound: an oddly hollow thunk, followed by a hiss. The tunnel they'd made jogged to the right to avoid a knot of bedrock, so Stax couldn't see straight ahead to where Tanner and Hodey were working. But he saw bright light beyond the turn, brighter than the soft glow of torchlight.

And he heard Hodey cry out.

"IT'S LAVA! TANNER! GET THE BUCKET! GET THE BUCKET!"

Hodey screamed.

Stax broke into a run, and tripped over something. It was the water bucket, left behind yet again by Tanner. Stax grabbed it and ran around the corner, but one look told him the worst had happened, and he had arrived too late.

CHAPTER 21

STAX STARTS AGAIN

Little house on the savanna *
Stax's new routine * Hejira's code

"You're sure you won't change your mind?" Mrs. Taney asked, for the fourth or maybe even the fifth time.

"I'm sure," Stax said. He was sitting in Mrs. Taney's office with his gear packed.

"Stax, it wasn't your fault," Mrs. Taney said. "I have eyes and ears down there, you know. I know that right before it happened, you warned all the crews about safety. I know how many times Tanner forgot the water bucket. And I know it was Barnacle who insisted on digging too low, despite your warnings. I don't know what else you think you could have done."

"I don't know either, but whatever it was, I didn't do it. And now Hodey's dead."

"Yes, he is. But going off on your own won't bring him back. It was an accident, Stax, and accidents happen—to solo miners as well as to full crews. In fact, they happen even more often to solo miners, because when you get tired there's no one next to you reminding you of the dos and don'ts."

"If I make that mistake, I'll be the only one to pay the price," Stax said. "And that's the way I want it."

Mrs. Taney looked at him for a long moment, her eyes searching his face, and then she nodded.

"So your plan is to go into the outback and set up your own homestead," she said. "It's dangerous out there, Stax. There's no law, no neighbors, no one to help you if you need it."

"I know that," Stax said, patting the sword at his side and pulling the hilt a microblock out of its scabbard. "Actual iron. No more wood."

"Well, that's a start," Mrs. Taney said. "You've been to see Brubbs and Xinzi already, I suppose."

Stax nodded. "The rest of my equipment's waiting there for me. Along with the title to the land I've chosen."

The iron sword, equipment, and land title had used up more than two-thirds of Stax's earnings at The Tumbles Extraction Company, leaving him with little margin for error if something went wrong. But Stax didn't want to talk about how little he had left. If he had, Mrs. Taney might have tried to talk him out of doing the last thing he felt he needed to do.

He reached into the sack he carried at his belt and extracted three emeralds, which he placed in a line on Mrs. Taney's desk.

"Would you see that these get to Hodey's sweetheart?" he asked. "It won't be enough for that undersea palace he was always talking about. But it will help her get something a little smaller."

Mrs. Taney nodded and tucked the emeralds into her desk

drawer. "We'll take care of her. We do that for our own. Everyone on the shift has given some of their wages. Barnacle even tried to hand over half of his bonus from Brandywine Hill."

Stax hadn't expected that, and found his emotions threatening to get the better of him.

"I figured I couldn't talk you out of leaving, so I went to the general store myself," Mrs. Taney said. "I have something for you."

She ducked into the back room and returned a minute later with a large, T-shaped package, which she indicated Stax should open. He stripped the paper away to discover a brand new pickaxe—one whose head was the cold greenish blue of diamonds.

"That iron one of yours was looking a little worn, and that won't do out there by your lonesome," Mrs. Taney said. "If you measure the handle, you'll find it's exactly a block long."

Stax stammered his thanks and stuck out his hand for her to shake.

"Oh, come here, you ridiculous boy," Mrs. Taney said, embracing him and kissing him on the cheek. "I hate to lose you, but I've known enough ridiculous boys over the years to see your mind is made up. Good luck, Stax. Good luck and keep safe."

The little patch of land Stax had bought was several hours' walk from Tumbles Harbor, beyond the hills that gave the town its name. Away from the coast, the land turned to savanna, a vast flat expanse of grass that stretched to a line of mountains to the north and away into infinity to the east. The grass was broken by stone-lipped ravines, as if someone had struck the ground with a giant axe, and by tall, brooding acacia trees, whose sharply angled limbs made Stax think they were about to fall over.

Stax's land was in the middle of the savanna, atop a little hill. Using a shovel he'd bought at the general store, he built a simple cabin of sod like the one he'd built near the shores of Desolation Bay—big enough for a bed, several chests, a crafting table, and a furnace, and lit by a single smoky torch. The cabin had a door of acacia wood from a tree Stax chopped down, and sat in the center of a square of fencing made from the same wood. In the corner of his plot of land Stax had dug out a little pond and planted a few rows of wheat and a few pumpkins, which was enough food to sustain him without the necessity of caring for animals.

If you're thinking this all sounds a little depressing, well, Stax thought so too. But his last sight of Hodey haunted him and he'd vowed that he'd never let that happen again. His plan remained much the same as it had been in Tumbles Harbor: He'd collect enough wealth to see the Champion and set out alone to try to enlist him to find Fouge Tempro.

So Stax dug down in his yard, his shovel making quick work through dirt, until he hit rock and put the shovel aside in favor of his new diamond pickaxe. The tool was lightweight and felt good in his hands, and it bit through rock with satisfying speed. As he had done working with Osk and Hodey, Stax tunneled straight down, capping his new mine with a trapdoor of acacia wood. Several days' work brought him down to bedrock, but this time the hard work of digging down wasn't fruitless; he accumulated enough coal to fuel his furnace and make weeks' worth of torches, and hit several veins of iron.

Once he'd dug back to above the lava line, Stax carved out a headhouse belowground, connecting the stairwell leading back to the surface to the feeder tunnel he'd started excavating. The headhouse became another base of operations, with chests full of equipment and food and a bed so Stax could rest between shifts. And, increasingly, that was where he spent most of his time: digging out tunnels until he was too tired to work any longer, and then sleeping in the headhouse with his diamond pickaxe next to the bed.

Stax quickly developed a routine. Every week, he harvested food from his garden to sustain him while he mined. Every other week, he made the long trip to Tumbles Harbor to get new supplies—allowing himself some honey for his bread as a small luxury—and to check if Brubbs had heard from anyone who might know the way back across the Sea of Sorrows. (The answer was always no.) The rest of the time, he mined.

Stax had one visitor while he was setting up this new operation: Osk, who brought him a pair of gifts. The first was a pressure plate by Stax's front gate, which activated a redstone torch down in the headhouse, telling Stax that he had a guest. The second was a golden clock, which indicated whether it was day or night in the Overworld far above Stax's head.

He was grateful, but since he never had any other visitor, the redstone torch down in the headhouse stayed dark, except for the afternoon when it turned out that a wild pig had stepped on it while looking for a way to get through the fence and eat Stax's crops. The clock was useful, but after a while Stax no longer cared what time it was.

All Stax did was mine and sleep and mine some more, and his clothes became dirty and worn and his hair grew long and a scraggly beard sprouted on his chin. Though he didn't realize it, he once again looked like the pathetic, ragged figure Ramoa's caravan had encountered near the road to Tumbles Harbor. He'd also started talking to himself again, having conversations about the quality of ore and the most efficient use of a pickaxe.

He had fallen into a routine that wasn't particularly good for his health, with his world shrinking to the mine, his little vegetable patch, and the general store. Even the memories of his beloved cats and his beautiful house on the hill, the one made of gleaming diorite and granite and glass, started to become a bit blurry and indistinct.

Until something changed.

It was the day to till the garden, or at least Stax thought it was; he'd lost track of day and night, but noticed he was down to a few crusts of bread, which were getting hard, and a single piece of pumpkin pie that smelled a little odd. So he'd trudged up the winding stone steps to emerge in his yard, blinking at what felt like too much light, even though the position of the sun indicated it was late afternoon.

Stax was hacking away at the stem of a ripe pumpkin when he felt the back of his neck prickle and stood up, peering across the savanna. At first he thought his mind had been playing tricks on him, but then he spotted a lone figure in the distance, striding across the plains from the direction of Tumbles Harbor. Stax thought the traveler might be Osk, but the figure was far too tall to be the eccentric artificer, and the way they walked suggested both power and purpose.

Stax realized he had left his iron sword in the cabin and ducked inside to get it. He wished he had a bow, but what would have been the use? He had only two arrows, and was a poor shot anyway. All he could do was wait.

The traveler was dressed entirely in black, with nut-brown skin and black hair streaked with gray, pulled back and tied in a pony-tail. His face was weather-beaten, seamed and pocked. A sword hung at his belt, and a bow was slung over his shoulder. To Stax's surprise, the man was barefoot but never broke stride, marching across the savanna like he was being drawn by a string, without a care for thorns or rocks that might be lurking in his path.

The man came to a halt at Stax's gate and stood there, regarding him.

"Good afternoon, Stax Stonecutter," he said in a voice that surprised Stax, for it was rich and melodic, beautiful even. The voice of a poet or a singer, not a rough-looking wanderer.

"And who are you?" Stax asked curtly, in no way reassured by the traveler's polite greeting. Fouge Tempro had been polite—at least occasionally—and he'd turned Stax's life upside down. Plus Stax had once again fallen out of practice at talking to other people.

"My name is Hejira Tenboots," the man said. "And we have a friend in common."

That name was familiar somehow. Had Fouge told it to him while Stax was his prisoner? Stax's hand crept toward the hilt of his sword, though he doubted he would have a chance against anyone who'd marched across the savanna barefoot without so much as batting an eye.

The man saw Stax's hand on his sword, and raised his eyebrows. "I believe you know my good friend and occasional traveling companion Ramoa Peranze," he said. "She asked me to check on you. The gentlemen at the Tumbles Harbor general store told me I could find you here."

Stax felt his shoulders sag in relief. "Oh. I thought you were—well, never mind what I thought. Please come in. It will be dark soon."

Suddenly he was embarrassed by his little house made out of dirt and also by himself, seeing how he was pretty much made out of dirt too by now. But Hejira shook his head, smiling apologetically.

"Unfortunately, that is against my code," he said.

"Your code?" Stax asked, wondering what, exactly, Hejira was saying he couldn't do.

"I have vowed never to make use of shelter, whether for myself or for another," he said. "I have no home, and no supplies beyond what you see. And I never stay in the same place for two nights in a row."

Stax looked at him in disbelief. "No shelter? How do you survive the night?"

"Trees are very useful," Hejira said. "Typically I sleep in their branches. If a tree is not available, I remain awake, relying on my sword and bow for protection. Once, I was awake for six straight days while crossing the Desert of the Last Sigh. That was a difficult experience."

Stax imagined spending the night in a tree, surrounded by prowling zombies and skeletons. He knew there were many of them on the savanna. He often found chunks of rotten meat or lengths of bone in the tall grass, outside his fence.

"Don't things climb up after you?" Stax asked.

"Spiders do," Hejira said. "I have been bitten many times, and though they are only doing what is in their nature, I must admit that I am not fond of them. In my experience, neither skeletons nor zombies climb. Occasionally a skeleton will fire arrows at me, but fortunately they are poor shots."

"I see," Stax said, though the whole idea felt fantastical to him. "If I can ask, how did you develop this code of yours?"

"I had a moment of crisis as a young man. I realized I was

growing slothful surrounded by comforts, and that I knew nothing of the world. So I decided to discover if I had a true self worth preserving."

"It seems like you've more than proven that you do," Stax said.

Hejira smiled. "I like to think so, yes. But I find the idea of going back to that life unimaginable now. This is who I am, and this is how I live—and if I can help others discover the path to their true selves, I do so. If it will not bother you, I will sleep tonight in that acacia tree."

Stax managed not to laugh at the idea that someone sleeping in one of the great thorny trees could somehow bother him.

"But now please tell me of yourself, so that I may tell Ramoa. How fares your quest to find this mysterious Fouge Tempro, and take your well-deserved revenge?"

"Ramoa told you that?" asked Stax, not sure that he liked the idea.

"Of course she did," said Hejira, looking surprised. "How would I find your adversary, if she had not? I have traveled many lands since adopting my code, Stax Stonecutter, though I am afraid what I know about the area west of the Sea of Sorrows is just rumors. Everywhere I go, people bring me news and stories they believe to be true but that are only stories. I have asked about this Fouge Tempro since Ramoa told me your story, and I will continue to do so. But so far, I am afraid, no one has heard of this man."

"I'm grateful to you for helping," Stax said. "And to Ramoa. Where is she?"

"I am to meet her outside the Lost Fane of the Green Faith, in the Rain-Jungles of Jagga-Tel, two weeks from tonight. It is a long journey. I may have to sleep less than is ideal. And I do not know which route Ramoa will take. She dislikes taking the same road twice, and never rides horses, for reasons I have never understood. And because of these things, she is often late."

Stax had to smile at that, remembering Ramoa's restlessness and her distaste for the idea of spending even a single night at the caravanserai.

"You may accompany me, if you like," Hejira said. "Perhaps such a journey would help you discover your own path. Though fellow travelers often find my code hard to abide by."

"No, thank you," Stax said. "I am afraid my duties are—"

Thunk! Stax jumped as an arrow thudded into the fence between him and Hejira.

"Excuse me, Stax," said the black-clad man, shrugging his bow off his shoulder with his left hand while his right reached up, unerringly, and eased a long arrow fletched with brilliant red feathers from his quiver. He turned, the bowstring twanged, and Stax heard the rattling of bones coming apart somewhere out on the gloomy savanna.

"Perhaps you should take shelter, Stax," Hejira said. "The nights of the Overworld are beautiful, but they are the domain of things with teeth. Until morning, my friend."

He clasped Stax's shoulder, his grip firm, and then turned and walked off into the dusk, offering a cheerful wave. Something growled in the gathering dark and Stax retreated to his acacia-wood door. He tried to spot Hejira but failed, and shut the door behind him.

Stax had been working so hard that he'd grown used to falling asleep the moment his head hit his pillow, but that night his sleep was broken and restless, and he dreamed that Fouge Tempro was knocking on the door of the little sod cabin, telling Stax their business wasn't concluded. Stax opened it and saw Fouge standing at the head of an army of skeletons, all of them clad in strange spiked armor made of acacia.

He woke with a start to find moonlight streaming through his window.

"Just a dream," he said. "I'm awake and it was just a dream."

But he could hear someone outside, yelling and chanting. Stax opened the door a crack and peered out. The brilliant moon made the acacias' zigzag shadows even longer and stranger. Stax thought he spied odd shapes out there—a lone figure in frantic motion at the center of a larger circle.

"Madness," muttered Stax, now not sure if he was dreaming or not.

Stax hadn't been dreaming. In the morning he emerged, blinking and scrubbing a hand through his hair, to find Hejira leaning against the fence, gnawing on a chunk of meat. Objects littered the ground around him: strands of spider silk, bones, arrows, and heaps of gray powder.

"Good morning, Stax," said Hejira. "I hope I did not disturb you. It was a busy night. Please take anything here that you can use."

Stax accepted the bones, which he could grind into meal to fertilize his garden, and left the rest.

"We were interrupted last night, and I was talking when I should have been listening," Hejira said. "You said you had duties that prevented you from traveling with me to Jagga-Tel."

"Unfortunately I do," Stax said. "My mining. And my mission."

"Your mission to find Fouge Tempro?"

"Yes."

"Are these things not mutually exclusive?"

"Excuse me?"

"If you are mining, you are not searching for Fouge Tempro. And if you are searching for Fouge Tempro, you are not mining."

Stax thought Hejira was making fun of him, and was about to tell the strange traveler it was none of his business. But he realized Hejira wasn't smiling, but seemed genuinely puzzled.

"It's . . . well, it's not that simple," Stax said. "I'm not a warrior. Though *you* certainly are. Say, Mr. Tenboots—"

Hejira held up his hand. "This is your quest, Stax, not mine. I will help you discover your path if you want my assistance. But I would not steal your destiny from you, whatever it may be."

"If it means ridding the Overworld of Fouge Tempro, by all means steal it," Stax said. "I wouldn't mind in the slightest."

The idea seemed to offend Hejira, whose gaze grew stony. "That is against my code."

"Of course it is," said Stax, with a sigh. "That's all right. I had someone else in mind anyway."

And he told Hejira of the Champion, and how he performed services in return for people making the Overworld a better place, and how Stax had no idea what the price might be.

"I have heard stories of this man," Hejira said. "Though there have been no new stories in recent years. So this is why you mine, instead of pursuing your tormentor. You hope to meet the price of this Champion."

Stax nodded. "And I'm not there yet."

Suddenly, under Hejira's stern gaze, his plan seemed less certain than he would have liked.

"How will you know when you have reached your goal?" Hejira asked.

That was a good question.

"I don't know," Stax said. "I just know I don't have enough. Not yet, anyway."

The sun had fully risen, drying the dew from the grasslands. Hejira was peering at the distant gray shapes of the mountains and shifting from foot to foot.

"I must go, Stax," he said. "Or I will be late to meet Ramoa. If she is not late herself, of course."

Stax had to smile at the man's obvious longing for the horizon and whatever lay beyond it. And for a moment he wanted to tell Hejira to wait, that he would pack his things and come with him. Stax had survived on a bleak shore with nothing but a shipwreck and a broken tower nearby; surely he could learn to live in a tree.

But no. He had chests to fill with ore and gems, treasure that would allow him to hire the Champion. And then, once the Overworld was rid of Fouge Tempro, he would search for a way home, to put his life back together. That was the plan, not gallivanting off to some jungle with a barefoot fanatic.

"Good luck journeying to the Jungle of Jagged . . . of That Place," Stax said. "I, um, hope the treetops are comfortable."

"As do I," Hejira said. "I have heard Jagga-Tel has massive trees, in which people make their homes. I am eager to see this myself. Though I am undecided on the question of whether a tree people consider a home counts as a shelter."

"I suppose you'll have time to think it over," Stax said.

"Yes. A long walk always helps. Good luck to you, Stax Stonecutter. May you discover the path to your true self, and find the destiny you deserve. And if Ramoa should pass this way, remind her of our appointment."

Hejira clasped Stax's shoulder again and then strode off, his long steps taking him across the savanna almost as quickly as Stax could have run. Stax had work to do—he'd mapped out a new feeder tunnel in hope of finding lapis deposits—but instead he stood at the fence, one hand on the rail, until Hejira had dwindled to a small figure and then was lost to sight.

CHAPTER 22

LURKERS IN THE DARK

Gravel, gravel, and more gravel *
A miner's mistake * Someone at the gate

Two days later—or at least Stax thought it was two days, though he had to admit it might have been longer—Stax finished the new feeder tunnel and surveyed his work. The tunnel was perfectly straight and studded with torches placed at the correct intervals, all of them on the left-hand wall, as they should be.

That was properly orderly, but the walls were an unattractive hodgepodge of different types of stone—as Stax walked the length of the tunnel, he passed sections of gray andesite, pink granite, and white diorite, with no rhyme or reason. The places he'd found ore veins crossing the tunnel were now patched with cobblestone, which looked even uglier. At least in those cases Stax had removed something of value: stacks of coal and some iron. The patches in the ceiling were there because Stax kept running into gravel. Packed above the rock for eons, it came showering down when disturbed, leaving Stax no choice but to shovel it all out and fill the gap.

There was a lot of gravel around the new tunnel. Stax could only hope he'd seen the last of it. And perhaps it was his imagination, but his diamond-headed pickaxe was growing a bit dull. Stax had found seams of diamond, but disliked the idea of using those stocks to make a replacement tool.

"Need those riches for other things, now don't we?" he said out loud, his voice echoing hugely in the tunnel he'd dug out.

That seemed unwise, and he clapped a hand over his own mouth.

"Quiet now," he said in a whisper. "Don't disturb whatever else lives down here."

But then he shook his head. There was nothing down here, nothing except the unimaginable weight of the rock above him and around him, through which he'd poked a few tiny tunnels, like a worm chewing into something too huge for it to comprehend.

"Nothing! Nothing! NOTHING!" yelled Stax, his voice booming and bouncing crazily around the tunnel. He laughed, bent over with his hands on his knees. He felt himself unraveling, but rather than dwell on those feelings, he retreated to the headhouse to sleep, with his pickaxe clutched to his chest.

In the morning, he gnawed on a crust of bread and drank a little water from the bucket he kept with him while he worked. The water tasted stony and metallic, and left a little grit in Stax's mouth.

"Next time I see Brubbs, I'm going to get some milk," he vowed. "Milk would be good. Maybe I can bake a cake."

The idea of baking a cake seemed hilarious, suddenly. He could turn the headhouse into the Overworld's deepest bakery, selling cakes and pies and cookies to absolutely no one. He was still chuckling about this as he swung his pickaxe into the rock to dig out the first branch tunnel.

(At this point, you're probably a little worried about Stax, thinking that perhaps he's gone a bit crazy, working all by himself in his new mine. I'd like to reassure you that it's not the case, but I can't. Because it's *totally* the case.)

Stax had excavated only a couple of blocks of the branch tunnel before he hit a pocket of gravel. Grunting in annoyance, he switched to his iron shovel and cleared it out, frowning up at the dark opening in the rock from which the gravel had spilled. He saw only darkness, so he patched up the ceiling and kept working.

More gravel. And still more. Stax was starting to hate this new tunnel, which was so far proving a source of additional work rather than wealth. He kept shoveling, plucking out pieces of flint when he found them, and muttering terrible things about gravel and its fundamental uselessness.

His pickaxe bit through the rock and, once again, revealed gravel.

"Oh, you have got to be kidding me," Stax said. He shoveled the gravel clear, arms straining, glanced into the darkness above him, and reached for some rock to patch this latest gap in the ceiling. Ahead of him, to his disgust, there was more gravel.

"That's not a pocket up there, it's more like a cave," Stax said.

He decided to just dig the rest of the gravel out before patching the ceiling. That would save a little time. He could feel the cool air from the cave on the back of his neck and thought that it felt refreshing.

"Stupid useless gravel," Stax muttered. "Worst substance in the entire—uhh!"

The arrow whistled past Stax's shoulder, clattering off the rock. Another zipped over his head, from the darkness above and in front of him.

"Oh, you fool, you utter fool," he said to himself, his voice thick with disgust. He reminded himself not to move, remembering Ramoa's lesson that skeletons were better at hitting a moving target than a stationary one.

The skeleton in front of him jumped down into the tunnel with a bony rattle, empty eye sockets fixed on his face. As it raised its bow, Stax drew his sword and knocked it sideways. The tip of the sword scraped across the rock wall, leaving a trail of sparks.

Pain flared in the back of Stax's shoulder. An arrow had found its mark. Another slash of his sword and the skeleton in front of him shivered and collapsed into loose bones. Behind him, Stax heard the rattle of the other skeleton jumping down.

He had done something profoundly dumb, turning his back on a dark place he hadn't explored. But his enemies had failed to keep the advantage he'd given them, rushing to confront him instead of sniping at him while concealed in the dark. Wincing at the pain at his shoulder, Stax drove the skeleton backward, the blows keeping it unbalanced and unable to fire, until it fell apart into a pile of bones.

"Gotta patch it up," Stax said. "Before—"

He heard a small sound behind him: a hiss. He turned to find himself looking into the face of a nightmare with huge black eyespots and a yawning mouth in green, spongy flesh.

The creeper's flesh seemed to pulse. Stax smelled something acrid and burning. Then everything went dark.

The first thing Stax saw was a light, but it was faint and far away. He was lying facedown, surrounded by loose rock. He shoved the rock aside and wondered why it didn't make a sound.

Stax sat up, blinking and confused. His face and chest felt burned. He was sitting on the lip of a pit blasted into the rock by the creeper's detonation. Above him was the black mouth of the cave.

"Gotta seal it up," he said, but he couldn't hear his own voice, just a ringing in his ears.

He forced himself to his feet and trudged down the branch tunnel, stepping over a torch that had been blasted off the wall and lay extinguished on the floor. He stopped once he was in full torchlight, breathing hard.

"Seal it up," he said again, still unable to hear the words, and watched himself move cobblestone into place, until the cave and the pit had been walled off. By the time he was done he could hear the scraping of his pickaxe. Little by little, his hearing was returning.

Stax stared at the blank wall of mottled cobblestone and let himself rest against it. If anything else had been hiding in the gravel cavern, he would have been killed. Fortunately, the creeper had been the last monster lurking in the darkness.

But it had been close. Far too close.

Stax walked slowly back to the headhouse and sat on one of the equipment chests. It took him a minute to realize the redstone torch was lit. Something was at his gate.

"Another pig," he said in disgust, shaking his head.

It was all too much, suddenly. He was a careless miner who had nearly gotten himself killed, digging at the rock below a horrible little house made out of dirt, and his fancy doorbell didn't even work. He stalked up the narrow stone stairs, muttering with each turn, threw open the trapdoor at the top of the mine, and climbed out into his yard.

"Get lost, you useless pig!" he yelled, and then stopped in disbelief.

Ramoa was standing at the gate, her mouth a shocked O.

"Gosh, Stax," she managed after a moment. "It's nice to see you too."

CHAPTER 23

AN EXPEDITION

Of Ramoa's wanderings * Reunited with Hejira *
Lessons in the art of war

"Ramoa!" Stax cried out. "Sorry! There's a pressure plate, and it activates a . . . but I didn't . . . and there was this pig . . . and, and I'm glad to see you."

"I'm not sure I followed all that, or any of it, in fact, but it's better than being called a pig," Ramoa said. "But what's happened? You're hurt. Your face and hands are burned."

She unlatched the gate and hurried to him, poking at his blistered cheeks.

"Ow!"

"Does it hurt?"

"Of course it hurts, that's why I said ow," Stax said. "But I'm okay, really. And I really am glad to see you. You know you're supposed to meet Hejira Tenboots, right? In some jungle."

"Heji was here? Oh good. I asked him to check on you, but

you never know what that crazy code of his may make him do. So I figured I'd better come see how you were doing myself."

Stax ushered Ramoa into his cabin, though a moment later he wished he hadn't. It was small and dark and dirty, and he could tell Ramoa felt the same way.

"I spend most of my time down below, mining," he said. "I haven't really kept house much."

"Or at all," Ramoa said, and her eyes narrowed. "What's happened to you, Stax? Brubbs told me you'd done well at the mining company but then gone off on your own. He warned me you'd maybe gotten a little strange, out here by yourself, but I wasn't prepared for this."

"For what? Like I said, I've been working. And I wasn't expecting company."

"When I met you, you had been marooned and were wearing nothing but rags, and you looked better than you do now."

Stax started to object that he'd just survived a close encounter with a creeper, but he knew that wasn't what Ramoa meant. His shirt was stiff with dirt and sweat and his hair and beard were filthy. He hung his head as Ramoa's gaze took in the cabin, jumping from his unmade bed to the chests along the wall.

"What *have* you been doing out here, anyway, Stax? I hope you're at least killing yourself for some reward that's worth it."

So Stax told her about the Champion and his plan, hoping it would make her understand and stop looking at him like he'd done something wrong.

"So that's what's in those chests, gems and ore? The stuff you're hoping to use to hire this Champion?"

"Yeah," Stax said. "I've done all right, but I don't have enough yet."

Ramoa lifted the lid of the nearest chest to peer inside. She looked questioningly at Stax, then opened the next chest, going down the line until she'd seen inside all of them. Then she turned, her hands on her hips.

"Stax. There's a *fortune* here. Forget ransoms on princes, or whatever that story was you told me. With this stuff you could become a prince yourself."

"I don't think—"

"You don't think *what*? Just look!" And Ramoa took Stax by the hand and dragged him over to look with her. At the stacks of gold bars, and the piles of lapis, and the containers of redstone dust, and the mounds of emeralds. At the blocks of coal and gleaming iron and at the diamonds, glittering icy blue in the dim little cabin.

"It *is* a lot," Stax admitted. "I guess I kind of lost track of how much I've found. But there's more to excavate—"

"I'm sure there is," Ramoa said. "And there always will be. And you are not going down into that hole to bring more of it up. Because it's making you crazy. Your goal was to go home. Remember that?"

"Of course I do. It's just . . ." And Stax trailed off, no longer sure what he'd been going to say, and stared at the dirt floor beneath his boots.

And then he looked up at Ramoa.

"I hate it here," he said quietly, the words surprising himself. "I hate the color of the grass, and these horrible trees that are basically big thorns. You can't see the ocean, or smell the salt in the air. There aren't any sheep or cats. Cats . . ."

Ramoa put her hand on his shoulder. "Come with me, Stax. Come with me and meet Heji in Jagga-Tel. You need to see something other than this awful place, and do something other than bang away at rock. Come with me, and we'll figure out what to do next."

Stax hesitated, thinking of the mine far beneath his little yard, and everything he had to do there. Ramoa had stepped back, breaking their embrace, and was waiting for his answer.

She was right, he realized. He had become so focused on finding gems and precious metals that he'd lost sight of *why* he was working so hard to gather them. His goal had been to amass enough wealth to hire the Champion, see Fouge Tempro brought to justice, and find his way home. He'd reached that goal weeks earlier, probably, but continued obsessively pursuing it anyway. He wasn't quite willing to agree with Ramoa that he'd gone crazy down in his mine, but it was obviously and embarrassingly true that his quest had become something unhealthy.

"You're right," he told Ramoa. "I'll come to Jackbell."

"To where? Oh, you mean Jagga-Tel. Good. Though there are some things we have to do first."

Stax nodded. He'd already been thinking about that.

"Yes. I need to bury my gems and ore, and my equipment. And—"

"And before any of that, you need to wash. Because, wow, do you stink."

"I do?"

"Stax, you smell like a dead cow. No, like a dead cow that's been covered in clay dug up from the bottom of the ocean. And left to rot in the desert. At noontime. On the hottest—"

"Okay, Okay," Stax said, throwing up his arms in surrender. "I get it!"

"All right then. So you take a bath in that pond out there, and find some shears for that hair, and put on something you haven't been wearing for a month. And then we'll go from there."

———

It was dusk by the time Stax had finished bathing and shaving, harvesting the crops that were ready and burying several chests beneath his front gate. That meant it was too late to set off for anywhere, let alone some distant jungle. He gave the bed in his little sod house to Ramoa and slept belowground, in the head-house. It was cool in the mine, and for a moment Stax's thoughts crept to ore veins and branch tunnels. But no, he was finished mining here, beneath these strange grasses and trees. He'd go with Ramoa, and clear his head. That idea felt good, and Stax realized he hadn't felt good in some time. He closed his eyes and was asleep instantly.

In the morning he emerged from the trapdoor leading to the mine and found Ramoa standing in the yard, peering at the sun and then at the gray line of the mountains. She was between him and the rising sun, and the morning light seemed to touch her black curls with fire, creating a halo of radiance.

"Let's walk," she said, opening the gate and inclining her head for Stax to go first. "It's four days to the jungle, maybe five. Quicker on a horse, but I never ride them. I always wind up more concerned with the horse than with the land around me. Heji said he was going to travel via the Mortimer Gap, probably because there's an innkeeper there who makes a roasted chicken he likes. But I've been that way too many times, so I figured out an alternate route. And anyway, I never quite trust Heji's math, seeing how every step he takes is two steps for a normal person."

"You and Hejira are good friends," Stax said.

"Oh, absolutely," Ramoa said. "He's helped me out of some bad spots, and always seems to show up when I need him most."

"Are you two . . . ?" Stax wasn't sure how to put it and let his voice trail off with a little flurry of hand gestures.

"Are you making little smoochy motions with your hands?" Ramoa asked, grinning. "Like in a puppet show? The puppets are mashing their scrunchy felt faces together and all the little kids in the audience are going 'ewwwww'?"

"No!" Stax said. "No, not at . . . well, maybe. I don't know what I was doing, to tell you the truth."

"Ha! To answer the question you couldn't figure out how to ask me, no, Heji and I are not smoochy puppets. I don't think he's interested in that sort of thing, if you want to know the truth. He's more like my big brother, or maybe my best friend. I met him years ago, when I was traveling with a caravan that got ambushed by bandits. I was hurt pretty bad, and he brought me all the way back to River House to recover."

"What's River House?"

"My home," Ramoa said. "I built it out of birch wood, above the sea, at the mouth of a little river that winds through a forest. I go back there every couple of months, to rest and think about the places I've seen."

She frowned, studying the hills ahead of her, and shook her head.

"Every time I go back, I tell myself that this time I'm going to stay," Ramoa said. "And it works, for about a week. Then I feel myself getting . . . I don't know, *restless*. I'm thinking about the lava falls I saw in the moonlight, pouring into a steaming sea. Or the flower forest with bees the size of apples, where the air was so thick with the scent of pollen and honey that I thought I could float on it. Or a hundred other places I've seen. And then I think about all the places there must be like that, only I haven't seen them yet. I ask myself how many there must be. Thousands? Millions? And then a day or two later I'm packing up my gear."

They said nothing for a few minutes, walking side by side through the tall grass.

"My house was on a little peninsula, on the edge of what I guess was once a forest like the one near your house," he said. "Right off the coast there are ice floes, and towers of ice that gleam at night."

"Oh, that sounds beautiful," Ramoa said.

"It is. And if I get back there, I'm never forgetting that again."

By the afternoon, they'd reached the hills. It was cooler on the higher ground, with birches and oaks instead of acacias, and Stax smiled to see bright green leaves and white bark again. That night he and Ramoa made camp in a little cave that Stax hacked out of the hillside with his shovel and his pickaxe, evening off the walls inside out of habit.

After two days of walking, the hills came to an end. Standing on their edge, Stax and Ramoa looked down at a riot of green. Massive trees rose from the vegetation, so high that clouds drifted below their crowns of dark leaves. Long strings of vines hung from their limbs. Stax wondered if those trees were as tall as the spires of ice by the Stonecutter estate. He spotted brilliantly colored birds flitting through the vegetation, and the air was filled with the song of birds and the hum of insects.

"Is that Jagmell?" he asked.

"Jagga-Tel," Ramoa said, laughing. "Honestly, Stax. If you could remember the names of places, maybe you'd be home by now."

"That's not funny," Stax said.

Ramoa raised her eyebrows, but kept quiet as they walked down the hill.

"All right," Stax said. "Maybe it's a *little* funny."

The Lost Fane sat in a low valley, on a grassy plain dotted with pools of clear blue water. The valley was ringed with stalks of bamboo, standing like sentinels. They made a hollow *thunk* when Stax rapped on them.

The fane itself was a low, pyramidal structure of cobblestone, green with creeping moss. Hejira Tenboots was sitting on its front steps, sharpening his sword. He looked up as Ramoa and Stax emerged from the bamboo and smiled widely.

"You are not late," he said.

"Why do you sound surprised?" Ramoa asked. "It's super annoying when you do that. Anyway, I'm never late. You're always early."

"Call it what you like. I am glad to see you regardless," Hejira said. "And you too, Stax Stonecutter, though your arrival is a surprise to me. What do you think of the Rain-Jungles of Jagga-Tel?"

"They're beautiful," Stax said, and meant it. He'd never imagined there were so many varieties of green, ranging from the dark traceries of the vines to the brilliant squares of melons that grew in the underbrush.

"I think so too," Hejira said. "Unfortunately, the Lost Fane was plundered long ago, and its treasury is empty. I had been curious about what would be inside."

"Guess it isn't so lost, then," Ramoa said, and Hejira shrugged.

"Things can be lost multiple times. But they have a way of getting found."

While Hejira and Ramoa compared notes on their journeys, Stax lit a torch and explored the inside of the temple. On the lowermost level he found trip wires that had been severed, rendering whatever trap they'd once triggered useless. Beyond them was a hole in the wall—raggedly cut, he noted with disapproval—and chests that contained only a few shreds of rotten meat.

Stax studied the carvings on the temple walls, wondering what they'd meant to the people who'd built this place. Upstairs, he gathered fallen stone and walled up a corner of the temple as a refuge where he and Ramoa could sleep.

Ramoa heard the noise and came to see what he was doing and smiled, but shook her head.

"That was kind of you, Stax," she said. "But a good thing about traveling with Heji is you can sleep out in the open. As long as you don't mind being woken by the occasional grunt or stabbing noise, of course. I figured we'd set up our beds on top of the pyramid, so we can see the stars."

That did sound more appealing than sleeping in the temple— it smelled musty, anyway—and so Stax took apart his bed and followed Ramoa back down the stairs, where Hejira was testing the edge of his sword with one finger.

"What did you decide your code said about sleeping in the jungle treetops?" Stax asked Hejira, remembering their conversation back on the savanna.

"I debated that as I walked here," Hejira said. "And I concluded that it is forbidden. If people live in the treetops, they are a shelter, and I have foresworn shelter."

"But birds nest in acacias and other trees," Stax said. "Does that count as shelter?"

Hejira looked thoughtful. Ramoa punched Stax in the arm.

"Goodness, Stax, don't encourage him," she said. "His code is ridiculous enough as it is."

Hejira smiled and clasped Stax's shoulder. "Ramoa told me

what happened to you in your mine just before she arrived. I find creepers the most dangerous inhabitant of the night. They are stealthy creatures, with excellent senses. You must have performed very capably to survive that fight."

"I didn't," Stax said, wincing at the memory of the creeper's gaping black mouth and green flesh. "The explosion knocked me flat on my back. I'm no warrior, Hejira. I just got lucky."

"This is a strange conclusion to reach," said Hejira. "You also prefer to believe that you were lucky to survive being marooned. You might instead conclude that you are capable and resourceful in difficult situations, and take heart from that."

Stax shrugged and muttered something.

"Heji doesn't give out compliments casually," said Ramoa. "And neither do I. Though perhaps you could use some combat instruction. We could help with that."

"I suppose it couldn't hurt," Stax said.

"Excellent," Ramoa said. "Heji, you take swordplay and I'll handle archery?"

A few minutes later Stax was standing face-to-face with Hejira, sword held in front of him, touching the tip of Hejira's. Hejira brought his sword down, sweeping Stax's aside, and immediately was inside Stax's guard, blade against his throat.

"I guess I'm dead," Stax said, stunned by the speed and ferocity with which Hejira had moved.

"No, you are just at the beginning of the learning process," Hejira said.

Over the next hour he taught Stax to watch the way he was balancing, to sense which way he was leaning, and to sense when to give way before an attack to avoid being thrown off-balance and when to stand his ground and push back.

After an hour Stax felt a little more capable with a sword, but Hejira still made short work of him in their exercises. If Stax found a momentary advantage, he quickly proved too eager and left himself open for a countermove. And if his defenses started to crumble, fear and dismay overcame him, and he soon found the tip of Hejira's sword against his chest.

"Your body is learning, but your mind and heart are lagging behind," Hejira said. "A warrior never lets emotion direct the fight. Emotion will carry you to a place your body cannot follow, causing you to lose your focus. And with no focus, you are undone. Put aside your emotions, so that there is only the moment."

To his surprise, Stax found that that helped him. By the end of the next hour, he was breathing hard, but Hejira had repeatedly pointed out what he was doing right, instead of what he was doing wrong, and had said "good" several times.

"And now archery," Ramoa said.

"I'm too tired," Stax said.

"Oh stop, you barely have to move to fire a bow. Come here, Stax. Aim for the cocoa pods on the side of that tree."

Ramoa handed Stax her bow and Stax admired the weight of it and the way it fit in his hand. While Ramoa watched, he nocked an arrow, sighted down its length, and let it fly. The arrow went wide, speeding into the greenery.

"Don't move your hands when you fire," Ramoa suggested. "You line up the shot and then you let go of the bowstring. No more than that. The path of the arrow's already determined, and you just send it on its way."

"Easier said than done," Stax grumbled, but he tried again. This time the arrow went low, thudding into the dirt.

"You'll get it," said Ramoa. "Here, let me show you something that might help."

She took the bow out of his hands and nocked an arrow.

"Stand right behind me and put your hands over mine." He moved a step toward her. "Closer, Stax, I'm not going to bite you. There. Like that. Now feel what my hands do. Keep your eyes on the target and breathe out," she said, and he could feel her shoulders move against him as she said it. "Empty your lungs, so that you're still. And then . . . you let go."

Her hand opened under his and the arrow streaked from the bow to split one of the cocoa pods.

"Now you try it," Ramoa said.

Stax took the bow from her hands, nocked an arrow and drew back the string, waiting for the tip of the projectile to stop making little circles and hold still. He breathed out and opened his fingers.

"Yes! That's it, Stax! Perfect!"

Ramoa clapped her hands. Stax's arrow had hit the cocoa pod right next to hers.

"You have further lessons to learn, Stax Stonecutter, but you are more of a warrior than you think," said Hejira.

Ramoa returned carrying the two arrows in one hand and a cluster of cocoa pods in the other.

"I agree with Heji. Tomorrow, we're making you a bow. This jungle wood will be ideal for building one. But for now, since you brought some wheat, we can make cookies."

CHAPTER 24

THE ROAD TO THE CHAMPION

On journeys, and the reasons for them * Across the
Endless Dunes * A long-awaited meeting

Ramoa built the fire, Hejira made the cookies, and Stax was assigned to lookout duty. He paced around the circle of firelight, peering out into the dusk, convinced every bush was a creeper and every tree hid a skeleton archer.

But nothing challenged them and soon they were eating cookies, which were delicious though too hot, causing Hejira to hop around blowing comically on the overly large hunk of cookie he'd bitten off.

"The man won't wear shoes or sleep under a roof, but he loves cookies," Ramoa said, grinning at Stax. "He's an odd one, that Hejira Tenboots."

"We all are," Hejira said, with a small smile. "It is what makes us interesting."

"You're certainly that, my friend," Ramoa said. "So where are you bound next, Heji? I've promised to head down to Karamhés and guide a caravan south. That will bring me within a few days' journey of River House. Do you want to come with me? They could always use another capable guide."

"Perhaps. Though I am curious where our friend Stax sees his path leading him now."

Stax looked at them, curious. "My path led me here. Have we done everything we're going to do? I thought we'd at least explore the ruins to see if we missed anything, or . . . I don't know, *something*."

Hejira and Ramoa exchanged a look, one that made Stax feel like you do when two other people are enjoying a private joke.

"The object of visiting Jagga-Tel was to visit Jagga-Tel," said Hejira. "I wished to learn what had become of the Lost Fane, and now I have done so. Whereas Ramoa—"

"Whereas Ramoa can speak for herself," she said. "I wanted to observe the animals of the jungle—ocelots and parrots—and watch until I was confident I could imagine them with my eyes closed. Which I will do tomorrow at dawn, before Karamhés. Stax? What do you think of a trip to Karamhés?"

"If we've done what we came here to do, I need to go back to the savanna," Stax said, holding up a hand when Ramoa's expression grew grim. "Only to collect my gems and ore. Once I've retrieved them, I'll go find this Champion and see if he can help me."

"And how far would you travel in order to see this Champion?" asked Hejira.

"As far as I had to," Stax said.

"For revenge," Hejira said.

Stax shook his head. "For *justice*. My last night down in the mine, before I left the savanna with Ramoa, I thought about how there was nothing to stop someone like Fouge Tempro from taking away everything I'd worked so hard to collect. That happened to me, to the house my grandmother built. And it could happen again. To me. To anyone. I wasn't Fouge Tempro's first victim, you know. And I bet I'm also not his last. Someone like that will keep doing what he's done, until he's forced to stop."

"In my experience, justice is something easy to talk about and difficult to achieve," Hejira said.

"That doesn't mean we shouldn't try," objected Ramoa.

"Your sentiments, as always, are admirable," Hejira said. "Stax, what if you achieved justice, but not for yourself?"

"What do you mean?"

"Your house was assaulted by raiders," Hejira said. "Your possessions have undoubtedly been dispersed to the four winds. If you confront this Fouge Tempro, you may not find satisfaction for yourself."

"It would be worth it knowing he's been stopped," Stax said. "However far I have to go to make that happen."

Hejira nodded, his eyes narrowed.

"I know that look," Ramoa said. "What are you keeping to yourself?"

"Something I heard, about this Champion in whom Stax has placed such trust."

Stax scrambled to his feet. "What did you hear?"

"He dwells in a fortress in the Graypeaks, beyond the land known to traders as the Endless Dunes. Though it is far from endless; I have walked the entirety of it, and in both directions. From west to east it measures—"

"Heji," said Ramoa. "I don't think that's the important part."

"Ah. Perhaps not. Anyway, Stax, now that I know more about the path you intend to follow, I find it worthy. Should you wish to visit this man, I can point the way."

"You mean you'll come with me?" Stax asked.

Hejira looked surprised, and Stax realized that wasn't what the traveler had meant at all. But then he frowned and looked up at the stars, his mind clearly working.

"Go with him, Heji," Ramoa said. "I would if I hadn't promised."

"Very well," Hejira said. "If Stax wants me to."

"Oh, I most definitely do," Stax said.

On its eastern margins, the Rain-Jungles of Jagga-Tel thinned and gave way to grasslands and rolling hills, which soon grew patchy and sparse, until finally they became mounds of sand that marched away to the horizon.

Ramoa turned from staring across the dunes to regard Stax and Hejira, her face grim under her glossy black curls.

"I wish I were going with you," Ramoa said. "I feel like I'm making a mistake."

"You are keeping a promise," Hejira said quietly. "Like you always do."

"Well, maybe this time I shouldn't be."

Hejira said nothing, and the look that passed between him and Ramoa made Stax feel uncomfortable, like he was intruding.

"Hejira and I will be fine," he told Ramoa. "And you have a caravan to protect. Who knows, there might be some marooned unfortunate along its route, with nowhere to go and no idea how to shoot a bow. He's going to be glad you were there, just like I was."

And he patted the graceful curve of the bow Ramoa had shown him how to make, which was now slung over his shoulder.

"That's true, I guess," Ramoa said. She smiled and put her hand on Stax's shoulder for a moment, then sighed and looked off to the south. "Heji, I'll leave word at the caravanserai in Karamhés, or with Brubbs and Xinzi in Tumbles Harbor. Stax, I'm counting on you to look after Heji. Don't let him decide his code means he's only allowed to walk on his hands or something."

"You will be late," Hejira said. "Perhaps you should be going."

"Love you too," Ramoa said. She sighed again, hitched her shoulders, and began striding off to the south.

"We must go," Hejira said. "The Endless Dunes are perilous at night."

Stax reluctantly turned away from watching Ramoa and followed Hejira across the desert, having to hurry to keep up with the black-clad traveler's long, powerful strides. Hejira was silent as they crossed the sand, the grasslands behind them fading to a gray-green blur. Something was bothering him, Stax realized.

"You didn't want her to go either," Stax said, hoping he was right and Hejira was not, in fact, considering introducing some new element to his already punishing code.

"I did not want her to go," Hejira said. "But I knew she would. She broke a promise long ago, and she still carries the weight of what followed that decision. That is what drives her from place to place. Seeking peace, when she will only find it inside, once she forgives herself."

Stax said nothing for a few minutes, digesting this.

"What happened?" he asked finally, when it became clear that Hejira had said all he planned to say.

"That is Ramoa's story to tell or not tell," Hejira said. "Now come, Stax Stonecutter. Your own story lies ahead of us."

The Endless Dunes struck Stax as different from the barren shore where he'd been left by Fouge and his raiders. That had been a dreary place, but the dunes had a stark beauty. They also boasted a surprising amount of life, from the green cacti that rose from the sand like towers to the rabbits that scurried for cover when Stax and Hejira came too close for their liking.

While the sun was fierce during the day, the temperature plummeted as night approached. With the sun low in the sky, Hejira stopped Stax.

"I suggest you find a suitable place to camp for the night," he said. "I can neither utilize shelter myself nor help others create it. So you must build your own refuge. It is against—"

"Let me guess—your code," Stax said with a sigh.

He began to dig a tunnel into a clump of rock left uncovered by the dunes' endless reshuffling of sand. Hejira stood nearby, scanning the horizon.

"I have a question," Stax said. "If I started on my shelter too late, and something came to attack us before I got it built, would your code allow you to do anything about it?"

"I would test myself against the creatures of the night, as I always do. In doing so, I would be defending you. But I would not help you build. That would be interfering with your path."

Stax leaned on his shovel. "Yet you warned me I should make camp."

"You are an inexperienced traveler," Hejira said. "You could not be expected to know the hazards of this region. However, now you do."

"So tomorrow you won't warn me that it's time to camp?"

"I will not," Hejira said. "Because now you know."

"Your code is very complicated," Stax said. "The more I learn about it, the more questions I have."

"We should save those questions for tomorrow," Hejira said. "But yes, my code is a source of aggravation for Ramoa, and for other travelers who accompany me. Which I regret."

The warrior bowed, then turned to face the desert. Stax finished working on his shelter and slept snugged up inside, waking now and again to hear the clanging and grunting of combat outside.

In the morning, Hejira looked haggard, slumped over his sword with dark bags under his eyes.

"Did you sleep at all?" Stax asked, concerned.

"A little. The absence of trees makes crossing the desert difficult."

Stax hadn't thought of that and immediately felt guilty. "Tonight we'll take shifts. You sleep in the sand and I'll stand guard. Unless that's against your code, of course."

Hejira clasped his shoulder. "Your path is marked by kindness, Stax, and it does you credit. But I welcome this test. I have crossed the Endless Dunes many times, when I felt my code demanded it. If we make good time today, by sunset we should be in a more kindly country. And in another day, I believe, we should reach the abode of your Champion."

Stax felt his breath catch, barely able to believe that he was so close to meeting the man who could bring Fouge Tempro to justice. That thought sustained him during the day, and he almost kept up with Hejira for long stretches of the afternoon.

The sun was low in the sky when Stax spotted a cluster of dark orange buildings to the north and pointed them out to Hejira.

"That is the village of Patannos," he said. "They are a strange folk. Not bad people, but they prefer their own company to that of outsiders. Let us push on, Stax. In another hour we should reach the eastern edge of the dunes."

Hejira was correct, of course, and just before sunset he climbed up into the boughs of an oak tree as Stax finished hollowing out a shelter in the side of a hill bearded with fragrant grass. In the morning Hejira looked much refreshed, with only a single length of bone and a purple spider's eye for his night's efforts.

Stax found this new green country beautiful and welcoming, from its carpets of flowers to the sheep and cows cropping grass in the shadows of the trees. Other people apparently thought so too, as they began passing fences surrounding trim little farms, and walked through several small villages.

Around noon Hejira pointed to the north and said he could just see the shapes of the Graypeaks. Stax saw nothing, to his frustration, but an hour later they were visible to him too—only a gray blur in the distance, but definitely there. By evening they loomed over the meadows and forests, and the setting sun turned them a brilliant pinkish-orange.

"It has been a privilege to guide you here, Stax," Hejira said, as they sat by a fire and gnawed on mutton. "But the next step of this journey is yours to take, alone."

"You mean you're leaving too?" Stax asked, his chest suddenly tight with worry.

"No," Hejira said. "I will accompany you back to the savanna near Tumbles Harbor, if that is your wish, or to Karamhés or River House. Or elsewhere, if our paths intersect. But you must meet the Champion on your own. I sense this moment is key to your destiny. And by my code, I must not interfere."

"You see, this is the kind of thing I don't understand," Stax said. "You've helped me, and Ramoa, and many others. But how do you decide when to help and when to step aside, because you shouldn't interfere with someone's destiny?"

"This is a question I have asked myself as well, and I cannot promise that the answer I give you today is the same one I will give you tomorrow. You are discovering what you are, Stax Stonecutter, and what your place is in the world. I cannot walk that path with you."

"And if someone's found their path but strayed from it? You keep telling me I'm more of a warrior than I think, and you helped me learn how to use a sword. Isn't that walking with me?"

"It is your path," Hejira said. "Pointing the way back to it is not the same as walking it with you."

"But . . . you know what, never mind," Stax said, too tired to ponder the puzzles of Hejira's philosophy.

"Very well," Hejira said. "I saw a most excellent sleeping tree. We can continue this conversation in the morning."

But when morning came, Hejira had several trophies to show Stax, including a golden helmet, apparently very old, that had been on the head of a zombie who made the mistake of growling in his ear just before dawn.

Hejira was so cheerful about this gleaming headgear that Stax didn't have the heart to bring up his puzzling code again. He was also a little worried that Hejira might decide he'd already been interfering with Stax's destiny and depart.

Hejira showed Stax the road that led up away from the meadows to the top of the Graypeaks and the Champion's house. It was a stone road and well built, rising gently and switching back and forth across the face of the mountain.

Stax took a deep breath and started climbing.

As he neared the top of the mountain, Stax worried, once again, that he hadn't brought his chests of wealth with him. He'd debated going back to the savanna first, but decided it was too far away. If he went back, Hejira Tenboots would probably decide some aspect of his code dictated that he couldn't accompany him. And anyway, if the stories he'd heard were correct, the Champion routinely struck bargains with people who came seeking his aid. Surely some of those people arrived without chests of goods, negotiating and then returning with the Champion's price. He could find out what the Champion wanted in exchange for his help and return with whatever wealth that required. Or at least Stax hoped that would be the case.

Stax also wondered what he would find atop the mountain. An army in brilliantly polished armor, perhaps, or a dragon with hypnotic eyes and wings that glittered with every color in the spectrum?

Neither awaited him, however.

Instead, the stone road led to the edge of a green valley between two hills, cordoned off by a fence of iron. Stax could see animal pens beyond the fence, and rows of crops. In fact, the Champion's estate looked so much like his own home that he felt his breath catch and hitch in his chest.

The road was blocked by a gate of deep brown oak, nearly black. There was no sign, but looking more closely he saw a button by the gate.

So Stax pushed it.

"Hello?" he asked.

Nothing happened. Stax pushed the button several more

times, said hello even though he was pretty sure no one could hear him, and haltingly explained who he was and where he'd come from. There was no answer—no sound at all except the distant mooing of cattle—and after a few minutes Stax sat down with his back against the fence.

The breeze was cool on his face after the long climb up the mountain. Stax took the compass out of his pocket and looked down at it, wondering if his father's travels had ever brought him to the Rain-Jungles of Jagga-Tel, or the Endless Dunes, or the village of Patannos. He wished he'd thought to ask him, to have him explain what all those flags on the maps were, and tell Stax stories about the places he'd been and the people he'd met there.

In the distance, he heard the slow *clop-clop* of a horse's hooves. He scrambled to his feet and saw a horse and rider moving down the stone road that cut through the Champion's estate, making their unhurried way to the gate.

The horse was a handsome palomino, chestnut and cream. The man sitting astride it was tall and thin, with white hair and a steady gaze.

"It's an honor to meet you, Champion," Stax said, wondering belatedly if the proper address was actually something like *Mr. Champion* or *Sir Champion*. "My name is Stax Stonecutter, and I've come a long way to see you and tell you why I need your help."

CHAPTER 25

THE CHAMPION, REVEALED

The Champion at work * Lunch in luxurious
surroundings * A warrior's misgivings

"You address me improperly, sir," the white-haired man said gravely.

Stax wanted to kick himself. He knew he should have said *Mr. Champion.*

"I am not the Champion, Mr. Stonecutter," the man added. "I am his butler, and my name is Troyens."

"Oh. Um, hello, Mr. Troyens. It's good to meet you. So . . . is the Champion here?"

"I believe he's working in the back garden," Troyens said. "Is he expecting you?"

"No," Stax admitted. "I've never asked a champion for help before. I didn't know it involved appointments."

"I'll take you to him," Troyens said, and swung down from the horse to open the gate. He closed it behind Stax and climbed back on the horse. Stax walked beside him up the stone road, past the animal pens and the fields, a fish pond and a formal garden with a gazebo.

"What a lovely place," Stax said, thinking again of his home. He wondered suddenly if the Champion had any cats, but decided not to ask, as Troyens didn't seem like he entirely approved of Stax having simply shown up at the gate.

Troyens said nothing more and Stax walked along in silence, listening to the palomino's hooves clip-clopping on the stone.

The house was set on a rise at the back of the valley, looking west. It was made of gray stone—andesite, Stax thought—with accents of pink granite. Turrets rose from either end, with the sunlight reflecting off their windows. Troyens led Stax around to the back of the house, from which stairs descended to a carefully tended garden. There, he tied up the horse at a fence post.

"This way, sir," he said.

Stax followed him through an arbor of immaculately pruned rose bushes and past rows of tulips in a riot of colors. At the back of the garden, under a cluster of oaks, a man was standing in the middle of a lawn, facing away from them with his arms folded. He reached forward and snipped a stray tuft of grass with a pair of shears.

"Sir," Troyens said. "You have a caller. A Mr. Stonecutter to see you."

"Eh?" said the man, turning. He was two or three decades older than Stax, with chiseled features, piercing blue eyes, and long, powerful arms. He was wearing a luxurious-looking teal dressing gown.

"Mr. Champion, sir, it's an honor to meet you," Stax said. "I'm

Stax Stonecutter, and . . . well, I've made a long journey to explain why I need your help."

"Oh goodness me, don't call me that, Stax," the man said, nodding at Troyens, who bowed his head and glided away. "You can call me Abel."

"I see, um, Abel. Your estate is lovely."

"Thank you," said the Champion—who, Stax reminded himself, would rather be called Abel. "Been having some problems with the new garden plot, where the peonies are going to go. Dirt goes missing overnight. I suspect it's endermen, up to their usual mischief. Strange creatures. All the treasures of the Overworld, and they're fascinated by dirt?"

"Right," Stax said. "That happened to me back home too. In fact, my home is the reason I came to see you."

"Ah," said Abel, and wiped his brow. "Warm out here today. Let's discuss this in the dining room. I'll ask Troyens to prepare a light lunch."

"Um, okay," said Stax, who'd been about to start telling his story. "That sounds nice. Thank you, Cham . . . sir . . . Abel."

Abel led him up a flight of polished stone steps to a porch overlooking the gardens. Troyens, hearing his request, bowed his head and quietly withdrew.

"Polished andesite?" Stax asked, running a hand over the wall. "It's very fine work. My family used to cut and polish stone like this."

"Let me give you a tour," Abel said, and before Stax could object that it wasn't necessary, the Champion had ushered his guest into the house.

The Champion's living room was broad and airy, with walls of polished stone lit by lanterns set into the ceiling. Bright paintings adorned the walls above bookshelves crowned with flowerpots. A variety of fascinating objects had been mounted as trophies: a creeper head next to an iron helmet creased by a dent, a finely wrought bow beside a small golden idol, a compass set in a frame near a map of a coastline marked with a red X.

Abel looked around the room, as if seeing it through Stax's eyes.

"A lot of memories in here," he said, and for a moment he looked tired. But then some recollection made his eyes brighten. "That helmet belonged to Dark Ulric, before I ended his reign of terror. The idol was a gift from the people of Klatsorro Island after I drove off the Fispolu buccaneers. And that map shows the location of the Lost Horde of Ubnar, which I discovered after besieging that fortress."

Abel smiled, his mind clearly far away. Stax stopped before a stand displaying a full suit of diamond armor: helmet, chestplate, leggings, and boots. The armor seemed to glimmer and coruscate, a telltale sign that it was enchanted.

"Made for me by Philedon the Elder, the best enchanter of Tumbles Harbor," said Abel. "Nearly impenetrable. And enchanted against a host of perils, of course."

Unable to resist, Stax ran his finger over the helm as Abel said something about the Siege of Ubnar. He looked at his finger and saw it was coated with dust.

Abel opened a chest in the corner of the room. Over his shoulder, Stax saw the chest was heaped high with diamonds and lapis. Abel turned, holding a sword of diamond.

"This is Keen Justice," he said. "Do you know swords, Stax? Give it a try. You'll find it's perfectly balanced in the hand."

Abel reversed his grip on the sword and offered it hilt-first to

Stax. Dumbfounded, Stax took the weapon. The sword was not just balanced but also surprisingly light. Stax made an experimental slash through the air with it and the sword seemed to hum, all but radiating power and purpose.

Stax carefully handed Keen Justice back to its owner, who studied the sword for a moment, a faint smile on his face, and then returned it to the chest full of diamonds.

"Ah, here's Troyens," he said, looking past Stax. "Let us dine."

Abel led Stax into a dining room paneled with stripes of different woods. The floor was glass and below it Stax saw brightly colored fish swimming among spikes of purple, blue, and pink coral, lit by softly glowing blocks of stone.

"Have you seen the tropical reefs of the Great Eastern Sea?" Abel asked. "Re-creating them was a project of mine. A little indulgent, maybe, but I enjoy sitting here after dinner and watching the fish."

Two plates heaped with melon and cake sat on a long table, at opposite ends. Abel pulled out Stax's chair, then took his own seat. The melon was fresh, and Stax closed his eyes with pleasure at its taste, simultaneously tart and sweet. He eyed the cake with happy anticipation, then paused. He was sure it would be delicious, and it was a pleasure to eat fine food amid the comforts of a beautiful house. But that wasn't why he'd come all this way, was it?

"Thank you for seeing me, sir," he told Abel, who looked up from watching his fish, seeming almost startled. "I first heard about you in Tumbles Harbor—heard about you and all that you'd done for people who needed help. People like the farmers who bring you bread, and the kidnapped prince and princess."

Abel shook his head and muttered something.

"I'm sorry, sir?" Stax said. "I missed that."

"Brats, the both of them," Abel said. "The princess set my horse's tail on fire, and the prince spat out everything I offered him to eat."

"Oh," said Stax. "Still, they didn't deserve to be kidnapped. That must have been terrifying for them. You helped them, and the people of their kingdom. Just like I'm hoping you can help me."

Abel leaned back in his chair, which Stax took as permission to keep talking. And so he did, starting with Fouge Tempro stepping off his boat at the Stonecutter dock and ending with Stax's time in Tumbles Harbor.

"That's terrible," Abel said, and for a moment Stax saw indignation flare in his eyes. But then he settled back in his chair, fingers steepled on the table in front of him. "But these days, Stax, I'm more of a gentleman farmer than a warrior."

"I know a lot of people must come to see you, and a lot of them are more deserving than me," Stax said. "I've done a lot of mining, back at Tumbles Harbor. I have gems, and ore. Surely you could use wealth like that to help somebody."

Though as Stax said it, he looked around the room—at the sleek paneled wood, and down at the undersea world re-created beneath the glass floor—and thought that the Champion had spent several fortunes to construct this room alone. And how did eating lunch on top of a giant fish tank help anyone struggling elsewhere in the Overworld?

"Last time I left here, brigands ambushed me on horseback," Abel said. "I almost lost Keen Justice, and my armor was bashed and dented. Had to replace my helmet and shield, as they were too badly damaged for further use."

"And so you replaced them?" Stax asked.

"Well, of course I did."

"And the brigands?"

"I chased them off," Abel said.

"And because of that you've stopped helping people?" Stax asked. "I don't understand. The worst thing that's happened to you is your diamond armor was damaged, and so now you're going to stay home? When so many people need you? When there's so much injustice in the Overworld?"

"You're right. You don't understand," said Abel. "I can't rid the Overworld of ugliness. I've tried, and it hasn't made any difference that I can see. Here, at least, I'm creating a little beauty. You can see the wisdom of that, can't you?"

Stax shook his head. "I've seen a lot of the Overworld in the last couple of months. It's got plenty of beauty. Beaches and jungles, deserts and meadows. It's got so much beauty your heart wants to burst. It doesn't need more beauty, sir. It needs less injustice."

"But you can't get rid of injustice," Abel said with a sigh. "Just yesterday, a band of pillagers threatened the house. Came right up to the fence. I ran them off, but there will be more. Getting rid of injustice? That's like pouring water into a bucket with a hole in it."

"So fix the bucket," Stax said. "I thought that's what you were doing, with these quests of yours."

Abel looked at Stax like he didn't understand—or didn't *want* to understand. Stax felt anger begin to burn in his chest.

"What he did to me, Fouge Tempro will do to others," Stax said. "Innocent people. Maybe you don't think I'm worth fighting for, but surely some of the other people he'll hurt are. If you don't want to help me, think of stopping Fouge as helping them."

"I know people like this Foulge or Fourge or whatever you said his name was," Abel said with a sigh. "People who are vicious and cruel. Sometimes I wonder what made them this way. I've never found an answer."

Hope flickered in Stax. Was the Champion coming around, and remembering how he'd earned that lofty title?

"I don't think there *is* an answer, not with Fouge," Stax said. "For him, the cruelty is the point. I think he enjoys that as much as the valuables he steals. And that's why he has to be stopped."

"And if he *is* stopped?" Abel asked. "There will just be another one like him. That's what being a hero—or whatever they call me in all those little towns—has taught me. There's *always* another one. If I get rid of this Fouge, the Overworld won't thank me. It won't care. It will just demand to know what I'm going to do about the next Fouge. When do I get to say I've done enough? When do I get to enjoy the time I've earned?"

Stax felt the anger rising again. He tried to snuff it out, but it rose up again and he knew he wouldn't be able to.

"But the Overworld *does* thank you, and it *does* care," Stax said. "That's how I heard of you in the first place. And the Overworld *needs* you. You could walk out of here encased in diamond armor, swinging that sword of yours, and no one would dare face you in battle. You could help me, but you won't help anybody, because you've decided there's a limit to kindness. You won't risk any harm to your little playground, so you just sit here surrounded by beauty. Which doesn't do anybody any good but you."

Abel got up from the table and Stax thought he looked sad. He peered down at the fish below the glass floor for a moment, then walked slowly to the window overlooking his gardens. He stood there for a long time.

And then Abel spoke, so quietly Stax almost didn't hear him.

"I think you'd better go," said the man once known as the Champion.

"Yes," Stax said, getting to his feet. "I think I'd better."

CHAPTER 26

PERIL IN PATANNOS

Stax discovers his own code * A return to a not
particularly beloved house * Surprising news

It was after noon when Stax reached the bottom of the stone road
and the meadow where Hejira was sitting cross-legged at the foot
of his sleeping tree, examining the golden helmet he'd taken off a
zombie's head.

Hejira sat calmly, his face serene, as Stax told him of the
Champion and his decision.

"So what will you do now?" he asked.

"I don't know," Stax said, and slumped into the grass next to
Hejira. "Finding the Champion and convincing him to help was
my plan, and it's failed. *I've* failed."

"It is now apparent your path leads elsewhere," Hejira said.
"Perhaps it always did."

"What does that even mean?" asked Stax, his frustration boiling over. "If you see my path somewhere in this, this . . . *disaster*, could you please tell me, instead of tossing riddles in my general direction? Because I sure don't see my path. Or any path."

"That is against my—"

"Your stupid code," Stax said, and let out a bark of laughter. "Of course it is. You know what, Hejira? My path goes back to Tumbles Harbor. I hate the idea, but it's the only thing I can think of."

Hejira nodded and got to his feet. "We should go, then."

He tossed the golden helmet into the grass and began walking west.

"You're just leaving that?" Stax asked, scrambling to his feet and picking up the helmet.

Hejira turned. "It would just weigh me down. Like many people, I find gold beautiful. But it is also heavy."

And with that he kept walking. Stax studied the ancient helmet for a moment, then placed it gently on the ground and hurried after his companion. He wondered if the warrior would tell him to find his own way home, but Hejira just nodded at him, apparently having forgotten Stax's outburst.

As the meadows gave way to the sand of the Endless Dunes, Stax felt his churning emotions subside. Hejira said nothing, but simply walked along beside him, and Stax found his presence comforting. He didn't ask Stax for more details about the Champion's refusal to help, or pester Stax about his path, when Stax had no idea how to even think about picking up the pieces. He let Stax be, and for that he was grateful.

It was late afternoon when Hejira stopped, holding his hand up.

"What is it?" Stax asked, scanning the horizon. "Do you see something?"

"I hear something. We are near Patannos. Let us climb to the top of that dune and take a look."

Hejira gracefully ascended the dune, his bare feet finding solid zigzag pathways beneath the sand, while Stax struggled along in his wake. Before he reached the top, he could hear the sounds too: the tolling of a bell, the din of metal on metal, and yelling.

Hejira stood atop the dune, peering down at the orange cluster of buildings that was Patannos.

"Pillagers on a raid," he said. "An ill-tempered people, not to be reasoned with. They will loot Patannos and leave it empty and lifeless."

Stax could see the pillagers now, gray-skinned and dark-eyed, carrying banners and crossbows. The villagers were running in all directions, trying to organize a defense.

"What is your code telling you to do?" Stax asked. "Is this a destiny you'd interfere with?"

That came out with a little more bitterness than he'd intended, but Hejira took no offense.

"The villagers of Patannos lead simple lives," Hejira said. "They care for their animals and crops and try to make a better life for their children. The Overworld would be a better place if more people found that a worthy path to follow. But enough about my code, Stax Stonecutter. What is your code telling you to do?"

"My code? I don't have a code."

"Everyone has a code. The difference is most people never think about what it is."

Stax watched the pillagers advance, crossbows raised. He wondered if they were the same ones Abel had shooed away from the boundaries of his estate. He looked at the neat lines of crops and imagined them erased, the houses sitting silent and empty.

"Someone has to help them," Stax said. "And there's no one here but us."

"Very well then," Hejira said, and drew his sword. "I would suggest going in aggressively. We can catch the pillagers from behind, and use surprise to our advantage. It will be a tough fight. Are you ready, Stax?"

"I think so," Stax said, and Hejira looked over with an eyebrow raised. "Yes. Yes, I'm ready."

Hejira moved down the dune in a swift silence that Stax found both exhilarating and frightening. He hurried to keep up, wincing at the sand he kicked up and the noise it made. Hejira's long strides carried him to the edge of the buildings, and his sword flashed in the late-afternoon sun as he reached the rear ranks of the pillagers.

Stax heard them grunt in surprise and anger, struggling to turn in the narrow confines between a pair of houses. Then Stax had reached them too. He heard himself yell and an arrow zipped past his head, so close that the feathers on the shaft grazed his ear. He swung his sword, trying to remember Hejira's lessons about balance, and a pillager fell.

The villagers cheered at the unexpected arrival of allies, but soon fell back again, intimidated by the pillagers' ruthlessness and their weapons. Hejira had scattered the party of raiders they'd taken by surprise, and crossbows littered the ground around him.

"Stax! More are coming!"

Stax, breathing hard, followed Hejira's outstretched finger with his gaze and saw more of the raiders storming across the plains, marching beneath gray banners. An arrow struck Stax in the side, spinning him around. He clutched at the wound, wincing.

"Are you hurt?" Hejira asked.

"I'm okay," Stax said, wondering if that was really true. He drew his bow and lined up a shot, reminding himself to empty his lungs of air. The arrowhead kept wiggling in his vision and Stax stopped, forcing himself to breathe in and start over. It was a lot harder to keep still with arrows filling the air around him than it had been in the jungle, where the cocoa pods hadn't been shooting back.

He let an arrow fly and saw it hit home, knocking a pillager backward, but his next shot was high and went over their heads. Hejira smashed a pillager's crossbow aside with his sword, stepping into Stax's line of fire. Stax put his bow back over his shoulder and joined the fight, forcing himself to close the distance with his enemies so they couldn't shoot him from a distance. He didn't know what the pillagers were shouting at him, in their deep, gravelly language, but their breath was foul.

Hejira and Stax dispatched the pillagers, leaving their banners strewn on the ground, but Stax heard growls and a tramp of feet—yet more reinforcements. Stax charged at them, his breath loud in his ears. He was soon too tired to keep track of how many pillagers they'd fought, or how long they'd been battling. His arms and legs were heavy and his side hurt, but he couldn't worry about that, or let his emotions get the better of him. There was only his balance, and watching the pillagers' eyes and limbs for clues about what they would do next, and staying alive.

Until he whirled around and found no one aiming a crossbow at him, just the wreckage of battle. The sun had set and the first stars were out, with the moon peeking above the horizon. Was it over? No, Hejira was nearby, pressed by three pillagers.

"Heji! I'm coming!"

As he hurried to Hejira's position, the black-clad warrior risked a look over his shoulder and stiffened in alarm.

"A creeper, Stax Stonecutter. Look there, by the village smithy. I can handle these three. You must deal with the creeper."

Stax saw the creeper now, a green pillar of black-spotted flesh, scuttling forward on its multiple legs. He brandished his sword, trying to read the monster's unfamiliar body language.

"No, Stax," said Hejira, his voice strained with effort. "You must shoot it. Before it gets too close."

"Right!" Stax fumbled with his bow. He'd always thought of creepers as slow, but this one was moving far too quickly for his liking. He nocked an arrow and sighted down its length, but his arms were tired and the point of the arrow made crazy circles in the air.

He fired and the shot went wide. The creeper didn't even react. Stax hurriedly drew another arrow and forced himself to breathe out.

The arrow struck the creeper low on its body, knocking it backward and making it shudder. But after a moment's hesitation it kept coming, its alien gaze fixed on Stax and Hejira.

"Stax, keep firing," Hejira suggested.

Another arrow. Stax tried to calm his nerves, to breathe out, but he was so tired. The arrow went wide. So did the next one. He could hear the creeper's feet scrunching through the sand.

Breathe out. Breathe out breathe out breathe out.

Another arrow struck the creeper, but it kept coming. Stax fired wide, then high. He reached for an arrow and froze. He had only one left.

He drew back the bowstring, trying to keep his heart from

hammering. He emptied his lungs, but the arrowhead wouldn't hold still in his vision.

The creeper hissed. Stax closed his eyes and opened his fingers.

There was a clatter of metal behind him and a grunt that turned into a gasp.

"An excellent shot, Stax Stonecutter," said Hejira. "Ramoa would praise you as a fine student."

Stax opened his eyes. There was no sign of the creeper except a little mound of gray powder. Hejira had his hands on his knees and was breathing hard.

Behind him, the villagers of Patannos peeked out through doors and around the corners of their houses. After exchanging glances of disbelief, they hurried forward, surrounding Hejira and Stax. Stax was buffeted by claps on the back and spun around in hugs. Villagers pressed gifts into their hands—pies, and blue nuggets of lapis, and a single brilliant red poppy, offered shyly by a child.

"They are asking us to stay for dinner, it seems," Hejira said as a villager ushered him toward a house with a delicious smell wafting out from its window. "Are you hungry, Stax?"

Stax's side hurt and he could barely lift his arms. But the smell of pumpkin pie made his mouth water.

"I could eat," he said with a smile, tucking the poppy behind his ear.

The feast lasted until late in the night. When Stax finally convinced the villagers that he couldn't possibly eat another pork chop or slice of pie, they showed him to an empty house where he could sleep. If Hejira battled any monsters that night, Stax slept through the noise.

In the morning they said farewell to Patannos and headed across the dunes. After half a day's walk, Stax found the emotions of last night ebbing, replaced with anxiety. He was returning to the little sod cabin outside Tumbles Harbor, and he had no idea what to do once he got there. The Champion had failed him, and he didn't know how to find Fouge, let alone defeat him if he did.

Hejira was silent, but Stax sensed that this was a different silence than yesterday's. Rather than let Stax be alone with his own thoughts, Hejira kept glancing over at his fellow traveler, as if he expected him to start talking and was disappointed that he hadn't.

Finally, Stax couldn't take it anymore.

"What is it, Heji? I can feel you over there, wanting to tell me something."

"Me?" Hejira asked. "I am simply walking across the Endless Dunes, and thinking about whether we should skirt the Rain-Jungles of Jagga-Tel or go through them."

"Sure you are. I'll make this easier: I have no idea where my destiny lies right now. So if you see a path for me, and think I've strayed from it, by all means please give me a little nudge. Even if your code says you shouldn't."

"You fought well in Patannos, Stax," said Hejira. "Well and wisely. It can be difficult for someone who has not been in many battles to realize that. I hope that you do."

"Thanks," said Stax. "But I don't think that's what you've been waiting all these hours to tell me."

Hejira said nothing for several minutes, but Stax could tell that he was thinking—or wrestling with the knotty demands of his code. But then he turned and smiled at Stax.

"You have spent a great deal of time and effort, and were prepared to spend a great deal of money, to find a champion. But you did not need one at Patannos. You were that champion. And you do not need one to bring Fouge Tempro to justice. Your path is to be your own champion. And you are farther along that path than you realize."

"Oh, how I wish that were true," Stax said. "But that's kind of you to say. Thank you, Heji."

"You are welcome, Stax Stonecutter," said Hejira and they continued their journey in silence, because now it was Stax who had something to think about.

Hejira suggested they go around the borders of Jagga-Tel, to make their journey shorter. The days passed pleasantly enough, with Hejira not pressing Stax about what he would do next and Stax asking him about adventures from his past. When night drew close, Stax would carve a shelter out of a cliff or hill, while Hejira found a tree—or, sometimes, spent the night roaming around testing himself against the perils of the darkness.

After several days, they found themselves once again amid the acacia trees and grasslands of the savanna where Stax had set up his homestead. Stax thought he recognized the shape of the hills to the west, in the direction of Tumbles Harbor.

He was correct; from the top of a hill he saw a familiar pattern of trees, and even the little square of his sod house. There was home, or at least the closest thing Stax had to one now. Except the sight of it made his heart sink.

Stax peered at the little square below them. Perhaps something else was there too?

Hejira had seen it too.

"That is a horse," he said. "And I believe that is Ramoa."

"It can't be her," Stax reminded his friend. "She doesn't like horses."

"No, she does not. Nonetheless, that is Ramoa. I am curious as to what this means."

They hurried down the hillside and across the grassy plains, with Stax falling behind Hejira's long strides. Ramoa ran to meet them, hugging Hejira and then all but jumping into Stax's arms.

"Aren't you supposed to be in Karamhés, guarding a caravan?" Stax asked, once they'd disentangled themselves.

"I was," Ramoa said. "But then I heard something that you're going to want to know, Stax. I think I found Fouge Tempro!"

CHAPTER 27

ENCOUNTER IN KARAMHÉS

A project for Osk * Surveying a caravan town *
Directions are offered and promises are made

Stax looked at Ramoa in astonishment.

"You *what*? Did you see him?"

"No," Ramoa said. "Not him. But I . . . look, it's simpler if I just tell you the story from the beginning. I was at the caravanserai, and the innkeeper there said that a couple of months ago, the place was overrun with bandits who'd come back from looting and stealing on the seas to the west. She said they'd thrown around money and gems, going on a real spree. Most of them had moved on, but their leader was still around. She said he was a big bruiser with a black beard, named Miggs, and he was waiting for new orders from his boss. Miggs, that was the name of the raider you told me was Fouge's right-hand man, right, Stax? Please tell me I didn't come all this way—and on a horse, no less—for nothing."

Stax felt slightly dizzy, like he couldn't get enough air. Miggs was Fouge's lieutenant, and supposedly he was waiting for word from the man who'd destroyed Stax's life. And Ramoa could bring Stax to him.

"Miggs was his name," he managed. "Thank you, Ramoa. I . . . I can't believe it."

He needed a minute to process what he'd heard, and what was now possible.

"I've never been to Karamhés," Stax said. "Where is it?"

"About two days' ride to the southeast," Ramoa said, and Stax's hand closed over the compass in his pocket. "Probably five days' walk, if you're Heji. Six or seven for mere mortals like you and me."

"And is there any kind of law there?"

Ramoa pursed her lips, thinking. "Merchants' associations, things like that. But no, nothing that could handle a situation like this."

Stax nodded, leaning on the fence of his little homestead. Thoughts chased themselves through his head. The Champion, and the hope Stax had invested in him for nothing. The chests of gems and ore he'd buried in the yard. Fighting in Patannos at Hejira's side. Huddling miserably in the bottom of a boat with Miggs. Fouge Tempro laughing as the Stonecutter estate burned.

"If I go to Karamhés to track down Miggs and confront him, will you come with me?" he asked Ramoa.

"I'd go even if you told me not to."

"Hejira? Will you come?"

"Yes. This is a worthy path, and I wish to see you travel it. But I must ask: Do you intend to kill this Fouge Tempro, when you find him?"

"He certainly deserves it," Ramoa said.

"That is not your path, and I did not ask your opinion," Hejira said.

"I'll offer whatever opinion I want, Heji, whether you ask me or not. That's always been my path, as you know perfectly well."

While his friends argued, Stax imagined Fouge Tempro before him, helpless and at his mercy, and felt the familiar flare of anger. But then it dissipated, and Stax just felt sick.

"I'd rather not kill anyone," Stax said. "But I don't see how to stop Fouge without doing that—and I *am* going to stop him. That's a promise."

Ramoa nodded, but then frowned.

"Heji won't ride a horse, though," she said. "So we'll get there long before he does."

"You are mistaken," Hejira said. "My code allows me to ride horses."

"It does?" Ramoa looked surprised. "But I thought—"

"Why would riding horses be forbidden? A horse is not a shelter, unless you desire a shelter that will pee on you and kick you during the night. I do not ride horses when we travel together because you do not like them, and I do not wish to offend you."

"Huh, I never knew that," Ramoa said, looking embarrassed. She turned to Stax. "So, since that's unexpectedly not a problem, we can buy horses from Brubbs and Xinzi. What else do you need to do before we go?"

"Dig up some chests," Stax said. "And go see someone I know in Tumbles Harbor who likes to make things. She's the best enchanter in town. Or the third best, anyway."

———

It was dusk, with the sky gloomy and threatening rain when they arrived at Osk's house on the edge of Tumbles Harbor. The cube at the gate was glowing, which made Stax smile. While Hejira and Ramoa tied up their horses and a donkey carrying the chests of gems and ore, Stax thumbed the doorbell, remembering at the last moment to step back to avoid getting walloped by the iron door as it opened.

"Coming, coming!" yelled Osk from somewhere in the depths of her little house.

The red-haired artificer arrived out of breath, wiping smears of redstone dust on her leather apron.

"Well, hullo, Stax," said Osk. "Did you see I rewired the streetlamp to come on automatically at dusk? Thanks for that idea!"

"You're welcome," Stax said. "Let me introduce you to my friends. This is Hejira Tenboots and Ramoa Peranze. Heji and Ramoa, this is Osk Fikar."

"Hi," said Osk. "Are you new miners? I stopped working for Mrs. Taney, Stax, did you hear that? But I'm always looking for redstone, if you run across any. I'm telling you, it's the material of the future."

"Osk, can we talk?" Stax asked. "I have a project for you."

"Sure!" said Osk. "I like projects! Speaking of projects, Stax, you have to see the design I've been working on for an ore smelter."

"Maybe some other time, Osk. We're kind of in a hurry."

"Well, that's a nuisance," said Osk. "What kind of project did you have in mind?"

"I need you to make me some armor," Stax said. "And a sword. Here, come outside—it's simpler if I show you something."

Osk scowled and scrubbed a hand through her red hair. "Armor and a sword? You could get a smith for that. Xinzi could do it."

"I'll pay you, of course," Stax said, patting the donkey, who was standing stoically beneath the weight of the chests strapped to his flanks.

"It's not that, Stax," Osk said. "I mean, I'd like to help you, but making armor is kind of boring, unless—"

Stax opened one of the chests and Osk gaped at the piles of diamonds and lapis.

"Oh," she said quietly. "Oh wow."

"I need diamond armor," said Stax. "And a sword. Enchanted so it can take a lot of punishment, and deal it out too."

It began to rain. Osk took no notice, seemingly hypnotized by the wealth in front of her. Hejira glanced at the sky and retreated across the street to stand beneath the eaves of a house.

"That chest over there is full of redstone," Stax said. "It's yours. Can you do this for me?"

"An entire chest of redstone?" Osk asked, looking astonished. "Yeah, I think we can work that out. Let's get this stuff inside and get to it."

While Osk and Stax relieved the donkey of its burden, Ramoa cocked her head at Hejira, who was leaning against the wall across the street where it was dry.

"What?" Hejira asked.

"How does that not count as shelter?" she demanded.

Osk worked through the night, fusing the diamonds into plates of armor and discussing enchantments with Stax. Ramoa studied the plans strewn across her table for a couple of hours, then excused herself to find a hot meal and a bed.

"So are you going after that Fouge character, the one you were telling me about?" asked Osk, while Stax tried to make sense of one of the inventor's schematics.

"Yes," Stax said. "Ramoa thinks she's discovered where his lieutenant is. Hopefully that leads me to him."

Osk nodded. "Bet you can't wait to see his face when you show up with an enchanted diamond sword."

Osk looked up from her work and frowned when she saw Stax's face.

"What is it, Stax? Did I do something wrong?"

"No," Stax said. "It's just . . . I'm not a warrior, Osk. You know that. I never wanted to be a warrior."

"So why don't you ask that scary-looking guy who came with you to do the job? He looked like he could take on a whole army himself."

"Heji? I did, believe me," Stax said. "He's got his code, and that means he can't . . . oh, let's just say it's complicated. So I put my hope in someone else, but then that didn't work either. It's my path, as Heji would say. I just hope I can find my way along it."

"So maybe you're not on the right path," Osk said. "I mean, my mom was a sailor and wanted me to be one too. I did my best to please her, and never mind that I always got sick the moment we left shore. Took me a long time to figure out that was never going to work."

"Maybe I'm not on the right path," Stax said. "But someone has to stop Fouge. And it looks like it's me."

"Well then, we better make sure this armor does its job," Osk said, returning to her work.

Stax nodded and returned to examining the inventor's sketches. He looked up after a moment, not wanting to interrupt Osk, but overcome by curiosity.

"What's this one, Osk?"

Osk peered over at the schematic Stax was holding up.

"Oh, that? I was thinking of a way to produce obsidian blocks without needing to have miners work up close with lava. But I'm afraid it's not very practical."

Osk paused, and then her face brightened. "Or at least it isn't yet. But there's a good idea there, Stax. See, you start with a water source here, and . . ."

Stax smiled as Osk talked excitedly about water and lava and pistons at the same time her hands were shaping the diamond into armor. He didn't know if Osk was right that redstone would change everything, but he did wish more people were free to invent things that they thought could.

And if there were fewer people like Fouge Tempro, perhaps one day they'd be proved right.

Shortly after dawn, both armor and sword were finished. Yawning, Stax stood with his arms outstretched, feeling slightly foolish as Ramoa and Osk closed fasteners and cinched up straps.

They stepped away and Stax flexed his arms, then carved a figure eight through the air with his sword. The weapon was a blur of sorcerous purple, and seemed to sing in Stax's hand.

"Wow," said Ramoa. "You look . . . different, Stax."

Mildly embarrassed, Stax took off the helmet, marveling at how light it was.

"We both know that you're twice the fighter I could ever be," he said. "Diamond armor doesn't make you a warrior."

"That's true," said Ramoa. "But it sure doesn't hurt. Let's get moving."

"Can I come?" asked Osk. "I've never placed so many enchantments on armor before. I want to see if they all work."

"They'd *better* work," Ramoa warned her.

"Oh, I'm sure they will," Osk said hastily. "But after all this, I kind of want to know how the story turns out. And . . . all right, I'll admit it. If this Fouge Tempro has done all the looting and pillaging you say he has, he's probably got a big stockpile of interesting things wherever he's holed up. Interesting things that could never be returned to their rightful owners, and would just go to waste if left to rot there."

Stax exchanged a glance with Ramoa, who shrugged.

"We're going to ride fast and hard," she told Osk. "Can you ride a horse?"

"Not in battle or anything like that, but I can put my arms around a horse's neck and hold on."

Stax considered the little artificer and her workshop overflowing with plans for machines she thought could change the Overworld. The plans he'd been thinking about all night, while Osk measured and tinkered and hammered.

"You can come, Osk," he said. "I might even have another project for you. So bring your redstone, please."

"How much?"

"All of it."

Karamhés was a sprawling town at the intersection of a river running east-west and a caravan route running north-south. Its buildings were constructed from terra-cotta and crowned with graceful minarets. Banners flapped in a stiff wind that blew from the north, sending little funnels of dust across the marketplace.

Stax, Ramoa, Hejira, and Osk arrived after nearly two days of riding dawn to dusk, saddle sore and caked in dust.

"I will never be able to walk again," Osk protested after the hostler led their horses away to be stabled. She groaned as she leaned against a wall and tried to convince her knees to bend again. "What a nuisance."

"You'll be fine after a good meal and a bath," Ramoa said, sniffing unhappily at her clothing. "Which we could all use."

"I too am relieved to have my feet on the ground once again," Hejira said serenely, stretching leisurely.

But Stax was staring at the door to the caravanserai. The idea that Miggs might be on the other side of it seemed impossible. And yet it was true; for all Stax knew, Miggs could be sitting just a few blocks away, unaware that his past was about to catch up with him.

Stax's hand flexed, as if around the hilt of a sword. His diamond gear was stowed, to avoid attracting attention, but retrieving it would take only a few minutes.

Ramoa saw the gesture and immediately knew what he was thinking.

"I'll find out if he's here," she said. "Wait here for me."

Ramoa slipped through the front door and Stax waited nervously, imagining all the things that might go wrong. But a few minutes later, Ramoa reappeared to say that while Miggs wasn't there, he'd been around the night before, and the innkeeper expected him back again come evening.

That gave them time to bathe and rest in the caravanserai's rooms, though Hejira contented himself with a dip in the horse trough, with Stax tipping a very confused stable boy so he wouldn't ask questions.

Hejira also took his evening meal outside, telling a nervous Stax that if Miggs fled, he'd be in position to intercept him. That left Osk, Ramoa, and Stax, who took a corner table with a view of the inn's common room. Ramoa and Osk flanked Stax, who sat in the recesses of a booth, his diamond armor covered by a dark travel cloak.

The inn's food was good—perfectly prepared mutton and a beetroot soup—but Stax could hardly taste it and chewed mechanically, his eyes fixed on the door. Osk was chattering away about some invention that would revolutionize something, while Ramoa quizzed her about the details with what sounded like genuine interest, but Stax barely heard them. Every time the door opened, Stax's brain tried frantically to make the new arrival into Miggs, never mind if the person was much shorter, had different-colored hair (or no hair at all), or was another gender entirely.

When the actual Miggs walked inside, however, Stax recognized him instantly, remembering the thick black beard, broad shoulders, and muscled arms. And, just in case Stax had had any doubts, he was wearing Stax's shirt—the yellow one with the red dragons.

"Is that . . ." Ramoa began, and Stax nodded.

"Where?" demanded Osk, getting to her feet with a scrape of her chair across the floor that Stax was pretty sure could be heard in Tumbles Harbor. He grabbed the artificer's arm and hauled her back into her seat.

Miggs glanced around, his eyes passing over Stax's booth with no apparent recognition, and took a table by himself in the middle of the room.

Stax got to his feet, annoyed that his hands were trembling faintly.

Breathe out, he told himself. *Like you're firing a bow.*

"I don't believe it," Ramoa said, and Stax felt a surge of annoyance. Had she thought he'd just sit there while Miggs had a leisurely dinner and left?

"Heji's broken his code," she added, and Stax saw that Hejira had entered the inn and was standing near the door. He caught Stax's eye and nodded once.

"I'll be right behind you," Ramoa told Stax, standing up. Osk scrambled to her feet as well.

Stax felt like he was floating as he crossed the room to stand at Miggs's table.

"Hello, Miggs," he said, and drew his cloak back so the raider could see his armor and his hand on his hip, next to his diamond sword. "It's been a long time."

Miggs's eyes went to the sword first, and then up the glittering armor to Stax's face. Stax smiled as he saw the moment when the raider remembered.

"Yer that kid," he said. "From across the water, way to the west."

"I'm that kid," Stax said. "I bet you thought you'd never see me again."

"I didn't." It annoyed Stax that Miggs was calm, while his own knees kept knocking. "Yer the fancy boy, the one with the weird name. No, two weird names. Stax, that's it. Stax Stonecutter. Hmm. May as well have a seat. And yer friends too."

And Miggs pulled out the chair next to him with one foot.

Not quite believing it, Stax sat. After a moment, Ramoa and Osk did the same. Hejira came and stood at the table, looking down at them.

"So what do yeh want, Stax Stonecutter?" Miggs asked. "Revenge? I'm guessin' that's it, what with three friends for backup and that pig-sticker on yer belt. Well, if that's what yeh want, here I am."

"I want information, for starters. Where's Fouge Tempro?"

Miggs made a sound that was something between a laugh and a snort of disgust.

"Yeh want my advice, kid? Yer lucky to be alive, and—"

"I don't want your advice," Stax said. "Let's try this again. Where's Fouge Tempro?"

Miggs studied Stax's face and nodded. Was that respect Stax saw in the raider's eyes?

"Yer not the same kid yeh were then, though, back when yeh were huddled in the bottom of a boat retchin' and spittin'," Miggs said. "Yeh've changed."

"Yeah, a lot's happened to me. Where's Fouge?"

Miggs sighed. "East of here, upriver. In a fort atop a mountain."

"Which mountain?"

"Yeh'll know it when yeh see it."

Ramoa shook her head, glaring at Miggs. "At least make up a good story," she said.

"It's true," Miggs said. "It's unmistakable. Can't miss it."

Stax fished the compass out of his pocket and found it pointing due east.

"And the rest of your gang?" he asked Miggs.

"They don't matter. Brigands, sellswords, pirates. Who knows where that lot goes when a job's done."

"I'm lucky I found you, then," Stax said.

"I suppose yeh are. So now what happens? Here I am. Yeh gonna draw that sword, Stax?"

Stax considered it. On the one hand, he was sure Miggs had committed any number of other crimes. But on the other, he had been the only one of Fouge's crew to treat Stax with a bit of kindness, however grudgingly offered. And that suggested there was something in the man that might be worth preserving.

Stax looked at Ramoa, and Osk, and then up at Hejira.

"What do you think, Hejira?" he asked. "Oh, come on. You're inside an inn, and that's definitely a shelter. I'll leave it up to you."

Hejira's eyes narrowed and he studied Miggs for a moment.

"Let him go," he said. "But only so he can find a different path, one that does not hurt others. I travel many lands, Miggs, and I have eyes and ears wherever I go. If you leave your new path, I will know. And I will find you."

Miggs looked from Hejira to Stax, his eyes dark with anger. "And if I don't want no part of this new path of yers?"

"Think about why we're here," Ramoa said. "Is this really the life you want to keep leading?"

Miggs glared at her, and Stax's hand crept to the hilt of his sword. But then the bearded raider seemed to sag. Slowly, almost unwillingly, he nodded.

"There's one more thing," Stax said. "That shirt belongs to me."

Now Miggs really was angry. But then he started to unbutton the shirt, his fingers trembling slightly. As people at other tables looked on in disbelief, he stripped the shirt off, balled it up and set it in the middle of the table. Then he got to his feet and strode bare-chested out of the inn.

"I will be outside," Hejira said calmly, once Miggs was gone. "I may suspend my vow only when I absolutely must, and then only for the briefest periods."

"That was kind of intense," said a pale Osk, as the door closed behind Hejira.

Stax had to agree. In fact, he felt like throwing up. But Ramoa smiled at him.

"And now we find Fouge?" she asked.

"And now we find Fouge."

"Good. I only have one question: Why did you want this shirt back? In fact, why did you own it in the first place? It's *awful*."

CHAPTER 28

THE MOUNTAIN

A country of legends * Into the caverns *
An ignoble retreat and a noble end

The next morning, Stax, Hejira, Ramoa, and Osk mounted their horses, put a lead on the donkey, and headed east out of Karamhés, riding along the south bank of the river. The caravan town gave way to farms, and within an hour they found themselves riding through a green, pleasant country, the hills dotted with gray and black sheep.

But something felt off, and finally Stax realized what it was.

"There are no people," he said. "We're not far from a big town, the river's navigable by boat, and this land is ideal for farming and raising livestock. But it's empty. There aren't even other travelers."

"Why would that be?" asked Osk, who was clinging unhappily to the neck of her horse.

"I do not know this country," said Hejira. "But I have heard tales of it. Supposedly the Omphalos lies east of Karamhés."

"The Omphalos?" asked Stax. "What's that?"

"The World-Navel," Hejira said. "The place where life began."

"Right," said Ramoa. "The Overworld's origin point. Remember, Stax? That's why your compass points this way. But I've never been east of Karamhés either. These lands are new to me. Maybe it's taboo to travel here."

"We could ask him," suggested Osk.

Startled, Stax looked ahead and saw a lone trader on the riverbank, clad in colorful garments, leading a pair of shaggy llamas.

The trader saw them too, and drew back in alarm.

"We mean you no harm," Stax called out, slowing his horse and raising his hands to show they were empty.

The trader stood warily as they approached, and the llamas grunted in fright. When they were close enough, he began talking rapidly in his deep, rolling language, and pointing ahead of them to the east.

"What is he saying, Heji?" Ramoa asked.

"I do not speak his tongue," Hejira replied. "But I can guess. He has no trade goods, and is very agitated. I suspect he has been robbed, and that the robbers dwell to the east."

Stax nodded. "Something tells me we're going in the right direction."

"I believe Stax is correct," said Hejira. "We are traveling his path. And we are close to its end."

"I'm going to take that as a good sign," Stax said, but Hejira said nothing. The trader stared at them for a moment, shook his head, and pulled his llamas away from the crowd of adventurers.

As they rode along, they began to see ruins—first the stubs of walls, then the stumps of towers, until they were surrounded by the rubble and rack of tumbled structures.

"This wasn't just some town, but a major city," Ramoa said. "And it's old. Older than anything I've ever seen. Have you ever seen anything like this, Heji?"

"I have not," Hejira said. "I suspect it is connected to the Omphalos."

While Ramoa and Hejira exchanged theories, Stax tugged on his horse's reins and dropped back to ride alongside Osk, who was clinging unhappily to her mount.

"So what do you think of the project I suggested?" Stax asked. "Would it work?"

"Yes, I think so," Osk said. "As long as I have all the materials I need. But are you sure this is what you want to do, Stax?"

"No," Stax said. "I'm not sure about anything. Except that I'm not a warrior, no matter what Heji and Ramoa think."

"You may have to be," Osk warned him.

"I know," Stax said. "And maybe that's the right path. But maybe not. In which case, I'm going to need your help following one that's a little different."

Farther to the east, the river thinned until it was little more than a stream, then vanished into the side of a hill—the first in a line of hills that gradually rose ahead of Stax's party. The hills were green, but broken by patches of sand and more ancient walls, which zigzagged back and forth across the landscape.

The horses picked their way up and down the hillsides, but they were growing increasingly nervous. Osk's horse kept rearing and trying to unseat the little artificer, and Stax's kept trying to go sidewise, ears pressed back against its head.

Hejira, of course, was the one who saw the mountain first.

Soon they could all see it: a spike of stone rising from the tumbled hills. One side was strangely bright, and there was a cloud of white at the base of the mountain below it.

"Is that the mountain?" asked Osk.

"I'm pretty sure it is," Stax said.

The brightness they'd seen turned out to be lava, a torrent of it splashing down one side of the mountain and into a small lake, which appeared and disappeared behind veils of steam. And atop the mountain was a fortress of dark stone. To Stax's eyes it looked like a malevolent ruler, brooding over the surrounding lands far below it.

"I suggest we stop here and take stock of our surroundings," said Hejira. "It would not be wise to proceed without learning as much as we can."

"Agreed," said Ramoa. "We can tie up the horses here. Then we split up and circle the mountain. Heji, you take Osk with you and I'll take Stax. We can meet on the other side."

Ramoa kept low and Stax did the same. The sides of the mountain were steep and sheer, mostly dirt and andesite, speckled with outcroppings of diorite and granite.

"That would be a dangerous climb," said Stax, and Ramoa nodded.

"Fouge must get up some other way," she said. "Unless he can fly."

"We could get up there by building ladders."

"If you cut down a forest, maybe," Ramoa countered.

The lake was deep and dark, hissing and boiling around the brilliant orange lava. Stax kept a wary eye on the top of the mountain, alert for signs of archers or other guards, but saw only rock.

"I wonder if Heji's seen anything," Ramoa said.

"I was wondering what he and Osk could be talking about," Stax said.

"What do you mean?"

"Well, Osk sees the world in terms of machines she can build to improve it. But Heji leaves the world basically untouched. He never goes inside. I don't think he'd even grasp the idea of what a machine is, and they're definitely forbidden by his code. So that has to be a very strange conversation."

Ramoa grinned. "Maybe Osk has convinced Heji he's all wrong about this code thing. We'll find Heji wearing some kind of armor made out of pistons, swinging a redstone supersword."

"Or maybe Heji convinced Osk," Stax suggested. "We'll find her barefoot, wearing animal skins, and yelling that redstone is a perversion of the natural order."

Neither turned out to be the case. Ramoa and Hejira spotted each other at a distance, on the eastern side of the mountain. They also spotted a worn track leading through tumbled walls to the mountain's base, where a cavern lit by torches gaped like the maw of some hungry creature.

"At least we found the way in," Osk said.

"Do you see any guards?" Stax asked Hejira.

"No," the traveler said, after scanning the area carefully. "Which concerns me. A fortress like the one above us is unlikely to be unguarded."

"So what do you think we should do?" Stax asked.

Hejira considered the question carefully. "I propose that I take the lead, with Ramoa to my left and you to my right. Osk is not an experienced fighter and should stick close to us."

"I agree with that one hundred percent," Osk said hastily. Stax thought about pointing out that he wasn't exactly an experienced fighter either, but decided not to. The other three knew that already, and calling attention to it would help nothing.

"We will have to fight, perhaps against heavy odds," Hejira said. "But this Fouge Tempro does not have an army. From what Miggs said, they are more of a rabble. And a rabble can be its own worst enemy. If tested by determined foes, they may prove ill-prepared, or not particularly loyal to their leader. Confront them, and they may surrender. Press them in battle, and they may break and scatter, instead of fighting to the death. Or perhaps they will prove worthy opponents. The only way to find out is to fight. Understood?"

"All right," Stax said, removing his cloak, his diamond armor shining in the light. "This quest is my burden, so as long as there's talking to be done, I'll do it. We give Fouge's raiders a chance to abandon him. And then, if we have to, we fight."

The cavern leading into the mountain was hacked out of the rock, with torches at irregular intervals on the walls, and stairs leading up at the far end. At first Stax thought it was empty—he *hoped* it was empty—but then he spotted windows set into one wall, and a door. It opened and four ill-dressed men stumbled out, swords held naked in their hands. At first glance, Stax didn't recognize any of them from the long voyage across the ocean.

"You there, stop," said the leader, a wiry, tattooed bald man. "This here's private property. What's your business?"

"I demand to speak with Fouge Tempro," Stax said, in a voice he hoped was firm. "He robbed me, destroyed my home, and left me to die. Now he must answer for what he's done."

The thugs looked at one another.

"Boss is busy," said the tattooed man. "No one interrupts his studies, not until he says so. Get lost, or we'll put you to the sword."

"Your boss must answer for what he's done, but I have no quarrel with you. Go, and we will settle our business with Fouge ourselves."

The raiders looked at one another in mingled amusement and disbelief.

"I got a better idea, fancy boy," said one. "We give all four of you what you deserve, and me and the boys take that diamond armor and sword as trophies."

One of the raiders fell back, clutching at his chest—one of Ramoa's arrows had found its mark. Hejira was already in motion, his sword flashing. The tattooed bandit leapt at Stax, screaming, with his sword raised above his head.

Stax, caught off-balance, parried desperately, but his opponent shoved him aside and smashed his sword into Stax's unprotected back. Stax felt the blow, but his armor took the brunt of it.

"Stax! Balance!" he heard Hejira yell.

He turned to find the tattooed raider standing in front of him, surprised that Stax was still on his feet. Stax brought his diamond sword around in an arc, sending him stumbling away, hurrying after the raider Ramoa had hit with an arrow. As Hejira advanced, face a mask of grim determination, the others fled in a panic.

Osk appeared frozen with shock.

"Are you all right?" she managed to ask Stax.

"Fine," Stax said, somewhat surprised to discover it was true. His back hurt, but he was otherwise uninjured. "You make a good suit of armor, Osk. Thanks."

"Not even the best armor can stand up to too much punishment," Hejira warned Stax. "Be cautious."

Stax nodded gravely. "I know. I will be."

"What was that about Fouge's studies?" asked Ramoa.

"I have no idea," Stax said. "He never struck me as the studying type, to be honest."

"That was all of them, right?" Osk asked.

Ramoa shook her head grimly. "There will be more."

"More? How many more?"

"We cannot know," Hejira said. "But now the next ones will know we are coming."

"Oh," squeaked Osk.

"Just stay with us, Osk," Ramoa said, obviously impatient to get moving.

But Stax held up his hand, asking her to wait. He turned and put his hand on Osk's shoulder. His friend was quivering.

"Osk, you're scared and that's okay," he said. "I'm scared too. If it's too much and you want to go back to Karamhés, go. But I'd appreciate it if you'd stay, because I might need your help once we reach the top of the mountain. And we all might need your help before then. We're far, far stronger together than we are apart. When I get scared, I remind myself of that."

"Okay, I'll try," said Osk, who was still breathing hard. "I think I can keep going."

"Good," said Stax. "If you can, I can. Heji, let's go."

Hejira waited for the other three to join him at the bottom of the stairs. As they took their places, he caught Stax's eye and gave him an approving nod.

The interior of the mountain had been carved into a warren of rooms connected by stairwells. Most of the rooms were empty, and looked like they had been that way for many years. Fouge's raiders had apparently taken over a disused fortress, one that had been built to house much larger numbers.

Stax and the others met several more groups of raiders, but no organized defense. They fought their way past these gangs, climbing ever higher, until they found themselves in a large cavern whose ceiling was mostly packed sand, its contours jagged above their heads. Sand lay piled up around the perimeter of the cavern too. Beyond lay a cave with a lower ceiling of stone, with several doors on both sides, set in a band of darker rock, and another stairway leading up.

"We have to be near the top of the mountain," Stax said, pointing out the stairway.

He could feel his own anticipation rising, his eagerness to confront Fouge Tempro. Apparently Hejira could sense what he was feeling.

"Remember what you learned in the jungle, Stax: Do not get carried away by your emotions and lose your focus," Hejira warned him.

Stax nodded, forcing himself to take a deep breath.

"I would have thought there'd be more guards," Osk said.

"Me too," Ramoa said. "Behind those doors, maybe. Or maybe they're higher up, with their boss."

They started across the cavern floor. Ramoa had an arrow nocked, searching for targets. Stax kept turning from side to side warily. Only Hejira betrayed no anxiety; but then the veteran warrior never did. Osk hurried along behind them.

They were halfway across the cavern when a whisper of sand reached Stax's ears. He turned, hoping his senses were playing tricks on him. But they weren't. Raiders had emerged from hiding behind the mounds of sand around the edges of the cavern to their rear. Stax counted a dozen—no, more than that.

"Oh no," Osk breathed.

"Stay calm," Hejira urged. "We must work together."

There were more bandits ahead of them, swords out. And their leader was a burly, black-bearded man.

Miggs.

"You should have run," Stax said grimly.

"So should yeh," Miggs replied. "Now, let's not have a scene. Yeh've beaten long odds to come this far, fancy boy, but yer luck's run out. Yer outnumbered and surrounded. Put down yer weapons."

"Let my friends go and I will," Stax said. "I'm the one your boss wants anyway."

"Stax, no," said Ramoa.

"I refuse as well," said Hejira, studying the ceiling. "The rest of you go forward. I will handle the ones behind us."

Stax looked at the packed sand that formed the roof of the ceiling and suddenly understood what Hejira planned to do.

"Heji, don't!" he said.

But Hejira had already turned. Two quick steps and a spring and he was among the raiders to the rear of the party, sword flashing. Startled, the bandits tried to regroup, falling back before him.

"Take them!" yelled Miggs, ducking to avoid an arrow fired by Ramoa, who was running forward, reaching behind her for another arrow.

"I didn't expect . . ." mumbled Osk. "I can't . . ." And then the red-haired inventor broke and ran, back the way they'd come, past Hejira and the crew he was battling.

Osk dodged a bandit and raced out of the cavern. Stax started to call out to Osk, but had to turn his attention back to the battle, and specifically to Ramoa, who had driven away one of Miggs's men but was alone against a dozen more. He hurried to her side as Hejira broke through the line of raiders and scrambled atop the piled sand.

"Look out!" Stax told Ramoa, who had slung her bow and drawn her sword.

Ramoa glanced at him and her eyes widened as she saw Hejira chopping with his sword at the sandy ceiling of the cavern.

"HEJI! NO!"

Hejira's sword bit through the sand. The roof of the cavern seemed to shiver, and then it came down with a roar. Sand filled the air around Stax and Ramoa, getting in Stax's eyes and mouth. He coughed and spat. Behind them, all was silent and still. Sand filled the cavern. Stax saw no sign of the raiders who had been behind them when Hejira brought the ceiling down: They'd either been buried beneath it or were cut off behind it. But he knew where Hejira had been standing, and there the sand was silent and still.

"A foolish sacrifice," Miggs said, and Stax tore his eyes away from the mountain of sand. "There're still a dozen of us and only two of yeh."

"Let's see if we can even up those numbers, then," Stax said, teeth bared.

The raiders just laughed.

"Stax, there are too many of them. We don't know where Osk is, and we've lost Heji," Ramoa said. "Don't throw your life away. Not like this."

"Yer friend's smart," Miggs said. "Are yeh gonna be smart, kid?"

Stax looked from Ramoa's grim expression to the eager raiders and the weapons in their fists. He was willing to go down fighting—but not to make that choice for Ramoa.

With a sigh, Stax lowered his sword.

CHAPTER 29

PRISONERS OF FOUGE TEMPRO

A recollection of bygone perils *
Morning visitors * A confession

The doors Stax had glimpsed in the rocky cavern turned out to be jail cells. Miggs's raiders stripped Stax of his diamond armor, took away his weapons and Ramoa's, and shoved Stax and Ramoa into one of the little rooms.

Ramoa immediately began examining the walls and doors for a way out, but Stax told her to stop wasting her time. The cell walls were made of obsidian, leaving just enough room for two beds with lumpy, dirty woolen mattresses. It would have been a huge effort to dig through the walls even with proper tools, and the guards would have to be actually unconscious to ignore the noise it would make.

"You're right, there's no way out," Ramoa said with a sigh, sitting against the wall next to Stax. "Still, don't despair. I've been in worse situations than this."

"You have? When?"

"I was taken prisoner by the Priest-Kings of Dahver-Nod," Ramoa said. "For daring to look upon the sacred waters of the Great Cataract as a heretic. Totally worth it, by the way. But when that cell door closed, I thought I was a goner."

"How'd you escape?"

Ramoa's face fell. "Heji rescued me. Oh, Heji. I wish something in his crazy code had stopped him. It's forbidden to dig sand above your head, or something."

Stax said nothing, remembering his last look at Hejira's slim, black-clad figure before the ceiling came down with a roar.

"At least Osk got away," Ramoa said. "Poor kid. She wasn't really cut out for swords and bows."

Stax tried to imagine Osk getting help and somehow returning to rescue them, but stopped himself. The artificer would be lucky if she got back to their horses without running into more of Fouge's gang. Stax hung his head at the thought.

"What do you think will happen now?" Ramoa asked.

"Oh, I imagine Fouge will come to gloat. And have his revenge."

"Which will be what?" Ramoa asked.

Stax just shook his head. "I'm glad to say I don't know what it's like in that man's brain."

He thought about adding that he knew whatever Fouge came up with would be worse than anything he could imagine, but decided not to. Their situation was bad enough as it was.

"Heji liked you, you know," Ramoa said. "He said you didn't understand how resourceful you were, and that your instinct was to help others. He said lots of people figured out that first part, but people either helped others or didn't. He told me he really wanted to know what your destiny would be."

Stax smiled, but shook his head. "I'm glad he didn't get an answer, then. Because this sure wasn't the destiny I had in mind."

"Me neither," she said. "But I'm still glad I met you. It's like I told you, back when we met: People need people. I'm glad we got to be each other's people, Stax. I could have done without the Being Captured by a Psychotic Bandit part, but that's regret for you."

"Quiet in there, you two!" growled a guard.

"Or what?" demanded Stax. "You'll throw us in jail?"

Ramoa laughed, and a moment later, despite everything, Stax was laughing too.

Stax expected it wouldn't be long before Miggs or someone else came to bring them in front of Fouge Tempro, but minutes stretched into hours and nothing happened.

Finally, a bandit brought them some stale bread and a curt message: The boss would deal with them later. They should get some sleep, because they'd need it.

Stax didn't think he'd be able to sleep while knowing that in the morning he'd be at Fouge's mercy all over again. But to his surprise, after a few minutes of tossing and turning he succumbed to exhaustion.

He woke up because Ramoa was shaking him.

"Stax! Wake up already! Can't you hear that?"

A moment later, anyone in the immediate vicinity of the mountain could have heard it: steel on steel, accompanied by grunts of effort.

Something clattered to the ground outside their cell. They heard footsteps. Then heavy breathing.

The cell door opened.

Hejira Tenboots stood in the doorway, shoulders hunched, leaning on his sword. He was breathing hard, and he looked awful. His black cloak was streaked with sand and his face and arms were bruised and cut. Behind him, Stax saw Osk Fikar peering into the cell.

"You're alive!" he exclaimed.

"Heji!" yelped Ramoa, and threw her arms around her friend.

Hejira stumbled backward, dropping his sword and emitting gasps of pain until Ramoa realized how badly hurt he was and let him go.

Stax was stammering something that wasn't exactly a sentence, more a jumble of hows and whats, and Hejira was trying to answer him.

"Osk dug me out of the sand," Hejira said. "The other raiders had fled. I did not suffocate, not quite, but it was not an experience I care to repeat."

"I'm sorry I ran off and left you guys. I just got so scared. I was halfway to the entrance when I heard the ceiling come down and I realized I was the only one who could help," Osk said, looking down at her feet. "So I hid until the coast was clear and snuck back in, but you were all gone. I managed to find Heji, but I'm sorry I couldn't stop them from taking you two."

"You ran off, but you came back," Ramoa said, and hugged Osk, who had no injuries that would allow her to escape Ramoa's embrace.

"But how did you get past the guards?" Stax asked.

"Stealth is an excellent strategy," Hejira said. "Particularly when you are not capable of prolonged combat. The last guard saw me before I could sneak up on him, unfortunately. I persuaded him to depart. But now I am winded."

Hejira put his hands on his knees and tried to get his breath.

"We need to get you back down the mountain," Stax said.

"No," Hejira said. "We must press on. This may be our only chance to take Fouge Tempro by surprise. Unfortunately, they have taken your weapons and armor to the tower. I suggest you salvage any useful gear you can find."

"You're not going to go down the mountain, are you?" Ramoa asked Hejira before Stax could protest. "No matter what we say or do."

Hejira just shook his head.

"Impossible man," she muttered. "All right, then. Stax, let's see what we can find."

They were able to find a pair of swords abandoned by the fleeing guards, one of which was badly notched but useable. So armed, they stood at the foot of the stairs leading up.

"Before we ascend, I have a confession I must make," Hejira said. "It is painful, and you will think less of me. When Osk found me, I was badly hurt. So we found shelter a level below, and I slept. In a bed."

Ramoa, Stax, and Osk looked at one another.

"We'll never tell," Ramoa said. "That's a promise."

CHAPTER 30

THE MAN IN THE MOUNTAINTOP FORTRESS

The bandit king's hideout * Hejira, preceded by
his reputation * Fouge, at last

This time Stax was in the lead, with Ramoa and Hejira behind him. They took the stone steps slowly, out of concern for Hejira's injuries.

The stairs ended at a pair of doors made of dark oak. Stax pulled the ring on the left-hand door and found himself at the end of a long hall. There was a table in the center, lined with low chairs on either side and with two high-backed ones at each end, and windows on the far side of the room. Everything was covered with a thick layer of dust.

"This place is old," said Osk.

"So were the rooms in the mountain and the ruins around it," Stax said. "Fouge either found it, or took it away from somebody. I doubt he's ever built anything in his life."

"Stax, look."

Stax saw what Ramoa was pointing to: a path through the dust, made by a multitude of feet. They followed it to another door that led to a long corridor with many rooms off it.

"It would be good to find our weapons," Ramoa said.

"But bad to find more guards," Stax said. "Osk, wait—"

But it was too late. Osk, who had just been muttering about "something curious," opened one of the doors and stood in the entrance, mouth agape. A strange purple light played over her astonished features.

Stax looked over Osk's shoulder and peered into the room. The door opened onto a balcony with an iron railing, with ladders leading down to the lower part of the room. Below, a massive frame of obsidian enclosed roiling purple light, shot through with traceries and sparks.

"What is that?" asked Stax.

"A nether portal," Osk said. "A gateway to another dimension. That must be what those guys back in the mountain meant when they said their boss was studying. Stax, if Fouge has gone through there, you might never find him."

"Then let's hope he hasn't," Stax said. "Come on, Osk."

He heard a whine of hinges and turned to discover Ramoa opening another door.

"What?" she asked. "Our weapons might be around here somewhere."

"Seriously?" Stax asked.

"I am both tired and injured," Hejira said. "I do not think I will be able to free you from captivity a second time."

"Nobody open another door unless we all agree, okay?" Stax asked, and led them down the hallway. It jogged to the right, merging with another corridor to form a foyer. Behind them lay a door of oak; ahead of them, three broad steps led to double doors. On either side of the doors sat low columns topped with torches.

"That looks like an important place," Osk said.

"It does," Stax said. "Everybody ready?"

The doors yawned open. Beyond them lay a wide hall. There was another long table in the center, and one side of the room was piled high with objects—some scattered on the floor, some spilling out of chests and discarded on chairs. Much of the stuff was valuable, or at least looked like it might be; there were gems, bars of gold, paintings, maps, pieces of armor, banners, and many other things besides.

But at that moment, Stax didn't care about any of those fascinating objects. Because sitting at the end of the hall, in a high-backed chair with a velvet cushion, was Fouge Tempro.

Stax recognized Fouge's bright blue eyes at once, and his unnerving, intent stare. And he was wearing mismatched clothes, as he had when he'd first arrived at the Stonecutter estate. But he was pale and haggard, with deep bags under those hypnotic eyes.

Standing next to Fouge was Miggs, who'd been speaking urgently with him. Three other guards were lounging nearby, and sprang to their feet.

"What's this then?" asked Fouge crossly.

"Stax Stonecutter," said Miggs. "The prisoner I told yeh about, boss. But how—"

Stax had spent a number of sleepless nights imagining what he'd say at this moment. And he did open his mouth. But before he could speak, Hejira stepped forward, head high and sword held almost carelessly in one hand.

That was amazing enough, but then Hejira did something Stax found even stranger. He looked at Stax and *winked*.

"The man in black!" one of the other raiders said. "But the roof fell on him! Buried him alive! It can't be!"

"It is," Hejira said, his voice even and calm. "The mountain is empty. You are the only defenders left, and now I have come for you. Run while you can."

"What is all this bother?" asked Fouge, more crossly this time. His hand strayed to the diamond sword at his hip.

"A ghost!" yelled one of the raiders, running from the room. Hejira continued to advance on the others, his strides slow and deliberate, his eyes fixed on Fouge and his minions. He raised his sword, the point held unwaveringly in his hand.

That was too much for the other raiders. They ran as well, eyes wide with fear, leaving Miggs alone at the side of his master.

"Your luck's run out, Miggs," Stax said, following a step behind Hejira. "Now you're the one who's outnumbered. You'd better go, and this time you'd better stay gone."

Miggs's eyes jumped from Hejira to Fouge and back again.

"I lifted you up from nothing, Miggs," Fouge growled. "I can make you nothing again. And if you cross me, I'll do far worse."

"You don't have to be afraid of him, Miggs," Stax said. "He's never leaving this place again. That's a promise."

Miggs hesitated, and then he too hurried from the hall, and Stax heard him break into a run once he'd reached the doors. Hejira stopped a few blocks from Fouge, now sitting alone in his chair. His shoulders slumped and he lowered his sword.

"I think I need to sit down," he said, fumbling for a chair.

"You were bluffing!" said Fouge, admiration and anger chasing each other across his face.

"In my experience most brigands are weak people, easily led by anyone with enough bluster and bravado," said Hejira, slumping in a chair. "This also makes them easy to deceive."

"Hard to get good help these days," muttered Fouge.

"Stax," said Ramoa. "I think I found some things that belong to you."

Stax looked over and found Ramoa standing by a pile of diamond armor. She had already picked up her bow and was gathering arrows.

"Stax Stonecutter," said Fouge, his blue eyes studying Stax.

"Yes," Stax smiled with grim satisfaction. "It's been a long time, Fouge."

"Miggs told me your name, and how he had you and your friends locked away," Fouge said. "But I'm afraid I don't remember who you are."

At first Stax thought Fouge was lying in an effort to provoke him. But the confusion on his face was real. He had actually forgotten.

"I lived in a house of diorite and granite, on a little peninsula by the sea," Stax said, his voice tight with anger. "With my cats and my flowers. And my family's mine in the back garden."

Fouge's face brightened.

"You had a little pool above that mine!" he said. "Built out of that black-and-white speckly stuff. I remember now!"

And he grinned; not that predatory grin that Stax had found so unsettling, but a real smile of delighted recollection. As if he and Stax were old friends, meeting again after many years apart.

"You destroyed the pool," Stax said. "And the mine, and the house. And then you carried off everything that had belonged to my grandmother and father. And left me on a desert shore to die. Do you remember that now too?"

"More or less," Fouge said. "But that was so far from here, Stax. Did you come all this way for revenge?"

"For justice," Stax said.

"Oh, call it what you like. What a waste of time and effort. You've done all right for yourself since we parted ways, Stax. Diamond armor doesn't come cheap. I'm betting you could build four or five houses like the one I visited and fill them with more stuff than even my raiders could take away. But instead, here you are wanting to settle some boring dispute from a long time ago."

"It's not a long time ago to me," Stax said, and turned to wave at the gems and treasures piled up in the hall. "And I bet it's not a long time ago to all the other people you've stolen from."

"I see you're determined to be tedious. Very well, Stax. So what's it to be? A duel to the death? Or is your excitable friend here going to simply shoot me where I stand?"

And Fouge inclined his chin at Ramoa, who was standing astride Stax's armor with her bow drawn back and an arrow aimed straight at Fouge.

Stax felt his anger rise. It wasn't just that Fouge had forgotten him, it was the casual way he referred to all the misery he'd caused.

Fouge got to his feet, almost lazily, only to start in surprise when an arrow thudded into the back of the chair beside him.

"You missed," he told Ramoa mildly.

"I didn't," she replied. "Stax gets to buckle on his armor and take up his sword, and you're going to sit back down and hold still while he does it."

Fouge fixed Ramoa with a look of pure malice.

"Osk, help him," Hejira suggested.

Stax kept a close eye on Fouge as he crossed in front of the table and stood beside Ramoa. He nodded at her and knelt to pick up his diamond sword, then turned to face Fouge. Osk strapped him into his chestplate, cinching it tight, then knelt to affix his leggings.

"This hardly seems fair," Fouge said. "I have no such protection."

"Was it fair when you invaded my house with boats full of bandits?" Stax asked, picking up one foot so Osk could fit a boot over it.

"Oh, Stax, why so serious? You are unhurt, wealthy, and have made interesting friends. Was that really all so bad?"

With both boots in place, Stax took his helmet from Osk and tightened its chin strap. His armor felt light and strong. The sword seemed to hum in his hand.

"*Now* you can get up, Fouge," Stax said.

Fouge glanced at Ramoa, who nodded and released the tension on her bowstring. He stood and stretched leisurely. Stax glared as Fouge drew his own diamond sword, that predatory grin back on his face as he approached.

CHAPTER 31

DUELISTS

A long-sought confrontation * Hunting for very
specific treasure * A puzzle with maps

Now, you've probably read *other* accounts of the duel between Stax Stonecutter and Fouge Tempro. Some of them are very exciting, full of sparks flying off diamond blades and sorcerous fireworks. Muscles bulge and sinews strain and there's a lot of that sort of thing.

But I'm going to tell you what really happened—or at least, what really happened the way I heard it. (And my sources are pretty good.) And while this version has less in the way of sparks and sinews, I think it's pretty dramatic too, in its own way.

What really happened was this: Fouge Tempro took a couple of steps toward Stax, smiling that nasty smile of his. He made a few cuts in the air with his sword, to see what Stax's reaction was. Stax, remembering what Hejira had taught him, simply waited.

He was watching Fouge's feet, and the way he set his shoulders, and was ready for whatever happened next.

Or at least he thought he was.

What happened next was that Fouge laughed, opened his hand, and let his diamond sword clatter to the stone floor.

"You know what, Stax? I'm not going to fight you. You can do whatever you want to me. Didn't I teach you that nothing matters? That all this—our lives, the Overworld, everything we get so worked up thinking means so much—is just a big cosmic joke? When we first met, the joke was on you. Now it's on me. So do what you will."

Stax hadn't been expecting that. He looked at Fouge for a long moment, expecting some kind of trick—the revelation of a second sword, or a bunch of bandits rushing in from a secret entrance. But Fouge just shrugged and sat back down, crossing his legs at the knee.

Stax glanced at Ramoa, Hejira, and Osk, but Ramoa and Osk looked as stunned as he did, and Hejira had no reaction whatsoever, because he was Hejira. After a moment, Stax bent, which wasn't easy to do in his armor, and picked up the sword Fouge had dropped.

"You *did* tell me that nothing matters," he told Fouge. "And you certainly tried to make me believe that. But I learned something else, Fouge. You might be right that nothing we do matters to the sea or the stars, but we aren't either of those things. Our lives are only meaningless if we live them that way. The world can be cruel, I agree. But that makes it *more* important for us to be kind. For us to create a bubble, however fragile and short-lived it might be, against the world's cruelty."

Fouge chuckled and clapped his hands.

"Oh, bravo, Stax. When I found you, you were a lazy, spoiled child. And look at what you've become. A warrior, an adventurer, and even a philosopher. Really, you ought to thank me. Would you have become any of those things, sitting in your solitude and clipping lawns and petting cats? I *made* you what you are. I made your singularly useless life *matter*."

Ramoa, teeth bared, made to draw her bow again, but Stax caught her eye and shook his head.

"*I* did those things, not you. It wasn't your job to turn me into anything. And your cruelty isn't designed to make anything. It serves nothing except your own selfishness. And now, I'm going to make sure you can't ever hurt anyone else."

"Ah, finally," said Fouge, spreading his arms and thrusting his chest forward. "Very well, Stax. Strike true and try not to make a mess of it."

"No, Fouge. I'm not going to kill you."

"Too noble to do the deed yourself, eh?" asked Fouge, glancing at Ramoa and Hejira. "So who will it be? The hot-blooded archer? Or the mysterious swordsman?"

"Neither," said Stax. "I'm going to leave you to my friend the artificer. Osk, you know what we discussed, and you've now seen the fortress. Do you have everything you need?"

"Oh yes," said Osk, pausing to give Fouge a little bow. "It's a complicated design, relying on obsidian and lava and water and pistons. And I'll need lots of redstone. But I've been thinking about it since Stax suggested it on the way from Tumbles Harbor, and I'm pretty sure it will work. An impenetrable prison: claw through the obsidian, and *wham!* A new block of it snaps into place."

"Sounds ingenious," Fouge said. "But no thanks. I'd rather die."

"I'm sure you would, Fouge," Stax said. "But you aren't going to. You're going to live, and comfortably. But you'll spend the rest of your days alone. No minions to boss around, no victims to torment, no shiny stolen baubles to distract you for a minute or an hour or a day. It'll just be you, alone with yourself, which I think is the only thing that's ever really frightened you."

Fouge, for once, had no words. But Ramoa did.

"Total isolation?" she asked. "That's a lot, Stax. For anybody."

"He won't change. Don't make the mistake of thinking he will." Ramoa frowned, but Stax had already turned back to Fouge. "Ramoa and I will see that you're comfortable—and secure—until Osk's prison is built. Osk, is there anything else you need?"

Osk shook her head. "A drawing table, some paper, and help. All of which I have."

"Don't you want to know why, Stax?" Fouge asked, in an unnaturally quiet voice. "You asked me that, a while back. You didn't deserve an answer then, but you do now."

"I don't want your answer," Stax said.

"You don't want to know why?" Fouge asked, incredulous. "I find that impossible to believe."

"I don't. Because, to be honest, I don't care. I'm not going to let you invent some reason for what you've done, because it would just be another lie. You're like a hazard deep in a mine, Fouge. Like a lavafall or a dungeon full of monsters. It's a waste of time trying to convince lava not to burn or monsters not to attack. Instead, you wall those hazards up and put up warning signs. And once you've done that, you don't have to think about them anymore."

———

Fouge resisted briefly, but he was trussed up and watched by Ramoa while Stax found a pickaxe in one of the fortress's storerooms, dismantled the nether portal, and used the obsidian to construct a temporary cell.

With that unpleasant task completed, they explored the fortress, discovering it contained a courtyard open to the sky, with shaggy oak trees. Hejira, to everyone's relief, decided this didn't count as a shelter and immediately climbed into the tree's branches to sleep and heal.

Stax returned to Fouge's hall and all the loot it contained. He pawed through gems, looked through stacks of paintings, and examined banners for hours. In the corner of the room, he found two simple wooden frames: one enclosing a stone pickaxe worn down to a stub, and the other housing a dull and notched stone sword.

"Do you recognize those things?" asked Ramoa.

"I do," said Stax. "They were my grandmother's. They used to hang in the hall by our gardens. Once I wanted to get rid of them, but now I know better."

He put them aside to examine the next pile of things, and nodded. Here was a banner with the Stonecutter family crest, a blue triangle on an orange field. And below that were long rolls of paper.

"Could you help me spread these out?" he asked Ramoa, and they brought them to the table in armloads.

As Stax had hoped, they were his father's maps, with symbols for the outposts he'd set up on the ocean voyages he'd made to sell stone.

"They're all out of order," said Ramoa, frustrated. "It's like a giant puzzle."

"My grandmother and I used to do puzzles all the time," said Stax. "I'm sure we can solve it."

And they spent the next couple of hours rearranging maps, and turning them this way and that, and standing atop the table for a better view, and making suggestions that went nowhere and trying to convince themselves that coastlines fit together when they actually didn't. But little by little the right answers began to outnumber the wrong guesses, until finally the table was covered with a huge map of lands and seas.

Ramoa studied it, walking around and around it with her hand on her chin, until her eyes lit up and she laid her finger on a stretch of coastline.

"I think that's Desolation Bay," she said. "Which would mean you and I met about here. And if you go up the coast to the north —"

"—here's Tumbles Harbor," said Stax.

He smiled at Ramoa, but then the import of what they'd discovered hit him, and he felt his knees go weak. He brought his hand back to Desolation Bay, and this time he followed the coast west. To the wide body of water that had to be the Sea of Sorrows. And from there, farther west . . .

"Here's my little peninsula," he said, and felt tears start in his eyes. He knew he was right; there were little spikes of pale blue right off the coast, representing the ice floes, and an orange chevron next to them. "Here's home."

Ramoa nodded, and showed Stax where her own finger was resting on a patch of green adjoining the coast, some distance south of Desolation Bay.

"What's that?" Stax asked.

"River House," she said. "My home. Which you better come see."

It took a couple of weeks for Osk's prison to be finished and another couple of days to test it, to ensure Fouge wouldn't be able to
escape. The completed prison was striking, if a little odd-
looking—a seemingly solid block of obsidian covered half of
Fouge's fortress, with lava surrounding that, an artificial lake on
the roof, and a perimeter of pistons around the lava. Inside, two of
the rooms had been converted into a small farm and a pen for
cows and pigs, while the others retained their creature comforts.
Fouge would have a bed, furniture, some paintings, and books—
everything except the freedom he'd used to hurt others.

And the prison came with another layer of security. Osk announced that if it was all right with the others, she'd set up shop
in the rest of the fortress, as Fouge's custodian. The fort would
make an excellent laboratory and a sprawling home. When word
spread that the bad men atop the mountain had been run off,
farmers and traders would follow the river east of Karamhés and
become Osk's neighbors.

With a glance at Ramoa, Osk said she'd keep watch over
Fouge—and see if he showed any sign of repentance for what
he'd done. And, she added with a glance at Stax, she'd be alert to
his tricks—Fouge would find charming his way out of prison as
difficult as digging his way free.

Stax, Ramoa, and Hejira said their farewells to Osk on a crisp,
clear morning and walked back to Karamhés, where Ramoa said
a not particularly reluctant farewell to her horse. The donkey,
recently weighed down with chests of redstone, was now blissfully
unencumbered. Stax had taken a small amount of diamonds and
lapis, his father's maps, the Stonecutter banner, and the frames
with his grandmother's tools. The rest he'd given to Osk.

Stax and Ramoa had rented rooms at the caravanserai. It was dusk, and Stax's stomach rumbled.

"Goodbye, Heji," he said, embracing the black-clad warrior. "Thank you for everything you taught me."

"And I, in turn, thank you," Hejira said. "Your path has been a fascinating one to observe. And I remain keenly interested in where your destiny lies."

"So do I," said Stax.

"Farewell for now, my friend," said Ramoa, hugging Hejira. "I'll see you at River House. It's been too long since I've been home, and this time I think I'll stay awhile."

"I am glad your path is returning you there," Hejira said, and embraced her. "I hope it leads you to the peace you deserve to enjoy."

"Where *are* you going, Heji?" Stax asked, when the two old friends parted. "You haven't said."

"North," said Hejira, and his smile faded. "I will watch for signs that the raiders are regrouping. And I will seek word of Miggs. I believe he needs another nudge onto a better path."

"It might take more than a nudge," said Stax.

"It might," said Ramoa. "But Heji can nudge pretty hard."

CHAPTER 32

TWO SHORES

A tower revisited * A familiar peninsula, and a long-
awaited reunion * The future, considered

After parting ways with Hejira, Stax and Ramoa traveled through forested hills, sprawling meadows, and rolling grasslands. They set a leisurely pace, with Ramoa telling Stax about caravans she'd guarded, amazing vistas she'd always wanted to return to, and lands known to her only through travelers' tales. Each night, they'd look at one of the Stonecutter maps and try to trace routes Ramoa had walked, or find places she'd been.

The time passed pleasantly, but it passed, and one afternoon Stax stopped Ramoa, sniffing at the air.

"What is it?" she asked.

"The sea," he said. "I just realized how much I missed it."

Another hour's walk brought them to the caravan track that led north to Tumbles Harbor, not far from where they had met. And a few minutes after that Stax was standing in the shallow water at the eastern end of Desolation Bay, looking west to where the sun was already low on the horizon.

They passed the night in a little hollow hacked out of a rocky hill. Tomorrow they would be parted, with Ramoa heading south around the Shining Desert, and Stax heading west toward home. They talked of a number of things, like bizarre experiments Osk might actually make work and demanding new rules Hejira would dream up for himself, but mostly they simply enjoyed each other's company.

In the morning, Ramoa sat on a rock on the seashore, ignoring the bees humming around her head and shooing away curious sheep, while Stax built a crafting table and hammered together a little boat from old logs. They discussed the route Stax would take home—Stax had studied the maps so many times that he could almost see it if he closed his eyes—and how best to avoid the perils along the way.

Until, finally, the boat was finished and it was time to part.

They hugged each other for a minute, or maybe it was two, and Stax smiled.

"Don't worry about me," he said, because he could tell Ramoa was doing exactly that. "I have this."

And he showed her the compass he'd carried in his pocket for so many months.

"Is that the one you found on the beach? The one Fouge dropped?"

"It is," Stax said, looking down at it. "I was convinced it was his, and maybe it was. But at some point on the journey I stopped thinking about it that way. My father would have used one just like this. And who knows? Maybe this *was* my dad's, before one of Fouge's raiders stole it. Which would mean it came back to me."

"I like that," said Ramoa. "Let's tell the story that way from now on."

"Agreed," Stax said, and returned his father's compass to his pocket.

He checked for leaks one last time and pushed the boat into the sea, standing next to it in the shallow water with one hand on the gunwale.

"I circled River House on your map," Ramoa said. "When you're ready, come see me. And if I'm not there, I will be again soon. A girl does get restless."

"I will," said Stax, and clambered into the boat. He rowed for a minute, and looked back to see Ramoa's figure growing rapidly smaller on the shore. He raised his hand in farewell, and a moment later she did the same.

Stax stuck close to the southern shore and soon found himself rowing past the barren desert coast he'd come to know all too well. He now knew it was called the Shining Desert, and avoided by wise travelers, just as he knew he was rowing across Desolation Bay. Before, he hadn't had names for these places; now he knew what they were called and could look at his father's maps and find them sketched out in miniature.

At midafternoon Stax saw a little black dot on the shore ahead. He knew what it had to be, but it was still a strange sensation to discover that, yes, he had returned to the patchwork tower where Fouge's raiders had left him. It was the place where he'd thought he would die, but instead, became the place where he'd learned how to save himself.

Stax stopped rowing and let the boat drift for a moment. Ahead, he could just spot the keel of the shipwrecked boat offshore, the one he'd plundered for wood to make a boat.

Stax looked at the position of the sun in the sky and thought about his route through Desolation Bay, calculating how far he'd come and how far he might still go before needing to find shelter. When he realized what that meant, he frowned and started to do the calculations again—and then stopped.

"Oh, what the heck," he said, and rowed for the shore.

The tower smelled of salt and charred wood. Stax spread out his bedroll, relit the furnace, and pondered whether he wanted to eat a beefsteak or a couple of slices of pie. He decided on pie, and after dinner he stood outside the tower and watched the sun sink into the sea.

As Stax was getting ready for bed and considering his choices for breakfast, something growled outside the door, the noise ending in a gurgle of seawater.

"Oh, get lost!" Stax called out. "We've done this!"

He decided against dried kelp for breakfast, though.

In the morning Stax bid the tower farewell and rowed west. And, I am happy to say, for the next several days his story wasn't terribly interesting. Each morning he checked his route on the map, decided how far he would go, and figured out a likely stretch of coast where he should look for a place to rest for the night. Then he rowed, glancing at the compass he kept on the bench beside him to ensure he was on the right course.

He rowed past desert shores and shipwrecks and broken towers, and across long stretches of empty sea. He stopped for a moment to give thanks when he spotted the ice floes and spiky towers he'd failed to reach on his first attempt to return home. Then he rowed carefully among them, seeking a path through the ever-changing obstacles posed by the ice. Other than a polar bear snarling at him, he met with no mischance.

And then, around noon one day, he came through the ice and saw a spot of green ahead of him. It was a peninsula with a little hill behind it, green and dotted with white birches: only a small part of the Overworld, perhaps, but one that meant everything to him.

Stax brought the boat in at the end of the broad green lawn, now overgrown with tall grass and interrupted by the stumps of birch trees. To his left were broken fences, and a single pumpkin growing amid the weeds. But to his right, flowers were growing with wild abandon, turning the hillside into a happy riot of red and pink and blue and white.

Stax walked up the lawn, past a stagnant green pool with a broken fountain, and climbed a flight of polished diorite steps, now gap-toothed and sprouting weeds. The top of the hill was a jumble of shattered rock, black-and-white diorite, and pink granite. To his left, where the sea curled around the peninsula, was a splintered dock and the wreckage of a boathouse.

"Well, I'm back," said Stax, sitting on a hunk of diorite and surveying the ruins of the Stonecutter estate. His mind went back to that day of fire and horror, when Fouge had brought his raiders and Stax's life had come crashing down. But Fouge was locked away and the bandits were scattered, and looking at the wreckage around him, Stax started thinking about stone blocks that could be fit together, and tall grass that could be cleared, and trees that could be planted.

He heard a little noise somewhere nearby and got to his feet, wondering if his ears were playing a cruel trick on him.

But no, it was real. A tentative, quiet meow.

A black head and golden eyes peeked out at him from behind a block of diorite.

"Coal?" Stax asked. "Coal! Come here, kitty! Come on, it's okay."

Coal, always the boldest of his cats, emerged from a jumble of fallen stone to regard Stax suspiciously and interrogate him with further meows. Then her tail went up and a moment later she was twining herself around his legs, bedraggled but purring.

Stax heard more meowing and looked up from stroking Coal to see a gray-striped cat with green eyes and a Siamese with blue eyes poke their heads out of their own hiding places.

"Emerald! Lapis!" A moment later Stax was surrounded by cats, meowing and competing for pats.

"It's so good to see you, kitties," Stax said. "Funny, you don't look as skinny as I would have guessed. Seems like we all learned what we're capable of, huh? Though I bet a fish or three would be nice to have, am I right?"

Fortunately, Stax had a fishing rod—he'd learned something from his hungry days in Desolation Bay—so he retrieved it from his boat and stood on the splintered dock until he'd landed three cod, which Coal, Lapis, and Emerald quickly reduced to bones.

Emerald meowed for more, and looked doubtful when Stax assured him that the days of shameful neglect had ended. But he was looking at the burned-out boathouse, and thinking about shelter for the night. It would be beyond ridiculous to make it all the way home, only to be caught out of doors after dark and obliterated by a creeper on its nocturnal rounds.

And so Stax spent the rest of the afternoon making an improvised shelter where the boathouse had stood. It was a ramshackle construction—honestly, it made the tower in Desolation Bay look

like a palace—but it would keep out rain, wind, and hungry creatures of the night, which was good enough for now. Stax even
found a few squares of carpet that hadn't been entirely burned,
and laid them out to cover some of the floor. And in the morning
he woke up on the Stonecutter estate with Coal on his left and
Emerald on his right and Lapis stretched out on his chest, and
simply lay there for a while, smiling in happy disbelief.

A couple of days later, the employees of the Stonecutter offices
were stunned to discover that Stax Stonecutter was not, in fact,
dead. They were even more stunned when he arrived carrying his
father's maps and full of questions about outposts and trade agree-
ments, and a dozen other things in which he'd never before
shown the slightest interest. And they were absolutely flabber-
gasted when he thanked them for keeping the business in working order, not just while he was presumed dead but for all the
years he'd been alive and had barely noticed its existence.

The employees were also surprised to be invited out to the estate, along with many of Stax's neighbors. The estate had changed
too. The day after he returned, Stax started clearing away the debris of the house and cleaned up the lawn, ridding it of birch
stumps and weeds. Soon after that, he drained the water from the
mine in the back garden—now *that* was a big job—and patched
the mine's roof. But after thinking about it for a little while, he
chose not to rebuild the big house that had sat on the hill, the one
made of diorite and granite that had shone in the sun. Instead, he
cleared the hilltop of shattered stone, filled in the stagnant fountain, and removed the broken staircase, so that visitors found a
green hill with a little lake, and a garden with a small, well-kept
family cemetery.

What Stax did rebuild was the boathouse, as best he remembered it. It was cozy, but big enough for his bed, as well as a chest, bookcase, furnace, and a crafting table. Windows overlooked the sea, and Stax hung his grandmother's stone pickaxe and sword side by side on the wall. He rebuilt the dock, too, and visitors got used to landing there when they had business at the Stonecutter estate. Most of the time, they'd find Stax sitting at a table on the dock with the cats snoozing in the sun, reading a book about mining or studying one of his father's maps.

Stax would greet these visitors warmly, thank them for not coming to the old landing on the lawn that he no longer used, and prove quite able to talk about things besides cats and flowers. Though visitors did note that Stax talked to those cats quite a bit, and occasionally was found having conversations with himself.

For a long time—it was definitely weeks and might have been months—Stax was happy. But over time a certain restlessness crept into his thoughts. He found himself retracing the route from the Stonecutter peninsula to Desolation Bay, and from there to Tumbles Harbor, the Rain-Jungles of Jagga-Tel, the village of Patannos, and the caravan town of Karamhés. But the route he traced most often led to a place on one map, surrounded by a circle drawn by the hand of a friend.

Until one morning, Coal and Lapis and Emerald had to meow quite a bit more than usual to remind Stax that it was his responsibility to catch fish and deliver breakfast. Instead, he was packing up maps and trying on armor and sorting through chests, without noticing three cats who were becoming terribly hungry.

Stax apologized and caught some cod, but the cats had only just finished picking the bones clean when he carried them into the boat instead of rearranging the chairs on the dock so they could snooze in the sun.

The cats weren't sure about this odd break in their routine, but they were too full and sleepy to object strenuously, and before they quite grasped what was happening Stax had rowed the boat away from the dock and was looking back and forth between the sun and his father's compass.

"Come on, kitties," he told them with a smile. "Let's go see the world."

ACKNOWLEDGMENTS

Writing this book meant that when my wife asked why I was playing a videogame at 4:30 A.M. again, I got to look wounded, exclaim "I'm working!" and have it actually be true.

Thanks to the good folks at Mojang for that, and for creating such a fun, beautiful, and imaginative game and world. A special tip of the cap to Alex Wiltshire for keeping me on the Overworld straight and narrow.

At Penguin Random House, Sarah Peed was a warm, friendly editor and a generous traveling companion from start to finish, while Nancy Delia was her usual eagle-eyed self, saving me from mistakes, redundancies, and bouts of laziness.

At home, my son, Joshua, was a source of valuable *Minecraft* tips and even once told me Stax's house was cool. My wife, Emily, puts up with far too much of my nonsense even when it isn't videogame-related; she was admirably patient every time I announced I'd taken an *even better* screenshot of Stax's cats, and asked if she wanted to see it. Even when it was 4:30 A.M. Again.

ABOUT THE AUTHOR

JASON FRY is the author of *Star Wars: The Last Jedi* and has written or co-written more than forty novels, short stories, and other works set in the galaxy far, far away. His previous books include the Servants of the Empire quartet and the young-adult space-fantasy series The Jupiter Pirates. He lives in Brooklyn with his wife and son and about a metric ton of *Star Wars* stuff.

Jasonfry.net
Twitter: @jasoncfry

ABOUT THE TYPE

This book was set in Electra, a typeface designed for Linotype by renowned type designer W. A. Dwiggins (1880–1956). Electra is a fluid typeface, avoiding the contrasts of thick and thin strokes that are prevalent in most modern typefaces.